THE SAND GARDEN

Stan Jones and Mary Wasche

BOWHEAD PRESS

Paul Jones was also part of the *Sand Garden* writing team

Published by
Bowhead Press
Box 240264
Anchorage AK 99524

Print ISBN: 978-0-9799803-2-9

Ebook ISBN: 978-0-9799803-6-7

Library of Congress Control Number: 2023910186

CHAPTER ONE

— • —

The Chaplain comes by night.

He can't afford to be seen near anybody with law-enforcement ties. Not even an ex-cop and a cop's widow like myself.

If he was spotted at my place, his fellow Mogul bikers would plant him in the sand garden known as the Coachella Valley before the next sunrise painted the ocotillos yellow and orange.

So, the Chaplain comes by night.

This time, my clock radio reads 2:18 a.m. when I wake to hear his Harley mutter to a stop behind the house. My place is in the Cahuilla foothills of the San Jacinto Mountains overlooking Chapel City, Rancho Mirage, and—if you squint hard enough—the south end of Palm Springs.

It's remote enough that I can afford my house, which is critical since Frank, my husband, got himself killed on what should have been a routine domestic violence call and left me nearly broke. All I got was a mortgage in default, a zero balance in his 401K, and no explanation of where the money went.

Lucky for me California takes care of the widow when a cop gets shot in the line of duty. Eventually there was a death benefit that paid off the mortgage, and I get half of Frank's salary for the rest of my life.

But the 401K? Damned if I know what happened to it. He closed it with a cashier's check and there the trail ends. Someday I'll investigate and figure it out. But not yet. I can't make myself do it.

Oh, yeah, I almost forgot: Frank did leave me the Chaplain.

The Chaplain was Frank's confidential informant and he asked the Chaplain to look out for me if the worst happened to him.

Eight months ago, the worst did. A few nights after the funeral, the Chaplain showed up at my back door and told me the deal. Now he's my confidential informant, witness retriever, and secret go-to for things best done in the dark.

I peer out the window beside my bed, and I can see in the moonlight that the Chaplain has a sidecar on his Harley, and luggage carriers on the back. He's lifting something out of the sidecar.

A few moments pass and I hear stuff being set on the patio, followed by silence. Then he cranks up the Harley and vanishes into the night.

This is my arrangement with the Chaplain. I ask him to find something—most often an uncooperative witness—and bring him in. One time he explained to me how he does it.

The Chaplain's wanted, so he doesn't carry a gun unless he expects to need it, just a ball peen hammer. If a guy's uncooperative, the Chaplain will show him the hammer, give him a look, and wait.

The Chaplain is six and a half feet and two-hundred-plus pounds of beard, muscle, and biker menace, and who's to know what else is under those leathers? The guy usually becomes very cooperative, because the people I ask the Chaplain to track down are too deep into drugs, depravity, or gambling debt to go to the cops.

And when one doesn't cooperate, the Chaplain slams the hammer down on the table, drags the guy's hand out over the dent, raises the hammer, gives him another look, and waits some more. So far, that's always done the trick.

Except tonight there's a problem. The Chaplain's not working on anything for me at the moment, so what's he dropping off on my patio? I slide on my robe and slippers, and I'm halfway to the back door when my phone chimes from the nightstand.

I go back and pick it up. The caller ID shows the number for the Chaplain's current burner phone. It's always a burner with the Chaplain and he gets a new one every few weeks, then smashes the old one with his hammer and buries it in the desert. There's gotta be dozens of his old burners out there in the sand. Do the metal-detector people ever find them and wonder how they got there?

"What's happening?" I ask. "We've got nothing going on right - -"

"Look on the patio. And stay on the line."

"But what - -"

"Please, Dana."

The Chaplain's like that. Gracious but implacable.

I walk out of the bedroom trailed by Duke, my retired German Shepherd K-9 partner, and swing open the back door. The Chaplain has switched on the patio light before leaving, and it takes me at least thirty seconds to process what I see: twin toddlers, one of each flavor, two or three years old, asleep in car seats. Around them is a bunch of kid stuff in reusable shopping bags--clothes, diapers, toys, plastic kiddie cups and bowls, books with covers in bright colors. "Grumpy Bird" and "Emily's Balloon" are two that I can see. On their laps are a bedraggled stuffed pony and a one-eyed teddy bear.

"Jesus," I say into the phone. "What the hell is this?"

The Chaplain, for once, doesn't seem to know how to say what's on his mind. The seconds drag past.

"They're Frank's," he says finally. "Their mother was killed tonight. I didn't know what else to do with them."

I drop into a wicker chair, set my phone on the arm, pick it up, set it down again.

I study the kids in the car seats. The girl's a redhead, the boy has hair that reminds me of Frank. His hair was a beautiful black till it got streaked with gray, which only made him more beautiful. And the boy has Frank's nose and eyebrows, too. Duke sniffs his wrist and he wakes up. He peers around the patio, looks up at me with a sleepy half-smile, murmurs "Dukie." Duke licks his face and he falls back asleep.

The boy's smile nails it. Slightly crooked at the right corner, just like Frank's. Plus, he and Duke know each other. Frank must have taken Duke along when he was with his twins and their mother, the bastard.

"Dana?" the Chaplain says.

I go back inside and tap the phone onto speaker. "They're Frank's? My husband had kids with another woman?"

The Chaplain is smart enough to know when a man should keep his mouth shut.

I process for another while.

The Chaplain clears his throat and waits.

"What am I supposed to do with them?" I ask finally.

"I thought you'd know. Because you're..."

"Because I'm a woman, right? I'm a woman who couldn't have kids!"

More tactical silence from the Chaplain.

I sigh. "All right, I'll keep them till morning, then get hold of Child Protective Services. What are their names?"

"Rose and Sonny Williamson."

"Sonny?"

"Dana, I am so sor - -"

"Frank. She named him Frank Junior. Didn't she?"

Another silence. I figure the Chaplain's debating if he can get away with saying nothing this time. Apparently, he decides not.

"Again, I am so sorry."

"Who was the mother? It's not another cop, is it? If it is, I swear, I'd kill her myself if she wasn't already dead. And how did she die? And how did you get those kids?"

"She was Jennifer Williamson. She was not a cop," the Chaplain says. "But the rest is too much to tell right now. You deal with the kids. You get some sleep. You put up the signal when you're ready. Then we'll talk."

"No, dammit, we'll talk now. Who was this bitch?"

But he's gone. I fight off the urge to call him back. He's told me never to do that. I tried, once. He blocked the call, buried the burner in the desert, and got a new one.

You don't call the Chaplain. He calls you.

CHAPTER TWO

—·—

S unlight through the window blinds stabs me awake around eight. I'm huddled in the kitchen chair where I sank last night. I can't think, can't feel. Duke is curled against my feet. He wakes when I do and gives me the look a dog gets when things aren't right in the house.

I still pay the bill on Frank's phone, so I can call to hear him on the voicemail. He was a lieutenant in the patrol bureau, but he liked to take a shift from time to time and hit the street himself. One of those times was the last day of his life. Sometimes I'll leave him a message. "Why weren't you more careful? Why didn't you shoot first?"

I fish my phone out of my pocket and call his number. His phone warbles from its drawer in the kitchen, goes to voicemail.

"You asshole!" I scream.

That brings a stir from one of the car seats parked on the kitchen floor from last night. My God! Frank's kids!

One cries, the other joins in, they howl in earnest.

I shuffle over. The girl reaches for me. I bend down and wrestle her free from the car-seat harness. She flails into my arms. She's warm and heavy and settles against my chest. The crying subsides and I set her on the floor to unbuckle the boy.

They watch me, looking confused and wary. The girl's already beautiful, with her wavy auburn hair. The boy's resemblance to Frank stops my heart again.

I push over the toys the Chaplain brought last night. Sonny grabs the teddy bear, Rose the pony. They clutch them to their chests and continue staring at me.

Diapers, I think. Their diapers must need changing by now. I dig into a box of Huggies, take out two and point to the living room. They toddle with me to the sofa and lie still while I change them. I'm slow at figuring out front from back and making the adhesive tabs work, but I get it done. Duke sniffs the wrapped diapers on the floor.

Food. They must need breakfast. I rummage through their stuff and come up with applesauce in the little single-serving cups from the snack aisle. I grab some, rustle up plastic spoons from another Albertson's bag and set the kids up at the coffee table by the sofa. Soon they're eating, by themselves, thank God. They're messy, but they're eating. I have some applesauce myself, to set an example.

"Sonny," I say as we eat our applesauce, "don't ever become a cop. And, Rose, don't ever marry one."

They look at me when they hear their names, but they don't answer. I find a couple of sippy cups in the Chaplain's box, put two inches of orange juice from the fridge in each one. Rose handles hers just fine, but Sonny knocks his over and somehow manages to spill a little. I attack the spill with a wadded paper towel, wondering how I even know what a sippy cup is.

Breakfast finishes, I wipe their sticky faces and hands. They pick up the teddy bear and pony and wander the living room hand in hand.

"Mommy?" Rose calls.

What to say? Your Mommy is dead, just like your jerk of a father?

They pick up on the pain on my face and wail in unison, "Mommy! Mommy!"

I sprint for the bathroom, leave the door open so I can keep an eye on them and catch sight of myself in the mirror. Face pale as a Kleenex, hair a haystack, big bags under my eyes that drain away what Frank called their ocean blue color. Frank Forsythe, did I ever really know you? Are these twins and that woman where the money went?

I collapse onto the rim of the tub and break down in big, wet gulps. They hear me and soon a regular chorus of crying is going on.

I have to get control. I run cold water into a face towel and press it to my eyes, suck in deep, shuddering breaths. Duke paces between me and them, whining.

A plan. I need a plan. I'll take them to Child Protective Services, that's what I said last night. Let CPS find homes for them.

Lita will be here soon. Mondays she gets in early, so she's due any minute. She can help me get them ready and out the door.

Lita—Estrellita Gomez—is the part-time assistant at my little business, Jacinto Investigations. She comes from a huge Palm Springs family, with more *tias* and *primas* than I can keep track of.

She's taking paralegal courses and hopes to be a lawyer someday. She's the smartest kid I know, works harder than anyone I ever met, and keeps a framed eight-by-ten glossy of herself in a purple *quinceañera* gown on her desk. In the photo, as in real life, she's more beautiful than she can make herself believe: flawless skin, liquid brown eyes, and a shape that draws the male gaze like a magnet. Still, she frets about her hips and is somehow always between boyfriends. But that's how it is with girls. Hiring her was the best career move I made after I decided Frank's death was a message from the universe, took my retirement after twenty years with a badge, and started my business.

Duke follows me out of the bathroom and goes over to the kids. Their crying lets up when he noses between them. Rose says something that sounds like "Ookie."

Duke's tail swishes against Rose's cheek and she baby-giggles. She pets him and Sonny pulls his ear. He grins in dog bliss. Oh, yeah. They've spent time together.

Shit.

The kids move to the patio door as if to be ready to escape from this strange place and this angry woman. I let them be and start repacking their stuff. CPS should be open by nine.

There's a knock on the front door and Lita steps in with a bright 'Hello.' As usual she turns straight into the former den that now serves as the headquarters of Jacinto Investigations, Dana Forsythe, proprietor and licensed private investigator.

I hear a purse and folio smack down on the office desk and remember what she's working on: An attorney named Leroy Huggins has hired us to track down a Bill Davis who witnessed a car accident that paralyzed Huggins's client.

The problem is, "Bill Davis" is all the cop on the scene wrote down. No address, no full name, no license number, just "Bill Davis." Of whom there've turned out to be no fewer than eleven in Palm Springs and nearby cities.

So Lita's slogging through the list, hitting the databases we subscribe to, calling, messaging on Facebook, Twitter, and Instagram, even knocking on doors when nothing else works.

So far, nothing has, but Lita's a digital bloodhound. I suspect she knows more about databases than some of the people who run them.

And what she doesn't know, her autistic cousin Guillermo definitely does. He's fourteen, morbidly obese, never makes eye contact, and can take a computer to places I don't want to know about. Between him and Lita, it's just a matter of time till the right Bill Davis is telling us what he saw that night.

She comes into the kitchen for our morning scoping session, stops short when she sees the twins.

She turns to me and starts to speak but changes her mind at the sight of my face.

I step over to the Keurig and start a dark roast.

Rose whimpers. Lita kneels to the kids with a smile. "*Hola, hijitos.*"

Their wary expressions thaw a little. She opens her arms, they move in for hugs. She murmurs to them while I set out mugs, sugar, and cream.

Lita untangles herself and comes to the table. The kids slide to the floor, clutching the pony and teddy bear, lean together as if glued at the shoulders.

I pour coffee and stare into my mug. There's no place to start this.

Lita gets herself a mug of coffee and slips into the chair across from me. "Okay. What is going on?"

I turn away from Sonny and Rose and whisper, "These are Frank's kids. Their mother's been killed."

Lita's eyebrows shoot up, her mouth drops open. "What! They're Frank's?"

Sonny says, "Daddy?"

Lita drops her voice. "How did you...killed...how...Frank's... - -?" She sees I can't answer, goes quiet.

"She was killed last night," I finally manage.

"How? What happened?"

"I don't know."

"How did you get her kids?"

"Mm." I roll my eyes.

"Ah. The Chaplain."

That's all Lita knows about the Chaplain—the name. She knows nothing of his ties to Frank, or to the Moguls, and doesn't bother asking anymore.

"Yep."

"But you are gonna find out what happened, right? We're gonna find out?"

"Absolutely not! I don't want anything to do with Frank's woman or his damned kids! I just want all of it out of my life. Right now!"

"Whew!" She looks around the kitchen and at the gear by the patio door. "Why are you packing everything up? Didn't they just get here?"

We're not whispering now. These words are too big to muffle.

"I'm going to take them to CPS. No way am I keeping that bastard's kids."

"CPS? *Nunca!*" Lita says. "They'll have to live with strangers! They might get separated and never even know each other!"

"Not my problem."

She pushes her chair back and rises. "Dana! I can't believe this! You can't toss them out like trash."

"Well, I sure can't keep them. They're going to CPS. Today. Right now, in fact."

"They're your last link to Frank. You don't do right by them, how you gonna live with yourself?"

"Sorry, but no," I tell her. "I'm not keeping them. It's a legal requirement anyway. Orphaned kids go to CPS."

"Look at them, they're just babies. Helpless babies! You're all they have now. How can you even think of doing that?"

The twins are still watching us. They may not know what's going on, but they're old enough to read the emotion in grownup voices.

I storm over to the sink, fling the rest of my coffee down the drain, and hiss-whisper so the kids don't hear. "Screw Frank and screw her!"

"Let me call Mom," Lita says. "She's a licensed foster parent. I'm sure she will take them and work it out with CPS to keep them while we come up with a plan."

"Whatever. As long as they're out of my house."

Lita brightens, punches in her mother Yolanda's number, and there's a long conversation in machine-gun Spanish. About all I catch is, "*dos bebes*" and "*si, gemelos*" and "*su madre está muerta.*"

She hangs up with a smile. "She said she'll do it, and we should bring them over now."

"Really? I mean, two little kids that just lost their mom? You sure Yolanda is willing - -"

Lita waves it off. "You've met her. You know how she likes children. Being a mom, that's her life."

I'm startled at the wave of relief that washes over me. None of this is these kids' fault. I draw my first deep breath since last night. "All right. But I'm still letting CPS know."

Lita starts collecting the twins' things. "Mom will do that. She has fostered CPS kids before. They know her."

I get the fob to Frank's Crown Victoria from the bowl by the patio door and start it with the remote so the air conditioner can cool it off before we put Rose and Sonny in. Then I help Lita with the packing.

There's a minor crisis when we discover that Sonny has somehow lost his right shoe and one green sock. We scour the house, find the shoe in the toilet, but never do find the sock. I rinse off the shoe, put it in a big Ziploc, and we're ready.

Lita takes the car seats out to the Vic and straps them into the back seat, then returns for the supplies.

I lead the twins onto the patio and it's like walking into a sauna, even with the shade from the roof.

And when we step into the sun, it's like someone in the sauna just pointed a blow-dryer at our faces. The weather app on my phone says it'll get up to 117 later today, and the patio thermometer says it's already 101. Sweat beads on my forehead and my armpits feel sticky.

All part of another day in paradise, why desert people go nocturnal in the summertime. We scuttle from air-conditioned houses to air-conditioned cars to air-conditioned offices to air-conditioned shops and question our life choices.

As Lita lifts Sonny into his car seat, he pulls back and looks around. "Daddy? Daddy here?"

Rose toddles up beside him, eyes bright, and pats the upholstery. "Daddy?"

They've been in this car before. Lita and I exchange a stare.

"No Daddy today, *hijito*," Lita says. "You hop in now, okay?"

Sonny clambers into his seat.

Lita walks Rose around to the other side of the Vic. "Your turn, *Princesa*. You climb in, okay?"

Rose gets in and Lita buckles her up. The children smile at each other and look around Daddy's car.

Lita tugs my arm. "C'mon, Dana. We have to do this." She walks to her Subaru, which is parked behind the Vic, gets in, and waits.

I force myself into motion, slide in behind the wheel, start the car, and put the AC on max.

Frank loved the Crown Victoria. Like a lot of cops, even younger ones, he wouldn't drive anything else on duty. "Nothing says 'cop' like a Vic," he'd tell me.

He never forgave the Ford Motor Company for killing the Vic a few years ago, and he bought himself one of the last civilian models off the line.

I drive it instead of my Jeep sometimes because it's a piece of him, same as his phone. It still smells like his damned Partagas cigars. There's even a Partagas butt in the ash tray that I haven't been able to throw away. Today I gag on the smell and shove the ash tray shut. Maybe it's time to sell the Vic.

Or run it off a cliff. How often was she in this car, in the front seat beside him, with Sonny and Rose in the back seat like they are now? Did she put her hand on his thigh, like I used to do? Did he turn to her and give her that smile?

Shit.

I turn and check the kids behind me. They return my gaze, untroubled and ready for a ride in Daddy's car.

Suddenly I can't breathe. I open the door, stagger out, bend over and heave up coffee and what's left of my applesauce.

Lita bursts from the Subaru and rushes over. "Dana! What's happening? Are you...?"

I try to stand. Bright spots flash on and off in my vision. My chest is tight. I lean on a fender and suck in deep gulps of air.

Lita hugs me. "It's a panic attack. Just breathe, Dana. Breathe."

I try. It's a few minutes before I can stand up all the way. "I can't...can't do this. You take them, okay? Just take them."

"But don't you want - -"

I wave her off. "Just go."

She transfers twins and gear to her car, and takes off down the hill toward town.

Chapter Three

—·—

Back inside, I build myself a Moscow mule, see from the clock it's not even ten yet, and park the drink in the refrigerator. I brew another dark roast and rely on caffeine to get me through as I surf the websites of the *Palm Springs Herald* and the local TV stations.

They don't have much yet, just a brief release from media relations at the public safety department about a female gunshot victim named Jennifer Williamson being found along Gene Autry Trail a mile south of Interstate 10.

I try to push it away for some other day, after I've had time to sleep and process and maybe get good and drunk.

But Jennifer Williamson won't let me.

I search her out on social media. There are what seem like a million hits on Facebook and Instagram, nearly all with pictures of her.

The first thing I notice is the face.

It's not the cascade of auburn curls or the porn-star body that stops me. It's Jennifer Williamson's face.

It's not what I expected. It's not sultry and pouty to match the body.

No, Jennifer looks more like a Botticelli Madonna. A sweet, inno-cent face with fawn eyes that say, "Love me and take care of me and I'll love you back like you've never been loved before."

I shove the laptop away and take my coffee out to pace the patio. That lasts about five minutes, then the blast-furnace heat drives me back inside.

Where the laptop waits on the dining table, that face still on the screen.

I scroll past it and try to act more like the investigator I'm supposed to be. Jennifer's Facebook profile says she works at the Desert Chamber of Commerce, has two kids, and is "in a relationship."

Yeah, with my husband!

The photos roll past, with me daring a dead woman to have posted a shot of herself with Frank.

She didn't. Lots of pictures with Sonny and Rose from infancy through a week before her death, lots of selfies of that face and body, but none that show Frank.

Except one that I scroll past, then pull back into view. It's taken in front of the San Diego Zoo. The twins in a double stroller, Jennifer killing it in big mirror sunglasses, a white sun dress and sun hat to match, head tilted, beaming a love smile at the camera.

But who was the object of that love smile? That's not clear until I spot the photographer's reflection in Jennifer's sunglasses and zoom in for a closer look. He's too backlit to be more than a silhouette, but he's got good shoulders and a cowboy hat.

I recognize those shoulders and that hat. The shoulders were the first thing I noticed about Frank when we met. And the hat is the Stetson hanging on a hook outside my patio door right now. I bought it for him after he had a basal cell carcinoma removed from his neck and made him wear it whenever he went out in the desert sun.

The silhouette in that Stetson was my husband and he took that picture of his woman and his kids at the zoo, just like any proud father would. How many of the other Internet pictures of her did he take?

I think back and try to connect the date on that photograph with San Diego. Then I remember: He went there for a rally of the California Crown Victoria Club, and I went to Coachella with my reporter friend Liz Hernandez.

I slam the laptop shut, go out and grab the Stetson off its hook, throw it on the barbecue and light the gas. Blue-orange flames eat through the brim and climb up the crown, then the whole Stetson blazes and curls and stinks of burning wool. It makes me feel better, but not much.

I go out to the carport and climb into the Vic and start for the crime scene. The news didn't say exactly where on Gene Autry the shooting took place, but it shouldn't be hard to spot.

It's not, because it's surrounded by yellow crime scene tape, that and desert sand dotted with mesquite bushes and spiky ocotillo plants bowing before a ferocious wind howling down the Interstate from San Gorgonio Pass. There's no more than light breezes elsewhere in the area, but up here it's gotta be at least forty mph, maybe fifty in the gusts. The sky is khaki-colored with airborne grit and tongues of sand are licking out across Gene Autry. Visibility on the road can't be more than half a mile.

A unit from Palm Springs Public Safety is parked on the shoulder. It's occupied by a female officer I don't recognize. She's gazing at her phone and looking bored as hell as the wind rocks her SUV. Behind her is another unit with a male officer stowing a metal detector in the trunk.

I slow down to pull over in hopes of a cop-to-ex-cop chat with the two officers about what they've found. Then I realize that will shoot me straight to the top of the suspect list when Homicide figures out my late husband fathered the late victim's two kids, who just happen to have ended up at my house after her death.

This thing is starting to feel like a python around my neck. I speed up and hope neither of them recognizes Frank's Vic as I roll past and the wind rips away a ribbon of crime scene tape. A left turn at the first crossroad takes me to Indian Canyon Drive and back to the house without having to pass them again.

Once home, I open the front door and take a phone picture looking downhill toward Chapel City and Palm Desert and the grid of cities beyond. It's a pretty nice day so it's a pretty nice picture, with only a little blur from the haze kicked up by the wind.

I post the image on my Facebook page and caption it, "Another beautiful day in the desert," because that's how I signal the Chaplain when I need him. His rule, not mine, but that's how it works.

The thing is, there's no guessing how long it'll take him to call. Could be ten minutes, could be ten hours. Once it was three days.

The Moscow mule in the freezer is still thawed, so I pull it out and flick on the TV to drink and wait. Three or four more, I calculate, will get me through to bedtime without making me too drunk to talk to the Chaplain when he calls. I'm not going to accomplish anything useful today, so why not?

Twenty minutes later, I'm starting the second mule when the Chaplain's burner number comes up on my phone.

"All right, let's talk," I say. "Can you come up here?"

"Only in emergencies. You know the rule."

"So when? Where?"

"You know the Del Taco in Chapel City?" he says. "Meet me there at two a.m.. We'll go up to the windmills."

"Really? The middle of the night and you still can't come to the house for an hour?"

"Park in the back. Don't bring the Vic."

Then he's gone, and I've got a long day to kill. Luckily, I've got plenty of Smirnoff, lime juice, and ginger beer, so the mules won't run out.

Chapter Four

— · —

A few minutes before two the next morning, I'm headed for my rendezvous with the Chaplain. The hangover isn't nearly as bad as I expected.

When I turn my Jeep into the Del Taco parking lot, the smell of fat, grease, and refried beans lingers in the air. But the lights are out and there are no cars to be seen.

Nor is there a motorcycle. Where's the Chaplain?

As soon as I nose up to the rear of the building and switch off my engine, I hear a motorcycle cough to life. A headlight flashes from the deeper shadows behind a dumpster. A Harley pulls into sight, the headlight out now, with the Chaplain in his leather Moguls vest just visible in the moonlight.

He stops and hands me a helmet with a built-in headset. I put it on, straddle the pillion seat in back, and zip up my windbreaker. He switches on his headlight, and we're on our way.

Nighttime is when the Palm Springs summer redeems itself. This night, it's cooled off to about eighty with a full moon riding high in the sky, perfect motorcycle weather. Even better, Palm Springs bans street lights to preserve the night desert view. We ride through the darkness like we're in an Armageddon movie where all the humans are gone but the buildings remain. No light except the moon and stars and the cone of white from the Chaplain's headlight.

As he heads north up Indian Canyon Drive, I realize this is not just the first time he's let me on his bike. It's also the first time I've had my arms around a man since Frank died.

Plus, there's a big, loud Harley engine throbbing between my knees, and the moonlight doesn't hurt. At first the surge of heat seems like a betrayal of Frank. Then I remember Jennifer and the twins, and figure it serves him right.

But I shut the feeling down. Because this motorcycle is driven by a man so mysterious I don't even know his government name, much less which team he bats for.

He's just the Chaplain—the tattoos, the beard, the leather smell of his vest with a hint of male sweat, enough melanin in a hound-like face to tell me he's mixed race, but features so ambiguous I can't guess what the mixture is. A highwayman on a chrome horse who comes only by night and might as well not exist by day. A man who, when he reaches up to grab the Harley's apehanger handlebars, looks like Christ on the cross.

Focus, I tell myself. This meeting is supposed to be about - - well, about everything in the past twenty-four hours.

We're up in north Palm Springs now, the homes and industrial parks giving way to stretches of vacant land.

"So how the hell did we get here?" I say into the little mike on my helmet. "I feel like I'm living on a different planet."

"Are you sure you want to hear this?"

"I think I have to."

We leave Palm Springs behind and start across a stretch of desert between the city limits and the 10, which is what people here call the Interstate. The Chaplain throttles back and watches the left side of the blacktop. He finally spots what he's looking for, shuts off his head-light, and swings onto a one-lane road leading out into a wind farm. It dead-ends at a No Trespassing sign put up by the wind company. He eases the bike around it and continues on through the desert sand.

A quarter mile in, he stops the Harley, cuts the engine, and we're alone with the big blades whirling overhead. Windmills have their own sound--the low thrum of a diesel locomotive on a distant track, combined with the soft sigh of a window fan in another room. Under the jeweled sky, they're like an army of ghosts waving the departed along to...well, to whatever comes next. Which has to be easier than what's come lately.

We drop our helmets onto the sand and lean against the Harley. The Chaplain clears his throat.

"This is how Frank told it to me," he says. "I don't vouch for any of it."

"Understood."

And here's what he tells me.

One afternoon, Frank's on patrol on Palm Canyon Drive when a silver Toyota blows through a red light just south of the Sand Trap Roadhouse. Lights and siren, the Toyota pulls over, Frank walks up. The window whirs down and there's this face looking up at him.

"Yeah," I interrupt. "I've seen it."

"What?"

"Facebook, Instagram, she plastered it all over the Internet."

"You've been st- -"

"Yes, stalking her online. How could I not?"

"Of course."

The Chaplain resumes his story.

Frank tells the owner of the face she ran a red light and he needs to see her license and registration.

She fishes the paperwork out of her purse and the console and hands it over. Frank takes a quick look, tells her to wait while he goes to his cruiser to write the ticket.

When he comes back, she lowers the sunglasses, turns those eyes full on him and says, "I'm loud, I'm multi-orgasmic, and I've never had sex with a cop."

I have to interrupt again.

"A badge bunny? Come on, Frank got hit on by badge bunnies every day. All male cops do. He'd tell me about it and we'd have a good laugh."

"So he said. But never like this. She was inside his head before he knew what hit him. That's how he put it."

"Oh, bullshit!" I hiss. But at the same time, I believe it. I've seen that face.

"She said the same thing about him," the Chaplain continues after a moment.

"What?"

"Jennifer. I presented myself. I told her Frank asked me to watch over her. She came to trust me. After that, he was all she could talk about. He walked up to her car and she got a look at him. It was game over. She couldn't let him get away."

"Jesus." But what I'm thinking is, I know what that's like.

Frank and I met in Slab City, a sprawling squatter camp in the desert southeast of Palm Springs. The occasion was a joint warrant sweep through the Slabs by his employer, the Palm Springs Public Safety Department, and mine, the county sheriff's office.

After the roundup, we went for drinks and dinner at the Surf Inn in a crumbling resort town near the Slabs called Bamboo Beach. He drank his Manhattan, I drank my Moscow mule, we looked at each other, and that was it. We canceled the dinner order, rented a room upstairs, and screwed our brains out till we got hungry and ordered burgers from the bar. An Elvis impersonator married us in Las Vegas thirteen days later.

"Her exact words," the Chaplain says, "were, 'I was tired of following my crotch around, and my baby bell was clanging like a fire alarm. Then Frank came along and I didn't look back.'"

He fishes a match and a joint out of his vest, strikes the match with a thumbnail, and lights up. He takes a deep draw and passes the joint to me for a hit.

"Nice night," he says.

Which is true enough. Yesterday's gale has subsided to a pleasant breeze and the tang of mesquite laces the air.

But, all things considered, a nice night?

"Would have been forty-eight hours ago," I say.

The Chaplain is silent for a while. Then, "What'd you do with Frank's twins?"

I explain about Lita's mom taking them.

"For how long?"

"That's up to CPS. I just have to get them out of my life so I can get this out of my head."

"They're all we have left of Frank," he says.

"We?"

"He saved my life in Afghanistan."

"What?"

"We were both working security for Triple Diamond."

"He never told me about that. What happened?"

The Chaplain takes a hit on the joint and passes it back to me.

"Have you heard of moral injury?"

"Sure, in PTSD training. It's when you see a thing so horrible you think you should have stopped it, even if you couldn't, and it eats you alive."

"Or when you did it yourself."

"You did?"

"Another time maybe," he says. "It's hard to talk about."

Now the conversation has stalled out, and I try to think how to get it back to what I don't want to talk about, but have to.

"How'd you get those kids anyway?" I ask him.

"I heard the traffic on my scanner about Jennifer being shot. I headed for her place and picked up the kids from the babysitter. I brought them to you."

"The babysitter just let you have them?"

"Teenager from next door. The kids knew me. They called me Unca Harley. The girl had seen me over there."

After a long silence, I pick up the hard part again. "So it was love at first sight with my husband and that...that, woman?"

"They both said that. He got off shift after the traffic stop, he went to her place. They - -"

"Don't paint me a picture."

"Sorry."

"Go on, just not too much detail." I pass him the joint and he draws on it.

"They spent every moment together they could," he says. "Right away she was asking him to leave you and marry her."

"But he didn't."

"He really loved you."

"The bastard picked a fine way to show it."

"She stopped her birth control without telling him. She was three months along when he noticed. She asked him again. He still wouldn't leave you."

"Sonny and Rose are his for sure?"

"He got a DNA test."

So, the Chaplain tells me, one thing led to another. Jennifer's apartment was too small for the kids, and she talked Frank into buying her a condo. Also a car, a compact SUV, because it was safer for the kids and had more room for their stuff than her old Toyota. Then she went part-time at the Chamber of Commerce so she could be a better mother. Frank had to pay even more of the bills.

"So that's where the money went."

"Must be," he says. "You never suspected?"

"Never," I say. "He always handled our finances, so...and there was no funny business with his phone or his laptop, he was always where he was supposed to be when he was supposed to be there, and he acted the same as always with me. Even in bed."

"Huh."

"I'll say. Was he a sociopath?"

"I think he just got lost in this one thing. Otherwise, he was the straightest shooter I ever knew."

It takes me a moment to choke down my feelings and speak again. "Who killed her?"

"I don't know," he says. "But I worried about her. She was broken after Frank died. She drank a lot. She partied a lot. She did coke sometimes. She saw a lot of different men. She wouldn't tell me anything about them."

Another pause as he draws on the joint. "I supplied her with the coke. So she wouldn't have to be out looking for street scrapings. But...I was supposed to watch over her. Now look."

"Did you and she ever...?"

"She was Frank's woman." He offers me the joint.

"Pass. A couple more hits and I'll be dancing with those windmills."

He shrugs. If the marijuana has affected him, it doesn't show.

"You gonna take care of whoever did it?" I ask.

"Only if I have to. My handler isn't on the case, so he doesn't want me involved. I'll let Homicide take their shot. If they strike out I'll deal with him myself. Will you take a look?"

"Why would I wanna bust the guy who killed her? Good riddance if you ask me."

"Dana."

"All right, maybe I'm not my best self right now. But...no, I gotta stay out of this or I'll lose my mind."

A couple of minutes pass while he draws on the joint and contemplates the windmills.

"So," I ask, "am I a suspect?"

"No. I took care of it."

"How?"

"I checked the engines on your Jeep and the Vic before I brought the twins up. They were cold. I told my handler. You're in the clear unless they get a hit on Uber or Lyft or a cab."

"They won't."

The Chaplain falls into a silence that stretches on and on.

"What?"

He pulls a manila envelope from inside his vest and passes it over. "I got these from my handler."

I shake it, feel it. "You brought crime scene photos? Seriously?"

"She was shot once in the throat. And five times in...you'll see."

I throw the envelope at him. "No, I won't. I don't want to look at these. I just want that woman out of my life. And out of my head."

He slides the envelope back inside his vest, pinches out the joint, and tucks it back into his vest, too. "We're done, then."

We mount the Harley, he cranks up and nurses the machine through the sand to the blacktop and we start for the Del Taco where we left my Jeep.

A few minutes later he drops me off. I open the driver's door, then turn and stick out my hand. "Give me the damn envelope."

He hands it over and pulls away. He doesn't turn on his headlight till he's back on the street and headed west. I take that to mean he lives somewhere in that direction, but I have no idea where.

I drive home, throw the envelope on the kitchen table, wrap myself in a blanket, and drop down on an Adirondack chair on the patio. I gaze out over the scattered lights of the cities at my feet and the dark desert floor beyond and try to figure out who the hell I married.

Then I smell cigar smoke and there's Frank beside me in his own Adirondack, legs outstretched, ankles crossed. He's smoking a Partagas, he's dressed in his off-duty uniform of shorts and a Vic owners club t-shirt. And he's wearing the Stetson.

He's not a ghost risen from the dead, not a dream or hallucination. I call him Imaginary Frank. He lives in my head and shows up once in a while for a chat. Usually I don't mind. Having him there has helped me to get through it, to the extent that I have.

But tonight is different.

"I burned that Stetson," I tell him.

"I saw," he says.

"I'm not sorry."

"I wouldn't expect you to be."

"Bastard."

"Apparently so."

"The Chaplain says you really loved me."

"I did."

"Then how did this happen?"

He blows Partagas smoke into the night breeze coming up the canyon. "I only know what the Chaplain told you."

"Right, because you live only in my head."

"Yep." He takes a puff on the Partagas.

"I've missed you terribly, Frank. Your voice, your hands on my ass when we would make love, your weight on me right before you would roll off after, the way your hair curled over your ears when you needed a trim, which by the way you do now."

"I did love that ass of yours. I told you so, right?"

"Many times, but never mind. You have any idea who killed her?"

He draws on the Partagas. "How would I?"

"Right, right. You only know what I know. Which it turns out wasn't very damned much!"

"Love you, baby," says the empty Adirondack beside me. The smell of Partagas smoke slips away on the breeze.

Chapter Five

A shaft of white from the morning sun wakes me on the patio. I'm still in my Adirondack chair from the chat with Imaginary Frank last night.

As I hit the kitchen to make coffee, I spot the envelope of crime scene photos on the table where I tossed it when I came in. It's like plutonium as it lies there, radioactive and glowing.

I shouldn't, but I can't not. I slice open the envelope with a steak knife and dump out the photos.

They're harsh and stark under the police photographer's flash in the desert night. Jennifer is sprawled on her back on the shoulder of the road, arms outflung.

It appears the first shot caught her just above the breastbone and passed directly through her neck. The bullet hole is surrounded by a speckling of powder burns. Under her neck is a dark patch on the sand that must be blood.

And the other five shots the Chaplain told me about?

Jennifer's white jeans are bloody from a few inches below the waist to her upper thighs, and there's another dark stain on the sand below. The shooter, it seems, put the last five rounds between her legs.

I've seen crime-scene photos before, too many of them, but nothing like this. I push down a surge of grim satisfaction and try to look away.

But my eyes are locked on those photos. They're a cliff, and I'm about to slide over it into total madness. I slap them face-down, stuff them back into the envelope and toss it into the junk drawer.

I'm still breathing hard when my phone jangles the Star Wars theme and the caller ID says it's Ike Skogel, the lawyer who gives me most of my business.

Before I can say hello, words spray out of him like water from a loose garden hose, his voice going shrill as his delivery accelerates.

"Hey, Dana, listen," he says. "This guy from Slab City got arrested for that shooting up on Gene Autry and I drew the short straw under my contract with the city and now I gotta defend him. You got time to work the investigation?"

Jesus, will this thing never let go of me?

I fill Ike in on the dumpster fire my life has become in the past thirty-six hours--Frank, Jennifer, the twins, Lita, Yolanda, all of it.

When I finish, the silence tells me he's as astounded as I am. At last he manages, "My God. How you holding up?"

"How do you think? I'm upside down and I've got no idea how to flip myself back. So I want no part of this. I just want it to leave me alone."

"I feelya," he says. "I feelya. But really, this'll be a piece of cake. We just need to make sure they don't put the guy away without a fair trial."

"No," I say. "No. I don't want it and it has to be some kind of conflict anyway, right?"

Ike falls silent again as he thinks it over. I know from long experience he's about to say something terrible. He doesn't disappoint.

"Not if you want to get him off. This guy that gave this woman payback for what she did to you, you don't want to see him walk?"

"Hell, no!" I'm shouting now. "I don't want to think about it, much less investigate it. I'm out!"

There's another few seconds of silence, then Ike sighs and lets his decent side show a little. "Okay, understood. But I'll keep you posted, yeah?"

"Don't!" I tap the call off.

I look around the kitchen, see the sippy cups in the sink, notice I'm still in yesterday's clothes. How the hell am I in the middle of Frank's orphans, his dead mistress, and her murder?

A shower, that'll help me calm down. I make a break for the bathroom and stand under the hot, soothing spray far longer than usual. I step out, wrap myself in a towel from the warmer Frank gave me for Christmas three years ago, and let the tears come.

I'm standing there crying and dripping, nothing on but that towel, when those photos drag me back to the junk drawer like I'm on a wire. Somebody wearing my skin shakes them out onto the counter, flips through them again. The ones that show Jennifer's face over that little hole in her throat. And the ones that show what those last five shots did between her legs.

I tear my eyes away, stuff the photos back into the envelope, walk out to the patio, and toss it onto the remains of Frank's Stetson in the barbecue.

A click and a hiss, and the blue-white flames lick up around the edges of the envelope. It starts to brown and curl. Then I yank it out, throw it to the tile floor, stamp it out, and put in a call to Ike.

I'm still in my towel staring at the photos, now back on the counter, when he answers.

"Hell, yes, I'll help you get the guy off." I say. "In fact, I'll buy him a drink for turning that bitch into roadkill."

He's silent for a long moment. "If you're sure you can be a hundred percent. I mean it's so personal - -"

"You're trying to talk me out of it, now? If I say I'm in, I'm in. All the way."

"Well, okay then. We need to go see our client, I guess. A couple of detectives from Palm Springs Homicide arrested him out in the Slabs yesterday and brought him back up here and the fucking idiot gave them a statement."

I put on my investigator hat, try to be the professional I'm supposed to be. "Anybody we know?"

"None other than our old pal Johnny Bottemueller."

"Johnny B? From the arson case?"

"That's him," Ike says. "It just hit the news. You didn't see it?"

"Not yet. Did he do it?"

"I don't know and I don't wanta know. You've heard the mantra: He's innocent until proved guilty and our job is to make sure he gets a vigorous defense."

"Yeah, right."

"Ten o'clock at the Palm Springs jail then?"

"Roger that."

I'm about to tap off when I remember what I forgot.

"Frank's kids?" I ask him. "Am I in trouble just for having them overnight?"

"I'll make some calls. Let me worry about it for a while."

"Thanks," I tell him. "I owe you."

And I mean it. When I was a cop, I was always terrified when Ike stood up to cross-examine me. He's brilliant in his sleazy way and he's merciless.

But now he's what I want. If you sell out and go to work for the defense bar, you at least want it to be somebody who knows the game.

CHAPTER SIX

— · —

I start my day with a news cruise. The bomb has gone off.

The *Herald* web page has a big headline reading *Gene Autry victim shot five times in torso*. It's over a crime scene photo of Jennifer's body with the area between her legs blurred out. Somehow, that makes it look even more obscene. "Accused killer Johnny Bottemueller," the copy reads, "has denied the charges."

The reporter is my pal Liz Hernandez. We swapped information in my days as a deputy with the sheriff's office, eventually became close friends, and she was my rock during those first weeks after Frank died.

Liz has dynamite looks and dynamite sources, and not by coincidence. All the best crime reporters I ever knew were attractive women, because no man is more male than a male cop. When she turns on her smile, cops start talking.

I shut down my laptop and start for the meeting with Johnny B. It's the kind of Palm Springs day when you don't go out if you can stay in. As I pull in at the jail a little after ten, the Jeep's dash tells me the temperature's already at 103. And the *Herald* reported a couple weeks ago that, when it's 100 degrees outside a parked car, the temperature inside will hit 140 in fifteen minutes.

I crack the windows a half inch, spread silver sun deflectors across the dashboard, and make a break for it. I feel like a burger on a griddle as I hurry across the asphalt parking lot, briefcase tucked against my chest and sweat trickling down my temples and armpits.

Blessedly, the sidewalk is shaded by the building and made of white concrete instead of gray asphalt. Compared to the parking lot, it's an oasis.

I push through the entry door, pause in the vestibule for a few breaths of sweet air-conditioned oxygen, then push through a second set of heavy glass doors into the lobby.

A guard flicks her eyes from my ID to my face and back again, digs through my briefcase, doesn't bother to examine the envelope of photos stuffed amidst a thick packet of documents. She watches as I pass through the metal detector, then escorts me through a bank-vault style door with a power lock that cracks like a gunshot as it shuts behind us.

The guard's nametag says Hurtado. Her face is ruddy, her hair is a tired shade of blond, and she's got a muffin top that laps over her belt. Her brown uniform shirt is plastered against her upper body and her hair is damp where it curls against her neck.

"Long shift?" I ask.

"Since midnight." She grimaces. "They musta bought this AC from Canada. Another hour and I got a date with *mi novio* and a cold Dos Equis."

Hurtado swipes a hand across her forehead, rubs it on the side of her pants, and leads me down a block-walled corridor painted jailhouse green. Widely spaced windows, high up and covered with steel mesh, block more light than they let in, and a corridor that echoes with the voice of every jail I was ever in—keys and handcuffs rattling as the guards walk past, the clangs of doors opening and closing.

And today, this corridor echoes with the lamentations of an unseen woman. "I have to pick my fucking kids up at fucking school by five o'clock or CPS will take 'em again!" she screeches.

From somewhere, another door clangs.

"Hey, motherfuckers, it's my fucking kids!" the woman continues. "Is anybody listening to me?"

Hurtado mutters "Good luck with that, honey," and stops at the steel door of a conference room. She lets me in and locks the door behind me.

Inside, Ike and Johnny B sit at a gray metal table bolted to the floor. It's seen better days, as have the four gray plastic chairs around it. The two men sweat under a ceiling vent that blows out air that's only slightly cool.

The conference room has block walls, too, but they're gray instead of green. On one wall there's a big dark window that I know from experience is one-way glass. A poster beside it warns in large red print, "NO SMOKING. NO BEVERAGES. NO PHYSICAL CONTACT WITH INMATE. YOU ARE UNDER OBSERVATION."

To remove any doubt, there's a video camera mounted on the wall over the window. Protocol says it's not supposed to have audio capability, so the guards can't listen in on attorney-client conversations. But how do you know?

Ike waves me to the chair beside him and across from Johnny B.

Ike's a piece of work. Ridiculous bow ties, wiry hair, big ears, big black-frame glasses on a big-nosed face that looks like the contractor walked off the project halfway through. All sitting on top of hunched shoulders on a scarecrow body, with that voice that goes shrill when he's excited. Just now he's twirling a fidget spinner in one hand.

But he gives me most of my business, he's a magnet for weird and interesting cases, juries love him, and he pays. Promptly.

He makes a show of looking at his watch, then at me. "So you are working today."

It's true, I'm fifteen minutes late. I give Ike an apologetic wave, but only with one finger.

He grins, drops the spinner, and opens a file folder on the table in front of him.

"I need a minute with you first." I jerk a thumb at the door, Ike closes the folder, and Hurtado lets us out into the corridor. I show him my envelope. "Have you seen the crime scene photos?"

"Nah, but I heard the girl was hotter than a stolen Ferrari. What a waste."

I give him the hate stare he deserves and hand him the envelope. He pulls out the photos and flips through them.

He stops at the first one that shows the carnage between her legs. "Holy shit."

"Exactly."

As he flips through the rest, we go back in and slide into our seats. He lays the photos on the table face-down.

Johnny's in the standard jail uniform: orange scrubs and paper flip-flops.

He's gone downhill some since we defended him from the arson charges a few months back. His mud-brown hair looks like it was cut with grass shears and gives off an oily smell. He's bony, with a facial rash that says his last happy meal came through a pipe, and probably the one before that.

Meth is the curse of the Slabs, I suppose. Or maybe the blessing, if you're self-medicating for buried pain. I don't judge how people deal with that, not anymore.

But blessing or curse, the drug seems to like teeth. Johnny has lost another one, I see, and the holdouts look a little more yellow. Meth always goes for the teeth.

He says my name, I nod in recognition and pull out my notebook.

Ike opens his folder and gives Johnny a laser stare. "What did I tell you about talking to cops when I represented you in that arson thing?"

"Not to." Johnny twirls his fingers with intense concentration.

"That arson thing" started when Johnny sold five gallons of kerosene to another Slabber.

A Slabber who, it turned out, bought into the conspiracy theory that cell towers weaken the immune system. He used Johnny's kerosene to make a fertilizer bomb and tried to blow up the only cell tower in the Slabs. Johnny got pulled in as an accomplice.

The case was still dragging on by the time I hung out my shingle and started working with Ike, and we finally got the perp to admit he told Johnny the kerosene was for making meth, not a bomb. Johnny got off and the perp got a long stretch at Uncle Sam's graybar hotel in Victorville.

"And yet you did talk to them. You actually signed a statement." Ike taps the folder. "Johnny, Johnny, Johnny."

Johnny looks Ike straight in the eye. "But this time I am innocent!"

Ike leans back, massages his chin, shoots me a glance. I roll my eyes. Is it possible Johnny's telling the truth?

"You were innocent last time," Ike tells him. "The jury said so. I don't want to hear any more about that."

"No, this time it's for real," Johnny says. "I didn't shoot that lady."

Ike fans the sheets in his folder across the table. "All right, let's walk through what I managed to cadge out of the cops."

He scans the documents for a minute or two. "So there's this guy," he says. "A trucker name of Luis Reynoso. He's headed out to Solipatria to pick up a load of onions for a produce distributor in Palm Desert. He's coming up Gene Autry, about a mile south of the onramp to the 10, he sees something white off the shoulder of the road.

Ike pauses, runs his finger down the page, stops when he finds his spot, continues.

"So it's a little hard to see, this white thing by the road, what with the darkness and all, and Luis has a schedule to meet with his onions, so he tells himself it's just an old mattress somebody dumped."

Ike pauses again, and we study Johnny for his reaction. He looks interested, but that's all. Not freaked. Maybe the homicide detectives didn't tell him this when they questioned him. Maybe it's news to him.

Ike resumes his scan of the police report, and stops with a smile.

"You know what Luis has, Johnny? He has an inner voice that's never wrong. He apparently believes this inner voice is his late grandmother Maria Reynoso, his *abuelita*, and she never lies to him. So his *abuelita* tells Luis, and I quote, 'Luis, *eso no era un colchón*.'"

He looks at Johnny.

"I don't speak Spanish."

"You should learn, Johnny. This county's sixty-five percent Latino. Us gringos are the minority."

"*No comprendo*," Johnny says with a grin.

"'Luis, that was not a mattress'," Ike says. "That's what Maria told him. Not a mattress."

Ike pauses to scan farther down in the report. "So Luis pulls his rig over—he's two or three hundred yards up Gene Autry by now—and he walks all the way back down there through the darkness. Which is not easy for Luis because, as he tells the cops, his hips don't work so good after thirty-four years behind the wheel of a semi."

Ike pauses again and gives Johnny the eye.

"I can see that," Johnny says. "You don't want your joints to seize up, you gotta stay active."

Ike rolls his eyes and picks up the story.

"And what Luis finds is that his *abuelita* is right yet again. It's not a mattress there in the sand beside the road, but a dead woman, a beautiful dead woman, dressed in the kind of white pretty things a beautiful woman wears on a summer night in Palm Springs. And this beautiful woman, she's been shot to death. So Luis calls nine-one-one and here we are. You know where she was shot, Johnny?"

"Uh-uh, the cops wouldn't tell me. They wanted me to tell them."

"Which is why you should never talk to cops, but let's just see."

I turn the photos over and spread them before Johnny. Jennifer sprawled on her back in the sand, the hole in her throat, the blossom of red between her legs with the ugly patch of red-black sand below. I shuffle the photos into a stack with the goriest of the torso shots on top.

Johnny looks at me in horror or a pretty good imitation of it. "For real?"

"One shot through the throat, five between the legs, Johnny. The way I read it, she's standing at the passenger window of a vehicle, maybe talking to the driver, the driver shoots her in the throat. She falls back, he gets out to make sure she's dead, he loses it and puts those last five rounds between her legs. That about right?"

He jumps up. "Jesus, no! I didn't do this!" He flips the photos face down. "I was at music night in the Slabs, at the Range, all night. Sandrat was playing. Ask anybody, they'll vouch that I was there. I told the detectives all this, but they have it in for Slabbers and they hauled me up here anyway."

He looks at us for a reaction. We don't speak.

Johnny shifts, pats his scrubs like he's looking for cigarettes. Then he looks at the sign that tells him he can't smoke and says, "Crap."

He resumes twirling his fingers. "They should be looking for Smokey Hale," he says. "He took off with my weed and my truck while I was at the Range. My wallet, too. He brought my truck back the next morning with a broken headlight and no wallet so I kicked his ass out of my camp. You know how hard it is to get anything fixed in the Slabs?"

"That's all in your statement here," Ike says. "But lay it out for us."

"Like I told the cops," Johnny says. "Smokey gets in at four o'clock in the morning, drunk as hell. My damn truck has a busted headlight and he tells me he was headed to a party in Desert Hot Springs when he hit a road sign and knocked it out."

"What about your wallet?" Ike asks. "They found it under this lady's body. It's how they knew to come looking for you."

"Like I said, it was in my truck when Smokey took off with it. He told me he never knew the wallet was there, and somebody must have stolen it out of the truck at the party. I told that to the detectives. They should be looking for Smokey."

Ike checks the papers in front of him, registers a little surprise. "Which apparently they are," he says. "Any idea where he might be now?"

"Guy like that, who knows? Last I saw him, he told me, 'Screw you, Johnny' and said he's going to hitchhike to someplace less fucked up than the Slabs."

"Pretty low bar there." Ike checks his papers again. "So, you know this Jennifer Williamson at all?"

"Never met her."

"I see the police have your phone."

Johnny nods.

"They gonna find any calls between you and her, texts, pictures of your junk, her junk, anything like that?"

"I said I don't know her."

"They can check," Ike says. "They can tell if your phone pinged on any of the cell towers up around the Gene Autry interchange on the 10 that night. If you had your GPS on, it's gonna tell them everywhere you went. It's not gonna show you were up around there that night?" He gives Johnny his best laser stare.

"Hell, no, I - - hey, I took a video of Sandrat at the Range with my phone that night. That's gotta be worth something, right?"

Ike checks his police report. "Seriously? You tell the police that?"

"I forgot. But they were playing, what? Yeah, 'War Children,' that's it. I love 'War Children.'"

Ike and I exchange mystified glances.

"That Rolling Stones song?" Johnny asks. "'War children, it's just a shot away?'"

It takes me a moment to figure out Johnny's talking about "Gimme Shelter." His name for the song is better.

"'Rape, murder, it's just a shot away.'" I say. "That one?"

"That's it," Johnny says.

"Oh, yeah," Ike says. "I'm familiar with it. So they're gonna find 'War Children' on your phone?"

"With me singing right along."

Ike makes a note. "So this Smokey Hale. What's he to you that you let him stay in your camp?"

Johnny sighs. "He's my cousin, government name Brixton Lee Hale the Third. He's the black sheep of this real rich family back in New York. Trust-fund baby, drifts around wasting his grandfather's money on drugs and women, especially women. He looks like that short actor, what's his name?"

Johnny pauses, tries to pull it up. "Shit. Played the fighter pilot?"

That rings a faint bell. "You mean, ah, wait, Tom Cruise?"

"Yeah, him," Johnny says. "Tom Cruise. Smokey could be his twin brother, except younger. The ladies get one look at him and all of a sudden it's 'Daddy, take me home.' Fuckin' unfair, if you ask me."

"Life is like that," Ike says. "So other than being a lady-killer, what can you tell us about Smokey?"

"Yeah, he shows up at the Slabs sometimes, moves on when he pisses too many people off. A total asshole."

"Who saw you at the Range?" I ask.

Johnny brightens. "Just ask anybody. Monkey, Little Juicy. You know 'em from the arson thing, right? I smoked with 'em, and we killed a couple bottles of vodka while we listened to the music. But, wait, no, they split when the county mounties rolled in and arrested me."

"They split? Where to?"

"They're Slabbers, who knows? Maybe holed up in one of those ghost towns around the Salton, maybe headed for Vegas. Who knows?"

"So I guess we can't talk to them," Ike says. "Now, can we?"

Johnny twirls his fingers again, then brightens.

"Oh, shit! Yeah. I bought some weed from a new guy, this biker named Tick I think it was. His old lady, I can't remember her name, but her head was shaved on one side and she had a really nice ass with a tramp stamp of Tick's name right over the crack. That help?" Johnny's face contracts in alarm. "But don't tell Tick I mentioned her ass, okay?"

"This Tick," I say. "Any chance he has a government name?"

Johnny returns the incredulous stare I expect. "In the Slabs? Nobody has a government name. They all have warrants."

"He's a biker, though?"

"Yeah, he had his cut on."

"A cut? He was wearing a biker vest?," I ask Johnny. "You see his colors? Was he a Gitano maybe?"

The Gitanos run things around the Salton Sea, so they'd be the logical ones to be dealing drugs in the Slabs.

"Green patch," I continue. "With a red vampire kind of a guy on a Harley?"

"Nope, more of an A-rab riding a cross between a Harley and a camel."

"A Mogul? Tick's a Mogul?"

"Yeah, that's it," Johnny says. "That's what it said on his cut. 'Moguls MC.'"

"In the Slabs?" Ike asks. "And the Gitanos haven't stomped his ass?"

Johnny raises his hands with a pushing motion. "I stay out of biker business."

"Wise choice," Ike says. "So does Tick have his own camp or what?"

"I heard he has a rig he works out of when he's in the Slabs, but I don't know where he parks it. He's new." Johnny frowns, twirls his fingers and looks like he needs a hit of something. "When can I get out of here?"

"If Tick backs you up, I'll go for a bail hearing and try to get you OR-ed," Ike says.

"Get me what?"

"OR-ed. Released on your own recognizance, no bail required."

Ike shoots me a look and jerks his head at the door. Time to go.

Hurtado lets us out, and we pause in the vestibule to click our remote starts so the AC will cool off our cars before we get in.

"Whattaya think?" Ike asks.

"I think I'm buying it. Provisionally at least."

"Yeah," Ike says. "I'm used to Johnny lying. He's different this time."

We decide to start for the Slabs early the next morning. For one thing, it'll be cooler. For another, Slabbers tend to sleep in. It'll be easier to catch them in their camps.

"How do we find this Tick guy?" Ike asks.

"He's a Mogul."

"Ah," Ike says. "The Chaplain."

I pull out my phone, take a shot of the parking lot through the glass of the vestibule door, and put up the "beautiful day in the desert" signal on Facebook.

Outside, heat monkeys dance on the asphalt griddle of the parking lot. Not a cloud in the sky, a blue so bright your eyes hurt. The palm trees along the sides bow before a hot, dry wind that brooms sand across the pavement. We throw open the door and dash for our cars.

CHAPTER SEVEN

—·—

S lab City has been described as a combination of Mad Max and
Woodstock.

It sits between the Chocolate Mountains and the lower end of the
Salton Sea on a square mile of state land that was a Marine base in
World War II. When the Marines pulled out, they took down the
buildings but left the concrete slabs they stood on, along with several
empty storage tanks and a grid of streets now fading into the sand.

Squatters discovered the place, moved in to camp on the slabs and
in the tanks, and Slab City was born. Today it's home to a couple of
hundred permanent residents in the summer, plus a couple of thousand snowbirds in the winter who come in RVs for the mild weather
and free camping.

Which makes the opposite ends of the Coachella Valley like fun-
house mirror images of each other. Palm Springs Rolex-rich, the Slabs
spare-change-poor. Both seasonal with a big snowbird influx in the
winter, both nocturnal in the summer because of the soul-sapping
heat.

The year-rounders, the true Slabbers, live in tents, teepees, lean-tos,
dead motor homes, rotting camp trailers, scrap-lumber shacks and
even the abandoned military water tanks covered with wild murals of
heaven and hell, nightmares and dreams, angels and demons. Most are

too poor to live anywhere with rent, and too broken to live anywhere with rules.

I start my morning with a quick pass through the Slabbers' Facebook pages. If it's happening in the Slabs, it's on Facebook.

Joe Bob has put up a cartoon of Dora the Explorer with bug eyes and a meth pipe over a caption that says "when you accidentally explore Slab City."

A lady from Schenectady wants to move to the Slabs with her fiancé. Fishbait warns her about coming in summer: "Be prepared for extreme heat. The desert will kill you without remorse."

MoonBat posts a night shot of distant flames and says it doesn't look like somebody burning trash or brush; Bunny Harris comments it was probably that guy Raymie cooking meth again.

Another beautiful day in the Slabs.

I slap my laptop shut and am packing for the Slabs when the Chaplain calls.

"Took you long enough," I say. "I put up the signal last night."

He answers with a shrug in his voice. "I was in Mexico."

"Doing what?"

"Please, Dana."

If he answered, he wouldn't be the Chaplain, I suppose. After I brief him on our need to get hold of Tick, and on Johnny's report that Tick seems to be a dealer and a Mogul, there's a long silence.

"You didn't hear this from me," he says.

"You feel like you need to say that? Please."

"Yeah, he deals for us out there."

"Deals what?"

"You don't really need to know that."

"The heavier the drugs the heavier the hardware, usually."

"Fair point," the Chaplain says. "Tick does carry. He handles weed, meth, heroin. Whatever gets them through the night. There's a lot of pain out there."

"But Jesus, how does that - -"

"And Narcan," he says. "And kratom. And methadone."

All of which are used to treat addiction and overdoses. "Talk about working both sides of the street."

"If they want to get straight, we don't mind," he says. "There's always new customers. And dead bodies attract attention. Even in the Slabs."

"The druggies out there actually buy Narcan?"

"Sometimes their people do. Old man, old lady, kids, parents."

"So this Tick guy. How do we find him?"

"He works out of an old motor home," the Chaplain says. "It's up on blocks just past East Jesus. A Fatboy will be parked in front if he's there."

"He doesn't live in the Slabs, I take it??"

"Why would he? He just shows up from time to time with inventory. He does business till he sells out, then leaves."

"He got a government name?"

Silence.

"I had to ask," I tell a dead line. The Chaplain's already gone.

Duke wanders in from the bedroom, laps up some water, and noses at his food dish. I scratch him behind the ears, feed him, let him out for a run and his morning business, then start downhill to the offices of Ike Skogel and Associates on Tahquitz Canyon Way. It's already ninety-two, according to my Jeep, and my phone promises 109 before the day's out.

I meet Ike in the parking lot and we climb into his old red Chevy Suburban. He has a new electric Beamer, but that's to impress clients and women. It's the Suburban he loves. It was the first new vehicle he bought after he got his law license, and he thinks it brings him luck. He says he'll keep it till it dies, or he does.

We always take the Suburban to the Slabs, we never go alone, and we dress down. Today it's jeans and high-top sneakers for both of us, for me a faded blue short-sleeve pullover, and for him an adobe-colored polo that's seen better days, and not recently. You don't put on airs in the Slabs. No Verona loafers or three-piece suits for Ike, no bling or fancy hair for me. And no Birkenstocks, either. The Slabs, like the rest of the desert out here, is crawling with scorpions and fire ants. High-tops it is.

The first twenty miles are pretty civilized. We take the 10 and skirt the fringes of Palm Springs and the other snowbird cities that sprawl along the freeway in a patchwork of golf courses, gated resorts, and fancy shopping malls.

As we proceed south, the money shine gives way to strip malls, drive-through food joints, and neighborhoods of bungalows, cheap apartments, and mobile home parks where the year-rounders live. It's another reminder that this county has the third-lowest average income in California.

At Indio, we leave the 10 for Highway 111, pick up the smell of rotten eggs, and roll into the part of the Golden State that looks as if the end of the world has already begun.

Exhibit No. 1 is the slow-motion ecological disaster known as the Salton Sea. It starts about halfway to Slab City and runs southeast for thirty-five miles. As we drive along the shore, it's a beautiful sight—a shimmering expanse of lazy swells and sun-kissed blue that conjures up visions of marinas, ski boats, and the waterfront mansions of rich people from Palm Springs and Los Angeles.

And the Salton was all that for a while. Then the Colorado River that fed into it got diverted to farms and cities and the Salton began shrinking. Today, with no input except a polluted river coming up from Mexico and farm runoff loaded with fertilizer and pesticides from the American side, it's a toxic sump that sends that rotten-egg smell as far as Palm Springs when the wind is wrong.

All of which makes a certain amount of sense. California has a Death Valley, so why not a Dead Sea?

As we pass the turnoff to Bamboo Beach, Ike speaks. "I think Johnny might be telling the truth. This kinda thing isn't like him."

"Yeah," I say. "And his reaction when he saw the torso shots, that seemed real. He might stab somebody in a bar fight one of these days, or get stabbed himself, but this? I don't see it. The cousin, maybe?"

Ike's voice turns hard. "My bet. Another damned rich kid who never had to make his own bed or wash a dish or take responsibility for anything."

"What?" This is a new side of Ike.

His knuckles are white on the steering wheel. He doesn't look at me.

"Yeah. Entitled little asshole, good-looking, gets pissed when a girl shuts him down, probably the first time it ever happened to him. Drunk, maybe high. Yeah, I like him for this."

Ike switches on his radio and finds KXO, a famous oldies station out of El Centro. Axl Rose howls outside the gates of heaven as we continue up the shore.

CHAPTER EIGHT

—·—

S lab City may be the epicenter of anarchy and likely starting point for the End Times, but it's laid out in an orderly street grid like Anywhere, USA. East Jesus is at the northern corner.

We drive in past the abandoned Marine guard shack emblazoned with "SLAB CITY—THE LAST FREE PLACE" and work our way past the ragged camps. Most are fronted with dead refrigerators, sun-bleached sofas, broken-down lawn chairs, and dogs lazing in the shade or nosing through the trash.

Here and there a Slabber, probably a woman, is making an effort. The camp tidy and fenced, flowers on the stoop, solar cells on the roof, an awning of black shade cloth stretched over a tiny front yard, even a port-a-potty or wooden outhouse in the back.

Halfway in, we meet a fire engine and a unit from the sheriff's office coming out, no lights, no sirens, no ambulance. Apparently the emergency, whatever it was, is over.

What we don't see is any Slabbers out and about, not one. It's the heat of the day now—at least 110 in the shade, I'm guessing—and all sensible people are indoors and out of the sun.

The East Jesus camp lies on a dusty dirt track called Sidewinder Road. East Jesus is not a desert doomsday cult awaiting the Rapture like it sounds, but an artists' colony with a taste for irony. One exhibit is a life-size elephant made of car tires. Another is a fifteen-foot wall of abandoned television sets with slogans painted on the screens in big red letters. One reads "THE TELEVISION WILL NOT BE REVO-LUTIONIZED."

But this is not an art-appreciation tour. Ike and I are in East Jesus on business, and our business involves a guy named Tick who supposedly conducts his business out of an old motor home somewhere in the vicinity.

Or rather, formerly conducted business, as we discover when we roll farther down Sidewinder. What we see is a little crowd gathered in front of the smoldering skeleton of an old motor home. A Harley Fatboy with apehanger handlebars, not smoldering, is parked under the canopy of a blue-green palo verde tree.

Ike pulls the Suburban to a stop under another palo verde, one with two bicycles leaning against it, rolls down his window, and says, "Huh."

"Another beautiful day in the Slabs. Shall we?" I slip on a sweatband against the heat, we climb out of the Suburban and start for the only guy who's a contender to be Tick, because he's wearing a cut. He's facing away from us and we can see the Moguls logo on the back of the vest.

He turns at the "ch-chunk" as we shut the Suburban's doors and reads us before we've taken five steps. He waves the crowd around the ruined motor home to stay in place and heads over, right hand under the back of his vest.

He's maybe thirty, not tall but built big, especially in the chest and shoulders. He's gentle-faced and hard-eyed. He looks too healthy to be a consumer of his own product.

He wears a camouflage ball cap and a ginger beard that goes down to his neck tattoo. The tattoo's in blue ink, but I can't make out what it is because it's mostly covered by the beard and by the collar of his cut. His right arm sports a full-color portrait of a creamy blond in a barely-there blue teddy, and his left biceps bears a portrait of the official Moguls warlord.

Ike steps forward to greet Tick, but I grab his elbow. "Let me. You two get into it, this'll turn into a dick-measuring contest and we'll get nothing."

Ike steps back and I'm in front when Tick joins us in our patch of shade, the hard eyes narrow and careful.

"Help you?" he says.

"You Tick by any chance?"

"Who's asking and why?"

"We're not cops, and our business here has nothing to do with your business."

He chews on that for a couple of seconds, eyes flat. "And your business is?"

I explain who we are, hand him our cards. He studies them, passes them back, doesn't offer to shake. "Okay." He waits.

"So we represent a guy named Johnny B who got tagged for a murder in Palm Springs a couple days ago, and he says - -"

"We heard about that," Tick interrupts. "Girl was shot in the pussy up by the 10?"

"That's it. But Johnny says he was down here that night, drinking vodka with you at the Range. Band named Sandrat was playing?"

"I got no problem with Johnny," Tick says. "But we don't talk to cops."

"But - -"

"Ever."

"The death penalty could be on the table if the feds come in, and if he didn't do it..."

It's not likely the feds will come in on a case like this but I'm guessing Tick doesn't know that. He appears to be thinking things over. I tip my head at the motor home and try for an icebreaker. "What's this about?"

"Woman trouble."

He turns his back on us and returns to the gaggle of Slabbers watching us from in front of the charred motor home. He speaks to a girl with one side of her head shaved, ink-black hair on the other side, and what even I have to admit is a well proportioned ass. An ass, I'm pretty sure, with Tick's name tattooed above the crack.

Tick jerks his head at us and Half-Shave starts over. Tick pulls a rucksack off the back of the Harley and picks his way into the shell of the ruined motor home.

"Oh, yeah," Ike says as Half-Shave approaches. "I'd hit that."

"And then you'd die." I give him a dig with my elbow. "You see where Tick had his hand when he came over?"

Half-Shave arrives and says, "Tick said I can tell you about the guy was checking out my ass at the Range."

Up close, we see that she has twining black leaves tattooed on the shaved half of her scalp, black eye-liner, black mascara, black lipstick, too many piercings to count, and a spiked black leather collar. Plus low-rider jeans and a leather vest open at the front except for the middle button, with nothing underneath but chest. Ike is having difficulty maintaining eye contact.

I introduce us and show her a picture of Johnny on my phone and she confirms he was the guy checking her out at the Range.

When we tell her about Johnny's situation, her face draws in on itself and she looks like a scared little girl instead of a Goth biker chick. "That's horrible, a woman getting shot in the - - shot like that."

Ike wrenches his eyes up from her cleavage. "Yeah, that's kind of why we're here," he says. "The cops are trying to hang it on Johnny, but he's not the guy, which means the real guy is still out there somewhere." Ike waves at the part of Slab City visible from where we are. "Even right here in the Slabs maybe. So if you…"

"Fuck him!" Half-Shave says. "Fuck, that guy. Fuck, yeah, I'll stand up for Johnny. He was definitely with us at the Range that night, he had two bottles of vodka we were drinking. Oh, yeah, and he bought some weed from Tick, and Sandrat was playing."

"And you'll tell that to the cops?" Ike asks.

"Tick said I could, yeah."

I pull out my phone. "Okay if I get a video while you say it all again?"

"Hell, yeah," she says.

We make the recording and then she agrees to add not only her government name--Connie-Ann Carson, from Clinton, Indiana—but also her cell number and Social Security number.

By now, two more Slabbers from the gaggle in front of the burnt-out motor home have wandered over, presumably figuring that if Tick's old lady is cleared to talk, they are, too.

"Anybody remember a guy named Smokey hanging around Johnny's camp for a while?" I ask them. "Pretty hot, looks kinda like Tom Cruise?"

"Oh, yeah," says a lady Slabber. "Smokey. I'd knock boots with him any time."

This one looks like she's been in the Slabs too long—dirty bare feet, dusty snarls of brown hair, the meth head's facial rash, a rumpled, oversize tank top, and shorts that don't cover enough.

"We heard he cleared out," Ike says. "Any idea where he went?"

Tank Top shrugs. "I heard he got a ride out with that girl was in here taking pictures of the murals."

"Yeah, Cara, I seen her pick him up," says a guy who's wandered over. Sixty-something probably, long tangled white hair and beard like a prophet. He's wearing a cowboy hat, pajama bottoms, and flip-flops. His chest is sunburnt to the color of saddle leather and sports a tattoo of Jesus's face. "Car had Ohio plates, maybe."

"Lucky girl," Tank Top says.

"Maybe she's taking him home to meet the parents," the Prophet says.

Tank Top and the Prophet have a good a laugh at that, then fall into a discussion about whether they could get some 'product'—unspecified—at Mesquite's camp now that Tick is out of business for a while.

They grab the bikes from beside our Palo Verde tree and pedal away. The Prophet is on a girl's bike. Tank Top is on a boy's bike.

Ike points at the ruins of the motor home and looks at Connie-Ann. "Were you guys in it when this happened?"

"We never stay in the Slabs," Connie-Ann says. "Somebody called us and said the rig was on fire, so we came up. But the cops and firemen were still here, so we pulled in at East Jesus till they left a couple minutes ago."

"Tick gonna be taking measures?" Ike asks.

"Not Tick, me. It was that bitch Superglue set it on fire. And she took my dog Raven, too!"

"Um, Superglue is...?"

"Tick's old old lady. He kicked her out and moved me in and she blames me for it so she did this. Bitch is gonna pay."

"We don't want to know about that," Ike says.

Connie-Ann pulls out her phone and shows us a picture of a black Lab giving the camera the side-eye. "My soul mate even back in Clinton. Fucking Superglue took her."

"Thanks for everything" I say, "We're gonna go now. I don't know if the cops will want to talk to you about Johnny, but I'll try to give you a heads-up if they do."

"Tha' be good."

We climb into the Suburban and Ike cranks it up. It's less than sauna-like inside, since we not only parked in the shade of the palo verde tree, but also left the windows down. A couple minutes of AC and it's almost comfortable.

On the way back up Highway 111, we decide it's time to try for a talk with the cops about Johnny. I get out my phone to call a homicide lieutenant named Adrian St. Clair. He worked with Frank when they were both new recruits at Palm Springs Public Safety. We were something more than acquaintances but less than close friends with him and his husband, Barney. Close enough for backyard barbecues and beer, not close enough to vacation together.

My knowing him means he'll probably talk to us. If it was just Ike, or Ike and some other investigator, he probably wouldn't. With me in the picture, I'm pretty sure he will. Who's gonna turn down a grieving widow?

A tap on his contact, and he's on the line after the first ring. "Dana, it's been a while."

I agree it has, and explain the purpose of the call.

There's quite a long silence.

"You're working that case?" he says. "Is that a good idea, ah, considering, ah - -"

"Yes, I am working that case. Is that a problem?"

"Not for me, I guess. But, ah, you say you want to come in for a talk?"

"That's right, me and Ike Skogel. We've got some information that might be helpful to both sides."

"Yeah, okay, but no promises."

CHAPTER NINE

— • —

An hour later, we exit the 10, then work our way across Palm Springs to Public Safety headquarters. We're still sweat-stained and grimy from talking to Tick and Connie-Ann in the heat, and my mouth tastes like a sand dune. But if St. Clair is willing to meet, we can't pass it up.

We park, spread foil reflectors over the dash, and hurry across the asphalt griddle to the building.

Inside, Ike beats me to the fountain in the lobby and drinks from the sparkling arc for a full minute, Adam's apple bobbing in his scrawny neck. Then my turn comes and I gulp down what tastes like pure nectar after all those hours on the road in temperatures above a hundred. The bottled stuff beats nothing, but nothing beats water-cooler water.

The receptionist spots us and points her pen down the hall.

St. Clair rises from his chair when we enter the conference room, and straightens a shiny blue tie. He's as dapper as ever–razor-cut silver hair, a tan that might be real, and a pale gray jacket that, if I remember right, is from a fancy label called Canali.

He tilts his head at another man at the table. "This is Lieutenant Gary Avila. He's actually the one in charge of the Jennifer Williamson case."

St. Clair waves toward us. "Dana Forsythe, Ike Skogel."

We step forward, shake hands, and exchange business cards. Ike and I take the other two chairs at the table.

Avila, like St. Clair, is fifty-ish, but more rumpled. Loosened tie, the creases in his jeans far from crisp, loafers a bit scuffed. Sleek black hair combed back, caterpillar eyebrows over chocolate eyes, twenty or so pounds of gut, acne-cratered face with no hint of a smile.

Ike and I take turns telling Johnny's story. I hand over Connie-Ann's contact information, explain her willingness to testify if it can't be avoided, and pull out my phone. Avila and St. Clair trade glances. I tap the recording I made in the Slabs, and turn the screen to the men. Connie-Ann comes through loud and clear.

Ike speaks up when she's done. "So there's your alibi. She puts Johnny right where he said he was when you questioned him."

"A Slabber," Avila says. "And a Mogul's old lady." He looks at Ike, then me. "Some witness."

"Have you analyzed Johnny's phone yet?" Ike asks.

Avila grunts.

"Yeah," St. Clair says with a glance at Avila. "It was in the Slabs all that night."

"Which proves squat about where Johnny himself was," Avila says.

"He says he took a video with it of a Slabber band named Sandrat doing 'Gimme Shelter' at the Range," I say. "You find that yet?"

"Our techs didn't mention it, but they're still working on the phone," St. Clair says. "I'll alert them."

"Anybody can make a video," Avila says.

"But this one allegedly has Johnny singing along with Sandrat," I say.

"Any evidence on the phone that Johnny was ever in touch with Jennifer?" Ike asks. "Calls, texts, anything?"

"No." Avila's answer is curt and reluctant.

"Any gunshot residue on his hands or the truck?"

"No, but it was a while before we caught up to him."

"Well, then," Ike says. "Assuming that video is on the phone, either Johnny wasn't involved in this murder, or he set it all up, then cleaned up afterward like a pro. Which would make him a major criminal mastermind, am I right?"

"Which is not something you'd expect from a Slabber," I point out in an effort to be helpful.

"Right." Ike tents his fingers in front of his chest, and gazes at Avila. "So, you need to release him."

"When I want your opinion, I'll give it to you," Avila says. "Johnny's ours till we talk to the cousin. Probably afterward, too."

"We do have a BOLO out for Hale, the cousin," St. Clair adds. "He goes by Smokey, right? The sheriff's office went into the Slabs and asked around about him, but nobody knew anything."

"Of course they didn't," Avila says. "Fucking Slabbers."

"The Slabs always know," St. Clair says. "They tell you two anything about where this cousin might be?"

"Somebody thought they saw a girl with Ohio plates pick him up on Beal Road the morning after Jennifer was shot," Ike answers. "She was in the Slabs taking pictures of the murals."

"Well, that's something." St. Clair makes a note on a yellow pad.

"But not much." Avila crosses his arms and gives us a flat-eyed cop stare. "We done here?"

Ike and I meet each other's gaze. It's been a long day. We rise and start for the door.

"Hey, Dana," St. Clair says. "Got a minute?"

Avila shoots St. Clair a glance and walks out. Ike shoots me one and does the same.

St. Clair and I settle back into our chairs. He fiddles with a pen, picks up the black-rimmed half-glasses on his legal pad and lays them down. I wait.

He clears his throat. "So, I've been thinking," he says. "And one of my colleagues brought this up, also. About you being involved in this case. I mean, you're the widow of the father of the victim's kids, now you're representing the guy charged with killing her. You could see how this might look, right? It could complicate things. For you, for us." He clears his throat again. "For everybody."

I wait some more. He has no freakin' idea how complicated my life has become.

"And, you know, the press is bound to make the connection before long. You'll go viral."

Well, duh. How could I not have thought of this? Of course the media will be all over me. This thing just keeps growing. First the twins, now my work for Ike, pretty soon I'm a headline. The python's around my neck again and it won't let go. Or maybe it's me that won't.

"I heard Frank's kids ended up on your patio that night," St. Clair is saying now. "And now your office assistant's parents have 'em? How'd that happen?"

"You heard all this how?"

"Our mutual friend, for one."

"Ah. The Chaplain."

St. Clair nods. "Some people call him that."

"What do you call him?"

"Please, Dana."

"Okay then. My assistant's parents have been foster care providers for years. They've already registered the kids in the system."

St. Clair frowns, clears his throat again. "That doesn't raise my comfort level a lot, actually. What's the legal status?"

"The twins are safe. It's all good. No police involvement needed."

He raises his hand in a gesture that says "For now."

I study him for a moment. "Do you think I had a hand in what happened to that woman?"

"I do not. Our mutual friend checked the engines on your cars - -"

"So I hear."

"And we checked with the phone company," St. Clair goes on. "Your phone hadn't been anywhere recently, either. And of course we checked with Lyft and Uber and the cab companies to see if they were at your place that night."

"Of course you did."

I should leave now, but I can't. "Did everybody know about Frank and Jennifer?"

He sighs. "Pretty much."

"Why didn't you tell me?

"I didn't know how," he says. "And Frank was trying to leave her. I figured it would take care of itself."

I hate crying, but this is too much. I snuffle and sob and baw-haw like a child.

St. Clair fishes in his jacket, passes me a handkerchief, and walks to the door. Then he turns back.

"Take all the time you need."

CHAPTER TEN

—·—

I sleep in the next morning and wake up to a day to myself. The cops are shifting their focus to Smokey Hale. At least for now, nothing needs to be done about Johnny.

Lita's off because it's Friday, so I wander the house and enjoy the clear morning view of Palm Springs and the patchwork of small cities around it.

I feed Duke and load the dishwasher while he gobbles up his food like I've been starving him. I put on a wide-brimmed straw hat and big sunglasses and we go out for a walk before it gets any hotter.

Edgar, the metal-detector buff next door, is just coming in. He's an old guy with gray stubble and a desert cap with a flap in the back to prevent skin cancer of the neck. Edgar's widowed and his kids live back East, which explains why he spends his nights prowling the desert with a metal detector.

Today he's wearing an orange T-shirt with "I GOT SCALPED AT THE AGUA DULCE" printed over a picture of the biggest tribal casino in Palm Springs.

"Morning, Edgar," I say. "How you doing?"

"Killing time till it kills me."

"Copy that."

"Yourself?"

"Won't complain. Big night?"

He unshoulders his pack. "A horseshoe, a set of keys, and a seventy-two Eisenhower S-2."

"Edgar, I've asked you to speak English."

He opens the pack and pulls out an Eisenhower silver dollar. He brushes away desert grit hands me the coin. Duke sniffs at it as I inspect it.

"This is the S-2?"

"Yup," he says. "The seventy-two is the rare one. Worth thirty bucks easy at Jackie's Pawn. "

"Which will go straight into the slots at the Agua Dulce?"

"Man's gotta kill time somehow." He puts the S-2 back into his pack and goes into his little ranch-style while I try not to think about how I'll kill time when I reach Edgar's age.

I toss Duke's ball into the brush, he darts after it and brings it back with a look of triumph. The fresh air relaxes me and my teeth start to unclench for the first time since the twins arrived on my patio four days ago.

Back inside, I refill Duke's water bowl, toss in a load of laundry and listen to public radio while a dark roast clears the last traces of sleep from my head. The public radio call-in is all about what happened to Jennifer Williamson.

I move to the couch and tune in to KZOA, my morning TV news source. Jennifer is also the big story there. Prosecutors are saying there's no danger to the public. Yeah, right. Except that they've issued a BOLO—be on the lookout— for the guy who's probably the actual shooter.

Next I check the *Herald* website. Stories sprout headlines like "*Despite arrest, cops mum on status of Torso Shooter case.*" The lead story includes pictures of Jennifer, who's identified as a receptionist for the

Desert Chamber of Commerce. I slam the laptop shut and close my eyes.

Duke ambles in, flops down at my feet, I scratch him behind the ears. I flick off the TV, lay my head against the back of the couch, and try to push it all away. Then my phone chimes and Lita's face comes up on the screen.

"Hey," she says. "Mom's aunt fell again and she needs to go talk to the nursing home and I have my class today. Can she drop off the twins for a while?"

"God, no," I want to say but what would be the point? This thing will never let me go, no matter what.

So instead it's a sigh and, "Sure, have her bring them up."

Thirty minutes later, Yolanda's Mazda pulls into my driveway. I go out to help her unload the twins.

"Good to see you again, Yolanda. And thanks again for taking these little guys until...well, until."

"*De nada,*" she says. "We always have room for two more."

She's exactly the mother you'd expect Lita to have. Plump, with threads of silver winding through a loose, fat braid that drops over one shoulder, and kind brown eyes like her daughter's.

"It's *Tía* Dana," she tells the twins as we take them from the car. They're too bashful to say anything to this near-stranger they haven't seen in four days. And those hours we spent together after the Chaplain dropped them off weren't fun for any of us.

Yolanda rescues us by kneeling on the sand, spreading her arms like wings and pulling us all into a group hug. "It's your *Tía* Dana, *hijitos!*"

Rose folds herself into the hug, but Sonny stiffens, draws back, and gives me the toddler version of a side-eye.

We get them inside and Yolanda slips each of them an orangish lollipop. They lick with gusto, and Yolanda gives me one. And it's not bad. Different, but not bad.

"Vero Mangos," she grins. "Like a gringo lollipop, except chili-flavored."

She watches the twins with their lollipops for a few moments, then looks at me. "The foster care people have checked, it doesn't look like these kids have any relatives to take them. Jennifer's people, they don't want them and their father..." She stops to see how I'm handling it.

"Yeah, Frank didn't have any siblings and his parents are, well, they weren't close. At all."

"Verdad," she says. "Sonny and Rose have nowhere to go."

I can't think of anything to say, so I don't.

"Maybe we could take them," she says.

"Take them? You mean adopt them?"

She lifts a twin onto each knee. "I miss having babies of my own. A woman needs something little to take care of, I think."

"It's not really up to me. I don't have custody."

"Lo sé, but would you mind?"

"You sure?"

"Sí, muy segura," she says. "I already talked to Silvio. He likes babies, too."

Sonny offers Yolanda a lick of his Vero Mango. She accepts, murmurs "Mm," and ruffles his hair.

"I guess I need to think about it," I say.

"Claro," she says. "I know you want to do the right thing for them. But so do I."

As she heads down Cahuilla Drive in the Mazda a few minutes later, I decide to take our little gang for a walk. The patio thermometer says it's 105 now. But one advantage of living in a canyon is that one side or the other is always in the shade except for an hour or two a day when the sun shines straight into it.

We stick to the shady side. Rose and I pick the last of the season's blooms from pale green brittlebush shrubs. Soon we both wear garlands of yellow in our hair.

Sonny heaves rocks at a white-spotted hedgehog cactus that resembles a fat, squat sea urchin and I get a lump in my throat at how much Frank I see in him.

Duke darts from one of us to the other, and tears off after a roadrunner. It's just like the one in the cartoons except real ones don't go "beep, beep." These kids, this dog, their ability to live in and for the moment—they're finally getting me out of my own head. It's just what I've been needing.

We get back to the house and decide to watch *Frozen* on Disney. Rose digs a frilly pink princess dress out of the bag Yolanda brought along, holds it up to me. "On, *Tía*?"

Tía. She called me *Tía*. I tear up a little as we get the dress on her while Sonny and Duke wrestle in the hall.

I reach for the TV remote to turn up the volume on *Frozen,* but it's not on the coffee table where I keep it. We search until Sonny tugs me into the bathroom, points into the toilet bowl, giggles, and gives me a proud grin. I'm as much tickled as annoyed. I fish it out, take out the batteries and run the hair dryer over it until it's dry. And that does the trick. It still works!

Back in the living room, Princess Rose has found the box of cotton balls under the bathroom sink and is piling them around Duke's head as he lies on the floor. He thumps his tail in ecstasy but holds his head perfectly still.

After *Frozen,* lunch is sliced hot dogs from the microwave, with applesauce and juice in little cartons. Soon, Sonny's face scrunches up and he announces "potty." That's right, Yolanda mentioned she's working on getting them out of diapers.

As we start for the bathroom, Sonny spots the picture of Frank on the nightstand in the bedroom at the end of the hall. He rushes toward it, calling, "Daddy! Daddy!" Rose comes in from the kitchen to join him. They stop in front of the picture. Sonny touches Frank's face, then turns to me with a questioning look.

"Daddy's not here," I manage. Should I lie? Tell them the bastard's on a trip? No, then they'll expect him back.

"Daddy bye-bye?" Rose asks.

"Yes, Daddy bye-bye," I croak.

They turn away and wander back down the hall holding hands. They're so little. Let CPS adopt them out to strangers? What was I thinking?

"C'mon, Sonny," I say. "Potty time, remember?" We return to the bathroom.

They fall asleep after lunch, Rose on the couch, Sonny on an area rug with an arm around Duke's neck.

I study their faces for a few moments, then call Yolanda, get her voicemail. Probably still dealing with the nursing home, I figure. I try Lita and she answers

"Is your mother serious about adopting the twins?"

"Yes, very serious," Lita answers. "And Dad really likes the idea, so I called Ike and he will help us work it out. How are you holding up?"

"Thanks, I'm good," I lie. "Let your parents know I'm on board with the adoption, okay?"

"Of course. I could meet you halfway about four-thirty to get the twins back here," she says. "At the west edge of the Target parking lot in Palm Desert?"

I agree.

When the twins wake up, I build peanut butter and jelly sandwiches on white bread, pour milk into the sippy cups. We take another walk, a short one this time, and laugh as Duke chases the roadrunner again. As before, he comes back empty-pawed and empty-jawed, tongue lolling out in a big grin.

I load Rose and Sonny into the Vic at four and we start for the handoff to Lita. It's been a good day.

Back home, I check in with Ike to discuss the adoption.

"Yeah, I've got some calls out on it and it looks doable," he says. "I'll push on it some more tomorrow and then we can sit down and--oh, hold on a sec, I have another call coming in."

He's gone for a long time, so long I think of hanging up and letting him call back. He comes on just before I do.

"Listen, I have some good news and some bad news."

"The good?"

"Johnny's been released and the charges dropped," he says. "St. Clair called me about half an hour ago"

"Yes! It's over! I'm free of this damned thing!"

A long silence.

"I'm not?"

Ike clears his throat. "Well, the reason Johnny was released is that Hale got himself picked up over a bar brawl in Bamboo Beach. The county mounties down there recognized him from the BOLO and turned him over to Palm Springs Public Safety. And when they questioned him, he confirmed Johnny's story about borrowing the truck. That, plus our interview with Connie-Ann and the *Sandrat* video they finally found on Johnny's phone, it was apparently too much even for Avila. So they cut him loose."

"And?"

"And you are gonna stick with me on this, right? That was Hale's grandfather calling me just now."

"No."

"Hale asked him to hire me because we got Johnny off, and the old guy didn't even ask the fee, just said to do everything I can for his grandson."

"Won't Johnny have to testify against Smokey?" I ask. "Isn't that some kind of conflict, you representing both of them?"

"That's what I said. But Smokey's willing to sign a waiver, according to grandpa. We're drafting it now. And he's pretty sure he can bring Johnny around on a waiver, too. Between us, if anything was said about Grandpa replacing his truck because of the damage Smokey caused, I certainly didn't hear it."

"Replacing it."

"With a new one, hypothetically," Ike says.

"Ah."

"I know. Rich people, right? So we're drafting a waver for Johnny, as well."

"No, Ike."

"The court was probably gonna try to stick me with his defense anyway," Ike goes on. "Because we already know the file."

"There is no 'we.' I'm out."

"You don't want to meet the guy that probably actually did kill her?"

Ike knows me too well, damn his soul.

CHAPTER ELEVEN

—·—

This morning's banner headline on the *Herald* website shouts *New arrest in Torso Shooter case*. The suspect is one Brixton Lee Hale the Third, described as "a part-time resident of Slab City, where he's known as 'Smokey'." The original suspect, John Bottemueller, has been released and is no longer a person of interest, according to police.

Even in his mug shot, Hale is smoking hot. Already a smitten female from Joshua Tree has put up a "Free Smokey" Facebook page. It's drawing dozens of comments, including one that proclaims "Smokey Hale can take a shot at me any time!"

I climb on the Peloton for a half hour of self-abuse and surf the channels as I pedal. The local reporters are all over the Torso Shooter case. Public TV has a panel on toxic masculinity. An "expert" on another channel advises every white woman in Palm Springs to buy a gun.

The Jennifer Williamson case has even made the big time, sort of. A bottom-feeding online news site called *The Dragger* headlines its story, *Cops cuff Palm Springs Crotch Killer*.

Crotch killer? Number one, that's not what killed Jennifer Williamson. And number two, how crazy will this get before it's over?

I'm close to my personal high of 135 watts output on the torture machine when my phone lights up with Lita's face.

"Thank God," I pant. "You rescued me from the Peloton. And cable news."

"I don't know which is worse," she says. "Can you talk now or do you need more pain first?"

I climb off the bike, mute the TV, and flop down on the sofa. "I'm good. What's up?"

"I finally tracked down Jennifer Williamson's family."

"Hang on a minute, Lita." I dial Ike, add him to the call, and switch my phone to speaker. "Lita has news."

"Yeah," he mumbles through a yawn.

I woke him. Good.

"Go ahead, Lita. We're on with Ike."

"So Jennifer's family is back in Minnesota," Lita says. "Her dad's widowed, lives in a cabin out in the woods near Lake Superior, no real contact with Jennifer for years. She cut her family off after too many fights about money and personal responsibility. He didn't even know she had kids, There's a sister in Minneapolis with MS. Neither one knows anything about Jennifer's love life or who might want to kill her. It looks like a dead end."

"Thanks, Lita, nice work. Ike, can you stay on a minute?"

There's a click as Lita disconnects.

"We seeing Hale today?"

Ike stifles another yawn. "Yeah, ten o'clock, but I can't stay long. I'll introduce you, but you'll need to handle the interview yourself."

"Sure, but what's up?"

"A moneymaker just walked in the door."

"Another nursing home death?"

"Better," he says in a happy tone. "Lesbian divorce. Both richer than God, got married in that first blaze of passion, soon realized they hated each other, been fighting ever since. Now it's mutual assured destruction and legal costs be damned."

"Who gets the Subaru?"

"Very funny. We're talking a Lambo, an Escalade, and matching Ducati motorcycles, thank you very much. Not to mention a Pekingese and a Moluccan cockatoo, a beach house in Malibu and a walled estate in Old Las Palmas."

I give an appreciative whistle. Fancy cars are a dime a dozen in Palm Springs. But a walled estate in Old Las Palmas? That's where rich people go to feel poor.

"I could go on," Ike continues. "But I gotta prep for the meeting with my client, so I'll see you downtown, yes?"

Hurtado is on duty again when we meet at the jail two hours later. Ike hands me the case file and I leaf through it as she lets us through security and escorts us to the same conference room where we met with Johnny.

Hale lounges at the table, ankle on knee, arms crossed, radiating more cool than I would have thought possible for a guy in paper flip-flops and orange jail scrubs. He is indeed a dead ringer for Tom Cruise, so much so that I do a double take before I catch myself.

And Hale knows how he comes across. He brushes styled hair off his forehead with a frown. "You're my lawyers?"

Ike says "I'm Ike Skogel. I represented Johnny."

We take seats across the table from Hale.

"And this is Dana Forsythe," Ike says. "My investigator."

Hale gives me the eye.

I decide to start with nice. "A pleasure to meet you, Mr. Hale."

"Brick, if you don't mind."

"Brick?"

Ike looks as puzzled as I am.

"From Brixton. Smokey's for the Slabs. Nobody out there uses real names. Brick is what they call me back home."

"Let's stick with Mr. Hale out here," I tell him.

"Your grandfather has been in touch with me," Ike says.

"How is the First?"

"The First?"

"My grandfather is Brixton Lee Hale the First. He's the one who made the family fortune. He's footing your bill, right?"

"He is," Ike says. "And I gather not for the first time."

"I lead an interesting life," Hale says.

"I have another appointment and I have to run," Ike says. "Dana's gonna take the interview. Anything you'd tell me, you can tell her. Either one of us, it's covered by attorney-client privilege"

Hale shoots me a glance and another frown. "I have to talk to your assistant?"

"I'm not his fuc - -"

Ike stops me with a nudge to the elbow. "Dana's a licensed investigator, and an ex-police detective. You're in good hands."

"I hope so," Hale says. "Otherwise I'll be getting new lawyers."

"Strictly your choice," Ike says. "But I'm sure that won't be necessary."

He walks to the door and the guard lets him out as I open the case file and lay out a legal pad and two pens. "So, you know why we're here, right?"

"Obviously. They think I shot that girl the other night, when was it?"

"Sunday night, up on Gene Autry just south of Interstate 10."

"Right," he says. "The county mounties picked me up over a bar fight in Bamboo Beach and took me to the jail in Brawley, then the next thing I know I'm talking to a couple of Palm Springs detectives about a murder case."

"And you're wanting to plead not guilty, is that right?"

"Of course."

"You sure about that?"

"Absolutely. It wasn't me."

"And you told the police what?"

"The truth. I know better than to lie to cops. They said Johnny told them I borrowed his truck that night and maybe hooked up with Jennifer before she got murdered. So I told them, yes, I borrowed Johnny's truck and I went to a party I heard about in Chap City. And, yes, that's where I hooked up with Jennifer."

"Right, Jennifer Williamson," I tell him. He doesn't react.

"Mother of two small children," I add. He doesn't react to that either, he just rolls on with the story.

"That party was the walking dead except her, but she knew about another one up in Desert Hot Springs where they were supposed to have powder. So she put the address in my phone and we started up there. But then I hit a speed limit sign and she told me I was too drunk to ride with. She jumped out while I was checking the damage and wouldn't get back in. So I left her there and went on up to the other party."

"That's it?"

"Just like I told the cops," Hale says.

I glance at the paperwork in front of me. "Yep, that's what you told 'em." I give him the eye and wait.

He meets my gaze for a few seconds, then looks away.

I tap the papers in the folder. "You leave anything out?"

Hale shifts in his chair. "Okay, yes, I did have to straighten her out when she got in my face about hitting the sign, but I didn't really hurt her. It was just a love tap. To send a message."

"A strong enough message to leave a bruise and a cut on her cheek, according to the autopsy."

"She asked for it."

"And then you shot her?"

"No, I did not shoot her. She kicked me in the balls, I knocked her on her ass, then I left. She had her phone out when I drove away."

"Calling who?"

"How would I know? I thought it might be nine-one-one and I wasn't about to wait around to find out."

I flip through the papers in the folder and find the one I want. "There was no nine-one-one call from up there that night until a passing trucker found her body and called the police. So, again, who was she calling when you left?"

"I said I don't know. Maybe a ride?"

"She did hail a Lyft, except the driver couldn't find her. Apparently she was already dead when he came by and her body was partly hidden behind a mesquite bush and he didn't notice it. He figured somebody must have picked her up so he canceled the ride and kept going."

"Whatever," Hale says.

"And you told the cops all of this except the part about punching her?"

"That and getting kicked in the balls. I figured if they were already trying to pin her murder on me, I shouldn't admit to any of that. They obviously didn't believe what I did tell them, they made me go over it again and again, so I finally said I wanted a lawyer. They let me call my grandfather and I told him about your boss and how he got Johnny off."

"He's not my boss. He's my client."

"Okay."

"Anything else you didn't tell the police?" I ask.

"No, and why do you sound like you're on their side?"

I close the folder. "Look, if you seriously want to plead not guilty and Ike takes this to a jury, we can't afford any surprises. You need to tell us everything about that night. Like he said, it's all confidential."

"I know," Hale says. "Attorney-client privilege."

"So Johnny's wallet being found at the crime scene. How did that happen?"

"Beats me. I didn't even know it was in the truck till Johnny got on my case about it the next morning." He pauses in thought. "I figured it got stolen out of the truck at the party in Desert Hot Springs or maybe the one in Chap City. But I guess Jennifer must have found it on the seat or something and took it when she got out after I hit the sign. Then somebody came along and shot her."

"That's it?"

"Check with the people at the party in Desert Hot Springs. They'll tell you I was there." He crosses his arms over his chest and breaks eye contact again.

"The police did, and the people did."

"So I'm off the hook, right?"

"You see much about this on the news while you were in Bamboo Beach?"

"Not really," he says. "I was pretty busy with Cara."

"And Cara is—oh, the photographer from Slab City."

"Uh-huh."

"Did the cops show you the crime scene photos?"

"No, they had a stack of stuff I assumed they were planning to hit me with, but everything shut down when I asked for a lawyer."

I dig the photos out of my briefcase and lay them in front of Hale, face down on the table. When I flip them over, the goriest shot is on top.

"Jesus Christ!" he says. "That's not...she wasn't shot there when I --" He stumbles to a halt, turns the photos face down, and stares at his hands.

I wait, let the silence build, but he doesn't speak.

"She wasn't shot there when you did what?"

Nothing.

"Where was she shot, Mr. Hale?" I flip the photos back over.

Hale glances at the top one out of the corner of his eye and looks away.

"Come on, Mr. Hale. The jury sees these, they're gonna fry you like an egg. You have to come clean and let us handle this."

He sighs, faces the photo down again, and locks eyes with me.

"All I know is, when I left her she was fine, okay? I mean, other than where I hit her. Like I said, I took off up Gene Autry for the party in Desert Hot Springs."

"But you saw her again, is that right? So you came back?"

There's another long silence, then he looks from me to the backs of the photos on the table, then at me again. He lets out a long breath. "This will not get any easier to believe."

"Try me," I say.

"Okay. So I leave her there hailing the Lyft or whatever, and I'm headed up Gene Autry when this big fancy SUV cuts me off and forces me onto a side road. I get out and go up to straighten the guy out but when the window comes down it's a woman! Older woman, pretty good looking for her age, really nice rack. And she says, 'Get in, I have a proposition for you.' So I do."

He takes a look at my face and grins. "I said it wouldn't get easier to believe."

"I'm trying," I lie.

A deep breath and he's off again. "So, yeah, I'm in the passenger seat, the floorboard's covered with empty wine coolers and it smells like a brewery in there. It's obvious she's out of her gourd, and not just from the wine coolers, she has to be on something. And she tells me she's been following Jennifer all night to kill her, but she can't get up the nerve, so now she wants me to do it."

"How did she - - oh, she followed the two of you from the party in Chapel City and saw you beat Jennifer up by the road, is that it?"

"Yeah, apparently she pulled over and cut her lights after I hit the sign and watched the whole thing. Anyway, she tells me she knows from that I'm just the man for the job. I'm about to get the hell out of there because I may be drunk but I'm not drunk enough to get tangled up with somebody this crazy, especially if I have to kill a woman. Straightening a girl out, you have to do that sometimes. But kill her? No way."

"But you don't get out of the car, I take it?"

"No, I've got the door open, one foot on the sand, when I take another look at the situation. I mean, fancy car, well dressed lady dripping with bling who's obviously had some work, not just the rack but also the face. Everything I can see says money, and plenty of it. So I ask her what she has in mind."

Now I'm getting hooked. "And that was what exactly?"

"She pulls this gun out of the console and says she'll pay me five grand to go back and kill Jennifer with it."

"Jesus Christ."

"Exactly," Hale says. "What an opportunity, right? I can take her money and her gun and disappear, and then what's she going to do, call the cops? So I feel her out by telling her I want ten thousand, which would give me a nice cushion for a month or two, and she says 'Fine' and pulls out this gold money clip."

"She had ten thousand on her?"

"No, that's where it got complicated," Hale says. "She starts counting out bills and when she's done, there's only nine hundred and change on the console. When I say that's not ten thousand, she sticks out her arm and shows me her watch. All diamonds and gold, obviously serious bling. She says it's a Patek Philippe worth at least fifteen thousand and tells me she'll wait there and give it to me when I bring back the gun from shooting Jennifer. Then we'll meet the next afternoon and swap the watch for the rest of the ten thousand."

"Let me see if I have this straight," I say. "You're gonna get nine hundred bucks on the spot, you're gonna go kill Jennifer, you're gonna come back and give the SUV lady the gun, then she's gonna give you the watch for collateral until you can meet to swap it for the rest of the ten thousand?"

"Yeah, that was the plan," Hale says. "She wanted the gun back to make sure I actually used it. And she didn't want me to get caught with it and have the whole thing lead back to her. She wanted to get rid of it herself."

"And you believed all of this? I mean, what could possibly go wrong?"

"I didn't care. I wasn't going to kill Jennifer anyway, so I was never going to get the watch or the rest of the money. I was just happy to get the nine hundred for the fun up in Desert Hot Springs. I figured I could not only party pretty hearty on that, but also get back to the Slabs with enough left to make Johnny forget about his busted headlight."

"So you take the money and the gun but you don't start for Desert Hot Springs, you go back to where you left Jennifer?"

"Well, yeah," Hale says. "I was starting to feel sorry for her. First, I smack her in the face, then she gets left by the road, and now this crazy woman is trying to kill her. So I figure I should at least warn her. It was the decent thing to do, am I right?"

He looks at me for validation, without success.

"And also," he continues, "now that I've got the nine hundred dollars, I figure maybe Jennifer will want to go up to Desert Hot Springs with me after all. I mean she was one hot piece and nine hundred dollars, that's a party for two."

He glances at the photos, still face down on the table.

"So I drive back down to where I left her and at first I don't see her. I'm figuring she must have gotten a ride when I spot something white on the shoulder with my one good headlight. It's partly hidden behind a mesquite bush like you said so I get out to look and sure enough it's Jennifer in her white jeans. I think maybe she's passed out from all the drinking we did at the Chap City party. Or it could be a delayed reaction from when I hit her. Or both, I don't know. I call her name, she doesn't move, doesn't answer, and I bring up the flashlight on my phone for a better look. That's when I see she's just lying there on her back with a hole in her throat. Not breathing, not moving, not coughing or gurgling, just lying there. I checked her wrist for a pulse, nothing."

He shudders with what might be genuine revulsion.

"So you're saying it was just the throat shot when you were there? No torso shots?"

"Absolutely not," Hale says. "Just the throat."

"How can you be sure?"

"Look at the pictures." He finds a torso shot photo and holds it up to face me, not him. "See the blood all over her jeans there? There was nothing like that when I saw her. Just the phone on her lap, like in the picture, except no blood." He glances at the photo and bends for a closer look. "Her phone got shot, too?"

"Twice," I say. "So then what? You obviously didn't call 9-1-1."

"Of course not," Hale says. "She was already dead and there I was with the crazy lady's money, plus her gun. How was I supposed to explain that to the cops?"

He flips the picture face down again.

"So you leave her there and you take off for your powder party in Desert Hot Springs with the crazy lady's money."

"I started to," Hale says. "But then I got to thinking again."

"Of course you did. Thinking what?"

"I'm smoking a joint to steady my nerves as I pull away when I see there's a further opportunity here. Jennifer's dead. The next day, it's going to be all over the news that she got shot, and the SUV lady is going to think I did it, because how long will it take the cops to catch the real guy that shot her, assuming they ever do? And, again, if she does find out eventually that it wasn't me, what's she going to do, turn me in for scamming her on a hit job?"

"So you decide - -"

"What I do," Hale says, "I park and walk back down Gene Autry maybe forty-fifty yards and I shoot that pistol she gave me into the sand under another mesquite bush. Because she's probably going to check the gun to see if it was fired, right?"

"Did you fire from the shoulder of the road? Or did you walk out into the desert first?"

"In the dark?" Hale says. "You have Gila monsters around here."

"And fire ants and scorpions," I say. "And rattlesnakes."

"Definitely from the shoulder," Hale says.

"You think pretty good for a drunk guy."

"I've had some practice. Anyway, I shoot the gun into the sand, and I drive up and meet the crazy lady at the side road. I give her the gun, she opens the cylinder, checks to see that the bullet under the hammer was fired, gives me the watch and says to meet her at three o'clock the next afternoon in front of the Macy's at the Westgate Mall to swap the watch for the money if the story's in the news by then. She pulls away in her SUV and takes off down Gene Autry. I head up to the party in Desert Hot Springs and - -"

"And Johnny's wallet." I say. "You really had no idea Jennifer took it?"

"Nope. Otherwise Johnny wouldn't have been arrested and I wouldn't be mixed up in it now."

I've got a million questions about Hale's story at this point, but i make myself wait. there's one more chapter to go.

"So you hitchhike out of the Slabs, you catch a ride with this girl Cara and you end up staying with her in Bamboo Beach. What about the meeting with the SUV lady?"

"Total bust," Hale says. "Cara and I christen the bed in her trailer for a couple hours, I crash for a few hours, then I start back up here in her Honda. But the SUV lady's a no-show. I must have waited forty-five minutes, an hour on that bench in the mall, and there was no sign of her. So I take off, get some pizza and a couple of Coronas at the Sand Trap, and go back down to Bamboo Beach with that watch burning a hole in my pocket."

"Just what I was wondering about. Where is it now?"

"I gave it to Cara and told her she could keep half the money if she sold it for me. Lucky thing, too. She was wearing it when I popped the guy for groping her at the Surf Inn and wound up in handcuffs.

Otherwise, the cops would have found it on me and then where would I be?"

"Right where you are now?" I wave at the conference room around us.

Hale chuckles. "Good point."

"So, Cara has the watch now?"

"Unless she sold it already."

"What's her last name?"

Hale opens his mouth, leaves it open while he thinks the question over, then closes it with a look of surprise. "I guess I never asked."

"You don't happen to remember the address of this trailer, I suppose?"

"Uh-uh. But it's got a big American flag that Cara painted on the side." He brightens. "Oh, yeah. And I think it belongs to the lady that runs the Surf Inn."

"Tanya?" I ask.

"Yeah, that sounds right."

"Useful information," I say. "She owns the Surf Inn and half the other real estate in Bamboo Beach. Even if she doesn't own this trailer, she'll know where it is."

"So you're going to go see Cara?"

"Duh."

"Tell her hello from Smokey, all right? And if she sold the watch, can you get my share of the money? I probably shouldn't trust her with it too long."

Rather than tell him where he can shove his watch money, I plow ahead.

"Anything you want to add here? Because I have some more questions."

He thinks for a few seconds. "I guess that's it. Except I did not shoot that woman."

"Noted," I say. "This SUV lady. She mention her name?"

"Nope."

"What kind of SUV? Mercedes, Cadillac, BMW...?"

"Sorry. I was pretty drunk and then she started talking about the hit job and the money."

"What about the license plate? You get the number, even just a couple characters?"

"Let me see... I can't, no, wait...CLOSEUP, maybe?"

"CLOSEUP?"

"Could be, I really was kind of drunk."

"What color was the SUV?"

"It was really dark out there," Hale says. "No moonlight or anything, I don't know. Not a bright color, like white or silver. Black, blue, dark red, dark gray, maybe?"

"What about the gun? Metal? Polymer?"

He flicks a hand. "No idea, sorry. It was a gun, it was little, it shot when I pulled the trigger."

"But it was definitely a revolver?"

He returns an annoyed look. "Again, it shot when I pulled the trigger. "

"You don't want to get convicted for this, you need to ditch the attitude, okay? Juries hate rich white assholes. Especially with names like Brixton."

He gives a little nod that might be his idea of an apology. "How would I tell what kind it was?"

"You said it had a hammer and a cylinder, so that means it was a revolver."

"Okay."

"Did you pull back the hammer before you fired?"

"No, I just pulled the trigger." He shows me by making a finger-gun, pointing it at me, and pulling the trigger. "Ka-pow!" he says with a grin.

I don't grin back. "So we're talking about a small double-action revolver?"

He grins again. At my earnestness, I think. "If you say so."

"What did the SUV lady look like?"

"Nice rack, like I said. Blond hair, I think." He studies me for a moment. "Like yours, but blonder and a little longer, down to the shoulders. She was kind of built like you, too."

"How old?"

"Sixty? Year or two more? Pretty good looking for her age, probably a babe back in the day. Also kinda like you?"

"I'm fifty-one!" I can't help saying. How is it possible that I give a damn about what this sleazeball thinks of my looks?

"Sorry, ma'am," he says.

"And don't call me 'ma'am'"

"No, ma'am," he says with that damned Tom Cruise grin. "But seriously. You got nothing to apologize for. Little work on the forehead, the neck, you'll be a babe again. For a couple years."

I clench many my teeth, flip back through my notes and check the paperwork Ike gave me.

"One loose end here," I say. "The Lyft driver, guy named Oscar Littlefield. Saw the news about the murder, realized it sounded like a no-show rider he had the night before, and walked into the police station in Palm Springs. He didn't notice Jennifer's body when he came by but he told the detectives he did see a vehicle, possibly a small sedan, pulling away as he approached the pickup point, which is why he figured she got another ride somehow. You see anything like a small sedan when you were back and forth between Jennifer and the SUV lady that night?"

"Nope," Hale says. "Nothing like that."

"The question is, did the Lyft guy come by between the two shootings, or after them?"

Hale reflects on that for perhaps a minute, as do I.

"Well, whoever he saw pull away, that had to be the guy that shot her in the throat, right?"

"Which would mean Oscar had to have been there between the two shootings," I say. "A few minutes after you dumped her, and right after the driver of the unknown vehicle shot her, but before you came back after your meeting with the SUV lady."

"Sounds right to me."

I check the file again and see that it's mined out. "I guess we're about done here, Mr. Hale. Do I need to remind you again what not to do?"

"No talking to police, I swear." He flashes a V-sign. "Scout's honor."

I sweep the file and the crime scene photos into my briefcase.

"Can your friend Skogel get me out of here?" he asks.

"Your bail's a million dollars and your grandfather has refused to put it up. Ike will try for a reduction, of course, but it's a tough sell. You're the famous torso shooter now. And judges don't like rich assholes, either."

"But I come from a good family." He puts on a grin that says he lives on Money Island and knows the moat around it will protect him from riffraff like cops and prosecutors.

"We'll see."

Before I go, I have to ask him a couple more questions. Not that I really need to. I just have to get the obvious on the record.

"Any guesses who shot her down there?"

"Had to be the SUV lady, right?"

"That's how I read it. You think she did the throat shot, too?"

He turns it over for a while. "Nah. Why would she hire me then?"

"Did she say why she wanted Jennifer dead?"

"No, but Jennifer had to be screwing her husband, right? What else?"

"Also how I read it. Anything else I should know about that night?"

He starts to shake his head, then stops and looks lost in thought. "Frank," he says.

"What?"

"When we made out in the bathroom at the party in Chap City. Jennifer said 'Oh, Frank' both times she came. Apparently she was hung up on some guy named Frank. Maybe he killed her. Maybe Frank is who you should be looking for."

Chapter Twelve

—·—

"Two shooters?" Ike's Adam's apple bobs as he tilts up a Dos Equis. "You're shitting me."

We're at the Sand Trap for lunch. It's the only decent dive bar in a town where most people are too fancy for music from a juke box and drinks from a barmaid named Rusty. With Rusty, you don't get a glass with your beer unless you ask for it. In which case it comes with a side of eye roll and attitude, no extra charge.

I've just led Ike through my interview with Hale, other than the part about Frank. That, I can't bring myself to mention.

"Yep, that's Hale's story," I tell him. "A throat shooter and a torso shooter."

We're interrupted by a visit from Rusty to take our orders. She's in her usual tank top, cutoffs, and cowboy boots, except the boots don't look familiar.

"New footwear?" I ask.

"New man." She cuts her eyes toward at a guy at the bar in boots and jeans, and smiles as a woman will at such moments.

He smiles back. I tell her, "Enjoy," and add with my inside voice, "while it lasts."

She takes our orders—a burger with fries for Ike, a Greek salad with grilled chicken for me.

Then there's the one Hale fired into the sand under the mesquite bush, which makes two. And there's the five torso shots which, if the SUV lady was doing the shooting, presumably came from the same gun Hale used to shoot the mesquite bush. And that makes seven all told."

"Of which the cops have just the five from the torso shots," Ike says. "We think."

"Right. They haven't found the bullet from the throat shot that we're aware of, and they don't know about Hale's mesquite shot."

Ike turns it over some more. "Let's say they find the bullet from the throat shot or they already did. There's two possibilities."

"Yep. Number one, it matches the torso bullets and there's no mesquite bullet."

"Which would blow up Hale's story."

"Right. Because if the SUV lady already shot Jennifer in the throat, why does she hire Hale to shoot her again and then go back personally to put five more rounds between her legs?"

"She doesn't," Ike says. "So a match on the bullets would pretty much have to mean Hale did all the shooting," Ike says. "And we have to defend a guilty client who's lying to us. I'm getting a headache already."

"And then there's possibility number two. The throat bullet doesn't match the torso bullets."

"Which would be very good for our side," Ike says. "Our rich asshole client would actually start to look innocent. So innocent it might never go to trial."

"The sound of heads exploding in Homicide you could hear in Slab City."

Ike smiles at the thought. "Uh-huh. Which takes us to Hale's mesquite bullet."

"Yeah. If we find that and it matches the torso bullets then we have six and that's a full load for a revolver and - -"

"And Hale's probably off the hook," Ike says.

Rusty brings our order, and we wolf down a few bites.

"So where is this mesquite bullet again?" Ike mumbles through a mouthful of cheeseburger. "Allegedly?"

"Forty or fifty yards down Gene Autry—south, that would be—from where they found Jennifer's body."

"Can we find it?"

"I might know a guy."

"A guy with a metal detector?" Ike asks.

"Uh-huh."

"Who's gonna say what, exactly, when Palm Springs Public Safety rolls up and asks why he's snooping around a crime scene with a metal detector?"

"He'll say nothing, because he won't have to. He's nocturnal."

"You mean the Chaplain?"

"Different guy. It's too hot to work by day this time of year..."

"Ah," Ike says. "So he works at night."

We have a few more bites of lunch before Ike continues.

"So here's my question. What if we just give all this to the cops and let them sort it out?"

"Seriously?"

"All right, call it a thought experiment instead of a question," Ike says. "But let's game it out."

"You're the lawyer, but do you really want to tell the police your client was at the scene not once, but twice? And the second time he not only had the money on him that he was paid to kill Jennifer, but also the gun he was supposed to do it with?"

"Just checking," Ike says with a grin. "The point is, we're not even close to ready to talk to your pal St. Clair again, agreed?"

"Or Avila. Especially Avila."

We apply ourselves to lunch. Ike orders another Dos Equis, takes a long pull, and makes an unsuccessful effort to suppress a belch.

"So," I say over a forkful of Greek salad. "The dueling lesbians."

A huge smile spreads over Ike's face. It's as if the perplexities and vexations of Jennifer Williamson's murder have melted away. "I'm thinking this is the case that buys me that Maserati. These ladies hate each other like you never saw two people hate each other before."

"Which one cheated?"

Ike grins. "We deny sleeping with our ex-husband, Your Honor. Underscore *ex*. And if we did, it was after the separation agreement was effectuated."

"So what's it about then?"

"I didn't tell you about the recipe box?"

"You didn't tell me anything except it's two extremely rich lesbians."

"So when Sylvia Webster, that's my client, turned twenty-one, she got this little cedar box from her Mee-Maw back in Kentucky. It had all of her hand-written recipes in it from, like, fifty years of Southern cooking. They were very close, Mee-Maw was the first person that Sylvia came out to. It seems Mee-Maw was also of the gay persuasion, but she never officially came out herself. Got married, had Sylvia's mom and two siblings, her husband passed away, she lived quietly with her best friend after that, which I guess is how you had to roll if you were gay in that time and place. Sad story, huh?"

Ike may have his faults, but he does commit empathy now and again.

"Very sad," I agree. "They should have moved to Palm Springs."

Ike lubricates his throat with Dos Equis and continues. "So, poor Mee-Maw dies in the pandemic and Sylvia doesn't even get to say goodbye. She could barely get through telling me about it. Twenty minutes of tears and mucus, I swear."

"Yeah, that's tough. But where are we going with - -"

"Guess what Miranda, that's the opposition, guess what she took with her when the big blowup finally came and she moved out?"

"How would I - - oh, no, not the - -"

Ike smiles like a great white about to swallow a baby dolphin. "Uh-huh. Mee-Maw's recipe box. Wants to cut it in two pieces and they each get half the recipes. A woman really knows where to sink the harpoon, am I right?"

"This should be a murder case!"

"I'd defend her pro bono," Ike says.

"No you wouldn't."

"I'd at least think about it."

"Please tell me there's a way Lita and I can help."

He grins. "Funny you should ask. Sylvia thinks Miranda bought a secret chalet up in Tahoe, but she hasn't been able to track it down to claim her half. You interested?"

"You kidding? What do we know about this chalet? Purchase date? Price range? Neighborhood? Realtor?"

"Some of the above," Ike says. "Plus, she might have used a trust."

"Why God made legal investigators. Email us whatever you've got and I'll get Lita on it."

"Excellent."

"So where is this recipe box?"

"We don't know," Ike says. "Sylvia checked their place here and the Malibu beach house, nada."

"Maybe at the Tahoe chalet, assuming it exists?"

"Dana."

"I could poke around."

Ike grins. "Don't tell me any more."

I wink and grin back.

He downs the last nacho, drains the Dos Equis. "Dessert? I wouldn't mind another beer."

I check my watch. "I should probably get to work on the Hale stuff."

"Good point," he says. "And I - -"

My phone cuts him off. It's Lita. I show Ike her picture on the screen and take the call.

Lita dives right in. "Mom needs some stuff for the kids. Maybe you can pick it up if you're coming into town?"

"I'm already here. At the Sand Trap. What does she need?"

"It's a long list. She said the Target in Chapel City should have all of it. Ready?"

I scribble as she talks. "Little juice boxes, the kind with the straws attached. Bananas, two gallons of milk, socks, pajamas, four shirts and four shorts for each - no zippers or buttons or snaps. And two boxes of pullups."

"Pullups?"

"Yeah. Diapers that are like little underpants so they can pull 'em up and down by themselves. The older kids there are teasing the twins about wearing baby diapers. Can you drop the stuff off?"

An hour later, I'm in the checkout line at Target and somehow a huge plastic jar of animal crackers has also made its way into my cart, along with Pop-Tarts, fruit chews, a half-gallon of chocolate milk and a six-pack of Kraft mac and cheese. The middle-aged cashier smiles as she folds the pink nightgown with a ruffled hem into the bag.

"Nietos, si?" she asks.

Nietos. Grandkids. That's not gonna be happening. Then I think, what if Sonny and Rose have kids someday? Maybe I'll get to be a great aunt, if not a grandma. I smile at the clerk and tell her, "*Sobrinos.* Rose and Sonny."

"Being a *tía,* that's almost as good," she says.

A few minutes later, I turn the Vic onto Yolanda's street in Chapel City. Clean sidewalks and well kept single-story homes in hot, bright colors say the folks here take pride in the neighborhood and look out for each other. The back yards are unfenced except for the occasional dark green hedge of ambrosia plants.

Yolanda's place is a bungalow with white stucco walls and a red tile roof. A bright red front door, set back into the shade of a stucco arch, is bordered by ceramic planters overflowing with green dwarf fan palms. Vertical white shades dress the front windows.

I park on a clean-swept driveway of reddish paver blocks bordered on one side by yucca cactus and the sharp spikes of agave plants. The other side is lined by Mexican evening primroses covered with yellow and white blossoms.

Lita comes out to greet me and we enter through the side door into Yolanda's kitchen, filled as usual with the smell of Mexican cooking.

The twins run in from the TV when they hear us arrive. Sonny hangs back but Rose charges me and hugs my legs. "*Tía! Tía!*"

I drop and hug back. "How about you guys come to my house again sometime? See Dukie? We can go for another hike, have a picnic."

Their eyes light up, then Sonny sobers and looks up at me. "Daddy come too, *tía?*"

My throat tightens. "No, *hijito.* Just Duke," I manage.

Rose chimes in, "Mommy come?"

I shake my head, Sonny joins the hug, and we huddle for a second. They're like me, still wondering where normal went.

Yolanda steps in. "Oh, look! Strawberry pop tarts! And cinnamon, too, with frosting!"

The kids turn. She holds up the boxes. "What kind you want?"

I slip out while she unwraps the pop tarts, and start for Bamboo Beach.

Half a block from Yolanda's, I smell Partagas smoke and there in the rearview mirror is Imaginary Frank. Sunglasses, Vic owners t-shirt, arms spread like wings along the seatback, cigar in hand.

"You again," I say to the mirror.

"Thanks for taking care of my kids."

"Go to Hell. And you're welcome. Rose and Sonny are great."

"Yolanda will raise them right," he says. "Probably better than Jennifer would have."

"Again, go to Hell."

"You would have made a great mom."

"Except I couldn't. Can't."

"I wasn't going to mention that," he says. "You shouldn't either. It's not your fault the medicos couldn't figure it out."

"Screw them."

"You should spend more time with the twins. It'll drain away the anger and pain."

"I'm not sure I want to let it go."

He lowers a window and flicks the Partagas out onto the shoulder. "Love you baby."

And then the mirror's empty.

CHAPTER THIRTEEN

—·—

Bamboo Beach is on the Salton Sea about sixty miles down Highway 111 from Palm Springs. A stiff wind is blowing in dust from that end of the Coachella Valley as I start south. The sky is the color of adobe and I pick up the Salton Stench before I'm even out of Palm Springs. At the north shore of the Salton, my eyes start to water from the mix of hydrogen sulfide gas belching off the sea bottom and the stink of rotting fish piled up on the shore.

It's one of those days when residents of Palm Springs call the mayor's office to complain. As if the politicians will do anything about the Salton Sea. Every idea anybody's come up with would cost too much. One example: fifty billion bucks, plus or minus, for a system to pump in ocean water from the Sea of Cortez, more than a hundred miles to the south. Like most desert dreams, it's too big to ever be real. There's no hope, but we complain anyway.

Bamboo Beach comes into view and I swing off the highway into town. The giant metal playground swing that someone set up thirty yards offshore is still there. So is the sea wall built to protect Bamboo Beach should the Salton ever rise up again as it did in the Seventies when hurricanes pushed water in from the Sea of Cortez. It doesn't hurt that the wall also protects visitors from the sight of fish carcasses, clumps of seaweed, rotting furniture, abandoned vehicles, and all the other detritus that litters the shores.

The dash tells me it's 104 degrees as I pull in at the Surf Inn, the town's chief watering hole. It's two wooden stories painted red and white, with a tile awning over the entrance and weapons-grade air-conditioning inside.

I take a deep breath and brace myself. Frank and I used to come down and spend the night here every year on the date we met during the warrant sweep in the Slabs. Our meetiversary, we called it. I'd rather be anywhere else right now, but it comes with the job. In I go.

There's a juke box with a guy complaining about his girl calling him a Coca-Cola cowboy and a pool table with only a few rips in the felt. The walls and ceilings are papered over with dollar bills signed and taped up there by customers. A few faded, curling, sun-and-sea posters from the Salton's heyday adorn the walls, pretty girls with curves to die for, hunky boys with abs to sigh for.

The place is empty except for an older couple having burgers and brew at a table in the back and a sturdy old broad in worn jeans and a frilled white top behind the bar.

This is Tanya Hoover. I've known her since that first night with Frank. Her eyes are framed by a lacework of wrinkles and she was here before the Stench.

"Long time no, Dana," she says as I take a stool at the bar. "Still drinking mules?"

I tell her I'm working and order an iced tea, which gets me a side-eye from Tanya. She sets a sweat-jeweled tumbler in front of me and a long silence develops.

Finally she says it. "Sorry to hear about Frank, sweetie. Sometimes life just serves you a shit sandwich."

I take a slow drink from the iced tea.

Another long silence and she gets the message it's not something I want to discuss.

"So," she says in a cheerful and businesslike tone, just two gals talking shop now. "You're working, huh? Anything I can help you with?"

"I'm trying to get in touch with somebody. Free-spirit artist girl named Cara. She was hanging with that Smokey Hale guy that got arrested over your bar fight a few days ago."

She snorts. "Asshole. He busted one of my chairs over a guy's back."

"I heard the guy groped Cara and Hale went Sir Galahad on him."

She sighs with a wistful look. "A girl doesn't mind that sometimes, I guess."

She studies me for a few seconds. "Cara in some kind of trouble?"

"I don't think so. I'm a legal investigator these days and I'm working with Hale's defense attorney."

"Oh, yeah, I saw on the news they think he's your torso shooter up in Palm Springs. Did he do it?"

"That's why I need to talk to Cara. He claims she can alibi him. Know where I could find her?"

She snorts at the stupidity of the question. Tanya knows how to find everybody in Bamboo Beach. But she does answer it. "You want Cara Levine. She's staying in the Jungle House. Couple blocks that way, south side of the street, first green trailer you come to.

"Thanks." I put a ten on the counter for the three-dollar iced tea, figuring Hale's grandfather can afford it and Tanya can use it.

I walk out into the blast furnace, hustle into the Jeep, and slam the door against the grit-laden wind.

The drive down Second Avenue takes me past the Bamboo Beach Drive-In--rows of dead cars facing a fake screen with a crude plywood billboard announcing that Hayley Mills is starring in "The Parent Trap."

The Jungle House is a dark green single-wide from the Sixties or Seventies, I figure, complete with the big American flag on the side that Hale told me about. It squats under a corrugated metal roof held up by wooden stilts. Sort of a parasol, except for a fifty-year-old mobile home instead of a fancy lady in bonnet and gloves. Without it, the summer sun hammering on that green aluminum would no doubt turn the place into a toaster oven ten minutes after dawn.

I park in the unsuccessful shade of a withered palm tree beside a Honda SUV with Ohio plates and knock on a rattly aluminum screen door.

The thirty-something who opens it wears a faded tee shirt a couple of sizes too big, no bra, and bib overalls with rips and tears that look to be a matter of style rather than wear. She has curves like a pro wrestler or a fertility goddess, and the first signs of a baby bump in front.

But what really sets her apart is the eyes. Big staring blue searchlights, like she just jumped out of a closet, shouted "Boo!" and wants to see your reaction.

"Hi." She lets the eyes work on me for a couple of seconds. "Can I help you?"

"You Cara?"

She taps a bare foot. Her toenails are sparkly silver. "And you are?"

Her voice is educated and composed. I can't figure this one out. She's not the meth head I half expected. She has all of her teeth, and they are extremely white.

"I'm Dana Forsythe." I pass her my card. "I'm a legal investigator working for Smokey Hale's lawyer."

Her smile turns fond and reminiscent and she extends her hand. "How's he doing?" she says as we shake. "Will he be released soon?"

"That may depend on you, actually. He said you might be able to provide some favorable evidence."

"Maybe." She slides one heel up the inside of the opposite leg, stops at the knee, and stands there in perfect balance, like a fleshy stork. "Care for some lemonade?"

"Sure."

She drops the foot off her knee and waves me in and I see why Tanya called it the Jungle House.

Every picture, rug, and drape, every stick of furniture, the tissue box cover on the kitchen counter, even a shower curtain visible through a bathroom doorway, is animal-themed. Lions, elephants, tigers, and zebras gaze from every surface. The table lamps are miniature coconut palms. One room features four single beds in a row, all draped with zebra bedspreads.

"Wow! Did you do all this?"

"No. My friend Ava. She's in Africa and I'm managing her B&B while she's gone."

She heads to the kitchen, returns with lemonade in tumblers with giraffes and monkeys etched into the sides. "Cheers."

We clink and drink. The lemonade has an extra kick I'm pretty sure is vodka. I set mine aside.

"You know Smokey is accused of being what they're calling the torso shooter up in Palm Springs, right?"

"Duh. It's all over the news. But he didn't do it."

"He says you have some evidence that could help clear him."

"Possibly."

"He says he gave you a Patek Philippe watch to, ah, hold for him?"

The blue eyes narrow. "I have a law degree so I know I don't have to answer that. You're not law enforcement anyway."

"A law degree?"

"Yes. Notre Dame."

I don't ask. I wait. I know she'll tell me the rest of it. People who come to the desert always do.

She does.

She bailed out of a job in the DA's office in Cincinnati after a tourist visit to Bamboo Beach, she says. She wanted to free herself from the pressure of city life, to be in a place where she could do her art and photography, practice yoga, and not be judged. Bamboo Beach, she says, spoke to her. She doesn't mention how she ended up on the road to motherhood and I don't ask. The tip of Cara's iceberg is enough for now.

She strides to the nearest wall, flips upside down and stands on her head, braced on her elbows and looking lost in thought as her t-shirt slides down. A band of tattooed vines circles her waist like a belt.

She bounces back up. "Tending bar for Tanya covers my nut. I paint every day, murals outside, oils inside, take photos of the art around here and in the Slabs, I sell a piece now and again. I'm living how I want to live."

"Congratulations. You're ahead of most people. So the Patek Philippe. Smokey did give it to you?"

She considers for a moment. "He did."

"What did he tell you about it?"

"He said it belonged to his late grandmother, which was obviously just a story to get me into bed." She grins. "So I said I'd only sleep with him if he gave me the real story. Then he told me how he really got it."

"And that was?"

"He picked up that girl, the one who got shot, at some party in what did he call it, Chapel Palms?" she starts. "But they left it to go to this other party in Desert...Desert...I don't know, Desert Something. But on the way..."

And she goes on to tell the same story Hale told me, right through the SUV lady's no-show at the Westgate mall the day after the murder. The fact that she can't quite pull up the names of Chapel City and Desert Hot Springs somehow makes it ring even truer.

"That's some crazy shit, huh?" she concludes.

"Seriously. And you believed him, I gather?"

"Of course. I can read people without trying."

"We need that watch for Smokey's defense."

"I need it, too." She pats her belly. "For when the Bump makes his debut. It's worth fifteen or twenty thousand dollars, I think. Half for me, half for Smokey."

"That watch is evidence in a murder case. You could go down for obstruction of justice if you sell it. The Bump there could be born in jail and end up in foster care."

She cocks her head and the blue searchlights lock onto my eyes. "You fight dirty."

"As needed." I put out my hand.

She goes to a kitchen drawer and returns with a watch. It's a Patek Philippe, solid gold with a slight pinkish cast except for a clear back that shows the clockwork inside. There's a ring of tiny diamonds around the face. Suddenly Hale's story feels as real as if I'd seen the events on Gene Autry Trail with my own eyes.

"Do you want a receipt?"

"Not necessary." She unsnaps a pocket on the bib of the overalls and pulls out a phone. "I have your card and I've been recording us ever since I opened the door."

"You may need to testify, too."

"And get involved in a murder trial? No thanks." She pats her belly again. "I do have this to think about now."

"Smokey did come to your rescue at Tanya's place."

She tosses her head with a laugh. "Only because I let him." Her right foot comes off the floor and flashes past an inch from my chin, almost too fast to see. "I'm a kick boxer. I don't need a man for protection."

"Point taken. But this one broke a chair over a guy's back for you."

She laughs again. "Yeah, that was sweet."

She gives me another dose of the blue searchlights. "Will I get it back? If it was given to Smokey voluntarily, there's an argument to be made that he's the legal owner. Or was, till he gave me a half-interest in return for selling it for him."

"You could be right, the watch might be yours and his once the legal system finishes with it. You can have it as far as the defense is concerned."

"I'll testify then, sure."

I collect her contact info, photograph the plates on her Honda, and drive out of Bamboo Beach past the Surf Inn to Highway 111. As I start north, I wonder for the millionth time, do people like Cara find the desert, or does it find them? And are they crazier than the rest of us, or saner?

As I speed through the Stench toward Palm Springs, mirage puddles shimmer on the asphalt like sheets of silver. The AC thrums at its max and I wish for rain. Nothing is green here. Everything is the washed-out khaki of sand and silt, everything but the poisoned blue loveliness of the Salton Sea.

I get home, feed Duke and let him out to do his business. He's back in less than two minutes. Palm Springs dogs learn to be quick on days like this. A wave of blistering air follows him into the kitchen. I toss some whites into the washer, and stack the mail for later.

Lita calls to report on the CLOSEUP plates. They belong to a wedding photographer in San Francisco who drives a Ford van, not a fancy

SUV. And, at least as of today, the photographer is in San Francisco, where he claims to have been since May. Another little miracle from my database queen, but another dead end.

"Oh, yeah," she says. "And Guillermo found the chalet at Tahoe, about four and a half million worth. She used a trust like Ike thought."

"Fabulous," I tell her, "absolutely fabulous. My love to Guillermo and email Ike the details, *sí*?"

"*Por supuesto*," she says, and we tap off.

I pull out the Patek Philippe, lay it on the kitchen island and study it. It tells me the time is a little past six. And this is a Saturday.

But you can't win if you don't bet. I ask Professor Google which jewelers in the area handle Patek Philippe. The professor reports just one, Sterling and Sons in La Quinta, and they're open till seven.

I call the number, connect with a Sterling son named Jacob, introduce myself, and describe the watch. Jacob is courteous and efficient and asks me if the finish is platinum or rose gold.

"Rose gold," I say.

Justin says that sounds familiar, he thinks they sold it, and he tells me to look under the clear crystal back for the serial number engraved onto the clockwork. I find the tiny digits, pull a little magnifying glass out of my junk drawer, and read the serial number to him. He puts me on hold to look it up. Can it be this simple?

He comes back, asks why I need information on the owner. When I explain I'm investigating a theft—which is within a few yards of the truth--he goes silent.

"Jacob? Are you still there?"

"Yes, ma'am," he replies. "But I'm sorry, Ms. Forsythe, I am unable to provide you that information. Customer confidentiality is at the heart of the Sterling and Sons guarantee. You'll need a subpoena."

Shit. Three dead ends in one day. Subpoenas take a while if the target fights back, and I'm guessing Sterling and Sons will do exactly that. Their business depends on rich people and rich people like their privacy.

I call Ike to report the day's developments. His phone goes to voice-mail. I leave a message, and flop down in front of the TV.

Chapter Fourteen

— · —

After breakfast, I go for a dawn outing with Duke. While he's off chasing the female coyote who torments him for sport, I see my neighbor Edgar unloading his metal detector from the back of his old Toyota pickup.

Which reminds me.

I whistle Duke back to my side and we stroll over. Duke lifts his leg and marks the truck's right front tire, then lies down to pant in the shade of the cab.

"Good hunting, Edgar?"

"Take a look." He opens his pack and shows me the haul: a rusty penknife, two old-school brass keys, a gold band, and about twenty cents in coins.

"A wedding ring, huh?"

He grimaces. "Worth fifty bucks at Jackie's, maybe. And I got some exercise."

"Where'd you go?"

"Poked around the hiking trails up there." He jerks a thumb at the Cahuilla Hills back of our houses. They're laced with such trails.

"There's enough light for it at night?"

"Yeah. We still got about a three-quarter moon and I got a head-lamp."

He pulls his gear out of the pickup bed and shows me an LED headlamp, then a Bounty Hunter metal detector.

"Bounty Hunter. That a pretty good brand?"

That's enough for Edgar. I ride out a five-minute treatise on the ins and outs of metal detecting, metal detectors, and metal detectorists like Edgar.

"That thing ever turn up any bullets?"

"Oh, yeah, all the time. It's as good for that as the ones you cops use. If it conducts electricity, the Bounty Hunter will find it."

"How deep?"

"A bullet? Twelve inches, maybe fifteen."

"Huh." I hand him one of the Jacinto Investigations business cards I keep on my person. "Think you could find one for me?"

He looks at the card, then me. "So you're a legal investigator now?"

"Yeah, I retired from the sheriff's office after...you know, after everything that happened."

He does know, and he just nods, bless his heart. No condolences.

"So I've got this case where my client says he fired a pistol into the sand under a mesquite bush. We need to find the bullet."

Edgar grins like a guy who hasn't seen much action lately. "Love to. Where is it?"

"Up on Gene Autry Trail, near where they had what the news people are calling the torso shooting?"

"And your client's the one that did it?"

"We don't think so."

"Hm."

"Don't worry, this is legal. You don't have to go into the crime scene they've got taped off. The spot I'm interested in is nearby, but not actually inside it."

"Yeah, okay, and how do I find your spot?"

I explain how he should start at the crime scene and work his way south along the shoulder for maybe a hundred yards, with special attention to any mesquite bushes near the pavement. "But thing is, we'd just as soon not have the cops get too interested in what we're doing, so wee hours would be good. Two or three in the morning, maybe?"

"Uh-huh."

"And maybe you could wear dark clothes and turn off the headlamp and walk out in the desert a few yards whenever you see any traffic coming?"

"This could be getting a little too interesting," he says. "If you catch my drift."

"Oh, yeah, I almost forgot. How does five hundred sound if you do find it and you're willing to testify about it in court, against fifty a night if you don't find it?"

"Now that is interesting," Edgar says. "I'll start tonight."

We shake on it, and Duke and I return to the house. I brew coffee in the Keurig and try to figure out what to do with the rest of my day. The case is such a snarl, it's hard to know where to go next.

I start with something easy and put in a call to Murphy Jackson, a former sheriff's deputy like myself, now head of security at the West-gate Mall in Palm Desert. He answers his cell on the second ring with "Hey, stranger!"

I respond with "Hey, Murph! How's retirement treatin' ya?" and we bring each other up to date for a couple of minutes. Finally we get around to business and I ask him if he can check some security video for me—the area in front of Macy's from around three o'clock to four o'clock last Monday, the fifteenth.

"That's a lot of video. What am I looking for?"

"Guy named Brixton Lee Hale. He's - -"

"Wait," he says. "Why is that name--not the torso shooter! I just saw him on TV!"

I confess that's the guy and say I'm helping Ike Skogel with his defense. "You're not gonna have to go into the office for this are you? I guess it could wait till tom - -"

"Not a problem," he says. "I can log in from here at home. They have this thing called the Internet now, maybe you heard of it?"

"Drop dead. You need me to email you his mug shot?"

"Nah, I know what he looks like. He is all over the news."

"Copy that," I say. "The main thing we're looking for is, was he actually at the Westgate like he's been telling us he was? And if he was, did he spend much time talking to anybody?"

"Right. You need the actual video or just a summary?"

"A summary will do unless you see something that rings your bell."

"Probably better if I don't send you the actual video anyway," he says. "I'm guessing there's a fair chance this could end up in court?"

"Safe bet. We can write up a subpoena if we actually need it."

"Tell you what, though, I can probably sneak you a frame grab of anybody he actually talks to if you need it. But we never had this conversation, right?"

"What conversation?" We tap off, and I go back to the main question of the day: What now?

When I'm dead-ended, it helps to put together what I call a tick-tock—a minute-by-minute timeline of who was doing what, and when, as the crime went down. Even if it's mostly guesses and hunches, it'll at least point in the right direction.

I grab my laptop from the office, tap it to life, flop down on the couch, and start typing. I think and I type, I type and I think, I rifle through the paperwork we got from the cops and my notes from the interviews with Johnny B. and Hale, then I type some more. I give

Hale the benefit of the doubt. I assume everything he said, however improbable, is true.

Two hours later, my timeline looks like this:

- 11:35-11:40 pm, Sunday, July 14: Hale dumps Jennifer by Gene Autry Trail.

- 11:45 pm, Sunday, July 14: Jennifer hails Lyft.

- 11:45-11:50 pm, Sunday, July 14: SUV Lady cuts Hale off near Interstate 10, hires him to kill Jennifer. He starts back to warn her.

- 12:00 pm, Sunday, July 14: Throat shooter kills Jennifer with single shot, leaves scene.

- 12:01 a.m., Monday, July 15: Lyft driver approaches pickup point, sees taillights as Throat shooter pulls away, assumes Jennifer got another ride home. Cancels Lyft ride at 12:03 a.m..

- 12:07 a.m., Monday, July 15: Hale arrives at murder scene, finds Jennifer dead of throat shot, no torso shots. Decides to con SUV Lady into thinking he carried out the hit. Shoots her gun into base of mesquite bush for when she checks if it was fired.

- 12:12 a.m., Monday, July 15: Hale returns to SUV Lady, returns gun, says he shot Jennifer in throat. SUV Lady falls for con, gives him watch, says they'll meet at Westgate Mall next day to pay him.

- 12:16 a.m., Monday, July 15: SUV Lady goes to murder

scene, shoots Jennifer in torso five times.

- 12:22 a.m., Monday, July 15: Onion trucker spots Jennifer's body by road, calls 911.

I print it out, make more coffee, and go back to the couch to step through it, minute by minute. I'm at the point where Hale's conning the SUV lady about having shot Jennifer when my phone chimes and Murph's caller ID pops up.

"Talk about timing," I say. "You got something already?"

"It's Sunday morning, too early to start drinking and what else have I got to do?"

"So...?"

"So, yeah, your guy was in the mall for fifty-six minutes starting at 2:58 pm last Monday. Spent all of it on or around the bench in front of Macy's except for a single three-minute trip to the john and six minutes getting a drink at an espresso stand a few yards down the corridor from the bench. Looked like he hit on the barista, got her number, went back to his bench, drank his espresso and played on his phone till he gave up and left."

"Didn't talk to anybody else?"

"Not that's on the video. We don't have cameras in the men's rooms, obviously, but he wasn't in there long. And the only other traffic through that particular one around the time he was in there was a Hispanic guy with a baby and a gay couple with mohawks."

"Huh."

"Is this good news or bad news?"

"This case is so effing crazy, I'm actually not sure."

"Sometimes they're like that," Murph says. "You want frame grabs of the men's room traffic or the barista?"

"Nah, might as well leave you with totally clean hands on this. If we need it, the mall will get a subpoena."

"All good," he says.

I thank him and we end the call.

Almost immediately, my phone rings and caller ID pops up the name of Liz Hernandez. Friend or not, something tells me not to take it.

I bump the call to voicemail and listen to it when the line clears. Yep, my best friend is working on a story about me for tomorrow's *Herald*. She apologizes, but has to ask, do I want to comment? At least she asks it as gently as possible.

I do not, of course. Instead, I make a dark roast and tell myself I will not read tomorrow's headlines.

I finish the coffee and call Ike. He answers in a not-quite-awake voice. Oh, yeah, it's not yet noon on a Sunday. Of course, he's still in bed. Good.

"Dana," he croaks. "What's up?'

"Who's Dana?" a muffled female voice asks in the background. "Is that a woman?"

"Sorry if I woke you," I lie, which we both know. "Say 'hi' to your friend for me. You get my voicemail?"

"Yeah, yeah, too late to call you back, hang on a sec."

There's a sound like he's covering the phone with his hand, then his muffled voice saying, "It's okay, baby, it's just work."

He comes back on in his normal voice. "Sorry about that. So it sounds like you scored the Patek Philippe in Bamboo Beach?"

"Big time. And I just confirmed Hale was in the Westgate when he said he was, but he never talked to anybody who could be the SUV lady. We need to meet."

I hear the rustle of bedding, then what sounds like a bathroom door being slammed. Ike clears his throat. "Okay, when and where?"

"Noon? The IHOP by your office?"

He mumbles an answer that I can't make out but sounds affirmative.

"See ya there." I hang up.

Ike is fifteen minutes late, probably as payback for my rousting him out of bed so early on a Sunday. His rumpled grey sweatshirt and blue jeans underscore the point.

The waitress brings him coffee and a menu. We order French toast for me, Rooty Tooty Fresh n' Fruity pancakes for him.

"Okay," he complains. "This better be good."

I pull the Patek Philippe from my purse and lay it on the table. He whistles.

"Exactly," I say. "Major bling."

"And Hale showed up at the Westgate like he said?"

"Definitely. Here's how it shakes out so far." I spread a printout of my timeline in front of him.

He stirs creamer into his coffee, sips it as he reads, ends with, "You've been busy. And on a weekend."

"I live to give, you know that, Ike. But point is, Hale's two for two now, counting the watch and the Westgate."

Ike sighs. "Just what I was afraid of. We really do have an affirmative defense on our hands."

"You're the lawyer, but...yep."

"All right," Ike says. "Let's make sure I caught the main points. Throat Shooter is a total unknown, correct?

"Correct."

"And ditto for SUV Lady."

"Correct," I say. "Lita struck out on the CLOSEUP license plate."

"But she's gotta be the torso shooter, correct?"

"Correct."

"Well, shit." He concentrates on his Rooty Tooty for a couple of minutes. "What next?"

"I guess you could work on getting the video from the traffic cameras in that area that night."

"Yuck," Ike says. "But, yeah, I'll put an intern on it."

"How about going after the jeweler on who bought the Patek Philippe?"

"Tough one," he says. "We don't know for sure if that watch helps us or hurts us. Until we do know, let's not rattle that cage and maybe alert the cops what we're up to."

"I thought you'd say that."

"And you?"

"Well, there's the SUV lady and the Throat shooter, obviously, but other than the traffic cams around the murder scene I don't see any way forward on either of them at the moment. Which leaves Hale's alleged bullet into the mesquite bush. My metal detector guy starts tonight."

Ike brightens a little. "I really like the bullets. I've always liked the bullets. We find that mesquite bullet, it might be time for another talk with your buddy Avila."

"Ick, but yeah."

"How much we paying your guy?"

"Five hundred if he finds the bullet, fifty a night if he doesn't."

"That seems eminently reasonable." The wheels turn in Ike's head for a moment, then he gives me a look. "All of which leaves you doing what, exactly?"

"Detecting 101. Track down Jennifer's friends to see what they know about who she was sleeping with."

"It's always money or monkey business, eh?"

"If not both."

CHAPTER FIFTEEN

—·—

My stomach knots when I see the lead headline on the *Herald* website: *Was Torso Shooter enraged widow?*

The victim, Jennifer Williamson, is now identified as the mistress of "slain cop hero Frank Forsythe." Police aren't saying if his widow, Dana Forsythe, is a suspect but that doesn't keep the *Herald* from speculating. Liz has dug up my official officer portrait from the sheriff's office. The caption says "Enraged Widow?"

I can't stop myself from checking The Dragger, which has managed to top itself: *Crotch Killer: Vengeful Virago?*

I slam my laptop shut. Will Sonny and Rose grow up knowing Daddy was a cheater? That Mommy was murdered? That *Tía* Dana was a suspect?

I knuckle away tears, open the laptop, and try again to get through the story. Unidentified sources say I had brief custody of the twins that Frank fathered with the victim, but their present whereabouts and status are unknown. I can't read any more. I slump down on the couch, dizzy and gasping for air. The laptop slides off my lap and bounces onto the hardwood floor.

My phone on the coffee table is boiling over with chirps, pings and buzzes, but I've been ignoring it. Finally I give in and tap it to life. Some of the traffic is from other reporters I knew when I was a county mountie. One is from outside the U.S. There are calls from Ike and Lita, and from cops I used to work with.

Duke alerts, hurries to the picture window at the front of the house, and rumbles in his throat. I force myself up and pull open the honey-comb blinds.

A TV news van is parked in my driveway, as close to the front door as it can get. The cameraman aims a monster lens at my window. Jack Sheridan, one of the reporters I worked with over the years, points his microphone like a service pistol.

Behind the van, my driveway is a parking lot. A small crowd is staked out in the front yard, cameras and notebooks in hand, shouting questions at my door. Edgar, the metal detectorist, is on his roof with binoculars.

I close the blinds and call Duke off alert with the *Platz!* command, which is German for 'Down!' Like every police dog I ever met, Duke was trained in German.

The shouts outside don't let up. "Are you the torso shooter? Did you kill Jennifer Williamson?"

What I want to do is hide out in the bedroom till they're gone. But no, I can't let myself become even more of a victim of this mess. So I do what I always do. I get to work.

I let Duke out the back door for his morning constitutional while I get dressed. I let him back in again, pull on a leftover covid mask to spoil the video the TV people will be shooting, and dash out the back door. The Jeep is still morning-cool so I jump in, careen around the house and speed downhill.

Two of the news crews take off after me, so I swerve off the asphalt of Cahuilla Drive onto a dirt track called Roadrunner Trail. It's barely more than a footpath, and a quarter mile downhill it crosses one of the arroyos that lace Cahuilla Canyon. It's too much for the news crews in their sissy vans and they soon give up.

The Chamber of Commerce is an office complex fronted by canted, full-height windows. A square brick planter at the entry hosts a little cactus garden, including a cottontop with a big yellow blossom the size of a silver dollar.

The Chamber receptionist is on the phone behind a high, curved, wooden counter when I come in, so I have some time to gaze around the premises where Frank's woman worked. How many times was he in this very lobby? Did he talk with her in the adjoining conference room? Sit beside her on one of the wheeled green chairs pulled up to the conference table and touch her forearm as they talked?

The receptionist finishes her call. I introduce myself and ask about Jennifer, whom she turns out to have replaced. She's pretty sure Jennifer didn't hang around with the other employees much, but she'll ask and let me know if she hears anything. She does recall hearing that Jennifer frequented the coffee shop next door. I give her my card and start over.

Of course the coffee shop is called Coffi, another example of Palm Springs cute.

Two baristas, one of each gender, rush between the polished oak front counter, the espresso machines, and the cash register. The place boasts real plants and oak chairs and tables that match the counter.

The male barista—skinny, with a man bun--notices me standing aside at the pastry case and points to the line of customers. I shake my head and wave him over. He's in khaki shorts, a black polo with "Coffi" embroidered in white on the pocket and under that a nametag that says "Patrick" with "Manager" beneath.

"Can I help you?" Patrick asks.

"I'll make this quick. I'm here about Jennifer Williamson."

He grimaces. "Yeah. We can't really believe it. She was in here almost every day. Nice girl. And so beautiful. You are?"

"I'm Dana Forsythe, a private investigator on the case."

A moment to process, a flash of recognition, and he takes a step back. God, does everybody know who I am? At least he doesn't say anything.

"We're talking to her friends and acquaintances," I say. "Trying to find anybody who might know why it happened?"

"You want Chelsea Miller, then. They were pretty close. She's in the back room right now, unpacking this morning's deliveries." He points at a closed door and starts back to his coworker.

I thank him and let myself into the back room.

A petite woman looks up from a cardboard box she's slicing open with a box cutter in her left hand. Eyes heavily rimmed in charcoal, crimson lips, dyed auburn hair in a spiky shag. She wears skin-tight black leggings topped by a matching tunic with a Coffi nametag. A spiked black leather necklace and silver rings on every finger complete the ensemble. She'd be cute enough if she throttled it back a little. As is, she looks like a Vegas dancer.

"Who are you?"

"Hi, are you Chelsea? I hear you were Jennifer's friend? I'm Dana. I'm an investigator in her murder case."

I put out my left hand. She looks at it and I tell her, "Us lefties have to stick together, right?"

She drops the box cutter into a pocket and clasps my left hand with hers. The surface toughness melts away and she tries without success to blink away tears.

"I just can't believe it! She was my best friend!" She covers her face and collapses into sobs. Her shoulders shake. I wait. Finally, she hiccups, fishes a tissue from a different pocket and blows her nose.

"Do you have any idea who'd want to kill her? Or why?"

"Don't they have the guy? Brighton...Berton...something like that?"

"It's Brixton. Brixton Lee Hale the Third, also known as Smokey and Brick. Did Jennifer ever mention a guy with one of those names?"

"No, but he's the one, right?" Chelsea asks. "He picked her up at a party and then, I mean, it's on the news, he, he - - I can't believe he shot her in the...where he shot her. Isn't he guilty?"

"Probably, but you know how it is, we really need to cover all the bases in a case like this. So I just have - -"

Her eyes narrow a little. "You're with the police?"

"No, actually, I work for the lawyer who's defending Mr. Hale. Again, sure, he's probably guilty, but a lawyer still has to do his due diligence under the canons of jurisprudence to make sure the accused gets a fair trial." Chelsea seems to buy the word salad, so I press on. "I just have a few routine questions to close the book on our investigation, like who Jennifer hung out with, that kind of thing. I hope you don't mind."

"No. Not at all. She was so cool, so gorgeous. I felt lucky she let me be her best friend. And now she's gone."

"Was there a man in her life? Maybe a, um...sugar daddy?"

"Oh, yeah," Chelsea says. "But she wouldn't say who. She kept her love life to herself after her cop boyfriend got shot. We talked about everything else, but she wouldn't talk about that. I don't know why she was so secretive. I wouldn't have gossiped about her private life to anyone. She knew that." Her face reddens and her eyes fill again.

She ducks her head and knuckles away more tears. "Some best friend, huh?"

"How about the cop boyfriend? She tell you much about him?"

"Jennifer loved him so much," Chelsea says. "She was never the same after he got shot, always drinking and partying, sleeping with any rando that hit on her. I think she'd still be alive if he wasn't killed."

"Was she getting money from this new guy? Apparently she lived pretty well."

"Yeah, she was squeezing him for all he was worth, she did tell me that much, but it wasn't going so good lately. He got fed up and cut her off and she got pissed. That's why she went to that party, that night," She sniffles back tears. "To make him jealous."

"And look how that worked out," I say.

"Yeah, poor Jennifer. Sometimes she had to borrow money from me. For day care, diapers, her mortgage, like that. And she liked to party, you know what I mean? As long as someone else was paying."

"You say she was borrowing money from you?"

"Yeah, I had to work overtime here and take on some, ah, other work, too, but that's what best friends do, right?" She begins to sob again.

"Would you mind telling me what you were doing the night she was killed?"

"I was home with my cat," she says. "You'd think she'd invite her best friend to go to that party with her, but, no. If I just would have been there, maybe she..." She starts sobbing again and digs for the tissue, which looks too soggy to be of much use now. "She called me for a ride after that guy dumped her off, but I was mad at her about the party and told her I wouldn't pick her up but if I would have then..."

They say the heart never graduates from high school, and this interview is starting to feel like an outtake from the *Mean Girls* movie. It even has a Queen Bee and a wannabe. I hand Chelsea my card. "Maybe you can call me if you think of anything?"

She apparently hasn't recognized my face from the news stories, and I'm praying she won't look at the card till after I'm gone. One thing I don't need at the moment is having to explain how Frank's widow happens to be investigating the murder of his girlfriend in which said widow is practically a suspect. I can barely explain it to myself.

Chelsea pockets the card without a glance, and I relax.

"Sure," she says. "If I think of anything I will. But I'm out of here. I'm going back to Nebraska and hire a lawyer and try to get my kids back. I've had enough Palm Springs to last a lifetime."

"Copy that," I say. "Best of luck."

Chapter Sixteen

— · —

I walk out into the blast-furnace day and skitter across the asphalt griddle to the Jeep. It has to be over 100 degrees already and at least thirty degrees past that in the sun-baked car. I turn on the AC, lower the windows, and pull the deflectors off the dash, then give the Jeep a few minutes to cool down. Finally the interior is fit for human habitation. I start to back out, but have to wait as an SUV eases past and pulls up to the curb a few spaces down.

Finally I make my escape and pull out of the parking lot. I'm halfway down the block when the hair on the back of my neck bristles. It's never wrong, but what did I miss?

Back into the parking lot I go and start circling. I've nearly completed my second lap and am about to tell my neck hair where to go to when it jumps to attention again as I pass the SUV that pulled in as I was leaving.

I brake the Jeep, back up, stop in the middle of the lane, and study the vehicle. It's empty, so the driver must have gone into one of the offices in the complex where the Chamber's located.

And the SUV itself? Unremarkable for Palm Springs—a big fancy Range Rover that drips chrome and shouts money. And boasts vanity plates, of course.

Vanity plates that say KLOZIT.

And it's blue. A deep, dark blue.

And what Hale said was that the SUV lady drove a fancy dark-colored rig with plates that said CLOSEUP. But Hale was not in full possession of his faculties. As he himself put it, "I was pretty drunk."

CLOSEUP, KLOZIT--close enough for a drunk and thank you, Brixton Lee Hale III.

I photograph the Ranger Rover and the rear plate, then get on the phone and ask Lita to track down the owner.

It's looking like a great day for Jacinto Investigations as I pull back out onto Belardo and start home. I tune the car radio to a country station and wail along to "Seminole Wind" cause I know the words and have a little crush on John Anderson. Maybe because he looks something like Frank.

My driveway holds an ancient Toyota pickup with Edgar the metal detectorist at the wheel. Rather than pull around back as usual, I park beside Edgar and we both get out.

He's wearing his "I GOT SCALPED" t-shirt and a huge grin. He holds out a Ziploc with a bullet in it. "You owe me five hundred dollars."

"Jesus, that was quick."

His grin gets bigger. "It was only a few inches down. Piece of cake."

I take the Ziploc and study the bullet. Its trip through the soft desert sand has left it almost unmarked. I've seen enough thirty-eight slugs to know that's probably what this is, though it could instead be three-fifty-seven or a nine-millimeter. They're all pretty close to the same size.

Edgar pulls out a big white iPhone and shows me the flash photos he took of the mesquite bush and the hole he dug to find the bullet.

"And I dropped a pin on the map where it's located," he says. He shows me that, too.

"You're pretty good with technology for an old fart. Can you email me that stuff?"

"Fuck you very much, but yes."

I give him one of my cards and he sends the photos and the map link on the spot.

"A check good?"

He clears his throat before I can even reach into the Jeep for my purse.

"Ah. Cash would be better?"

He raises his eyebrows. I get my wallet out of the purse and come up with only $280.

He whisks it out of my hand and disappears it into a pocket of his cargo shorts. "Down payment," he says.

"I'll hit the ATM today."

"I know where you live."

My phone goes off as I enter the house.

"I think I found our SUV lady," Lita announces at my hello. "Rachel Bartell. She owns a real-estate agency called RaBar Luxury Properties and she chairs the real estate committee at the Chamber. So KLOZIT must be - -"

"Of course, KLOZIT as in close the deal."

"Right. And she's married to Julian Bartell, that plastic surgeon with the billboards all over town that say 'Discover the New You!' You've seen 'em?"

"Who hasn't?"

"His clinic belongs to the Chamber of Commerce, too," Lita goes on. "So there's lots out there on both of them. They have a big place in Andreas Hills, market value $5.8 million, according to Zillow, and two sons in college. He drives a Porsche SUV, she has the Range Rover. There was a court case three years ago about their maid getting deported. Looks like she might have been pregnant, but I didn't have time to look into that. You want me to?"

"Sure. Thank you, Lita. Great job, above and beyond as usual. And on your day off, too. I'm lucky to have you."

I'm about to ring off when I remember what else I want to ask her. "Hey, while you're at it can you run a background check on a Chelsea Miller? Thirty-ish, barista at that Coffi by the Chamber office, apparently picks up other work from time to time, supposedly our victim's best friend."

Lita gives me a cheery "*Si, senora!*" and we tap off.

I hit the RaBar Luxury Properties website on my phone, find a place in La Quinta she's got listed for $2.8 million, and call her office as one of my undercover identities, a woman named Judith Kaplan. In a couple of minutes, "Judith" is set up for a walk-through at three-thirty.

Next I call Ike and brief him on the day's developments. He thanks me and, being Ike, also congratulates me on my good luck.

"The harder you work the luckier you get, counselor, and you're welcome," I tell him. "Can I borrow your Beamer? I need to go un- dercover as a rich lady if I'm gonna impress Rachel Bartell."

He says the car will be waiting at his office by three o'clock. I dig out a floaty sundress, slip into heeled sandals I haven't worn since Frank's funeral, put on earrings, and slide the Patek Philippe onto my wrist.

I pick up the Beamer on schedule, find the La Quinta address, pull through the gate past the "RaBar Luxury Properties" sign at three-thirty, and park beside the blue Range Rover with the KLOZIT plates.

The La Quinta property is what Palm Springs calls a mid-century modern, and they've been hot on the market lately. The term means the house is from the fifties, which means it's pushing seventy years old, but it's been seriously upgraded. This one looks like it started out as a modest bungalow, but grew in size as well as flash in the up-grade. Like most desert houses, it's white, with a low stone wall--also white--in front, and a big desert fan palm tree in the yard. The place speaks of ease and comfort. Even so, $2.8 million is barely a starter home in La Quinta.

She who can only be Rachel Bartell greets me at the front door. Fifty-ish, smooth banana-blond bob, designer dress, heels an inch higher than mine, a turquoise necklace that must weigh a pound. Her complexion shines, there's not a wrinkle in sight, and her eyebrows arch a little too much for their own good under a Botox forehead. It's what they call a plastic face around here, as much a Palm Springs trademark as agaves in the landscaping.

And Hale wasn't kidding about having some work on the boobs. They strain against the fabric of her bodice like too many volleyballs in a carry bag. Her posture tells of workouts, yoga, massages, probably a personal trainer, and anything else money can buy to make a woman think she still looks like she used to. And she pulls it off, except for the fifteen pounds of wine weight she carries.

She gives the Beamer a once-over, then me, and it's like being x-rayed. She extends a silky hand with perfect oval nails tipped in muted pink, and passes me her card. A whiff of expensive perfume wafts my way.

"Mrs. Kaplan? Nice to meet you."

"Not for long," I tell her. "I'm divorcing the cheating son of a bitch. Rat bastard bought his mistress a car and a condo and had twins with her, and now he's gonna pay. I want some real estate revenge."

She smiles like she's heard this kind of thing before. "And you should have it, Judith," she purrs. "It's only fair."

We exchange a warm handshake, sisters united against the patri-archy now, and she leads me through fifty shades of light gray into a dining room that has to seat at least a dozen. Through the patio doors, I see a hot tub and a sparkling blue pool.

And then there's the kitchen, all granite surfaces and polished wood cabinets and gleaming stainless steel appliances. I let her tell me about the end-grain butcher-block table and how the big silver refrigerator can be linked to my Amazon Echo, then I make a show of raising my wrist to check the time.

Her eyes widen and her spiel skips a beat. She clears her throat, gets her face under control, and starts to tell me about the pool cooler, an essential in Palm Springs if you don't want your afternoon swim to become a warm bath.

"How are the property taxes here?" I interrupt. "Ridiculously high, I hope?"

She smiles and starts to answer, but she's lost control of her eyes. They lock onto the watch, then my face, then the watch again. She reaches for it with both hands, then yanks them back.

I grin and hold out my wrist. "It's a Patek Philippe. More revenge on the cheating bastard. There's no such thing as too much of that, am I right?" I point at her wrist, which is bare. "You should get one."

Her smile becomes a scowl. "You're not here to see this house." She steps back and folds her arms across that chest. "Who are you?"

"Dana Forsythe." I hand her my card. "I'm working for the attorney who's defending the man accused of killing Jennifer Williamson. The torso shooter, they're calling him?"

"What the - - what does that have to do with me?"

"A guy named Brixton Lee Hale the Third, everybody calls him Smokey? Looks like Tom Cruise?"

"I never heard of him and I don't know who you think you are, coming in here like this - -"

"Hale says he ran into you up on Gene Autry Trail the other night and you gave him this watch and promised him ten thousand dollars to kill Jennifer Williamson."

She takes a step back, stumbles, and winces as her hip bangs into a corner of the kitchen island. "I have no idea what you're talking about. I do not know that awful man who shot that poor woman and that is not my watch."

"We'll see." I give her the shark smile I save for special occasions. "We'll be hitting Sterling and Sons with a subpoena for the ownership records on this watch."

"Subpoena? Are you working with the police?"

"When I need to. Do I now?"

"What you need to do is leave!" Her face is flushed and the real-estate lady purr is just a memory.

"Sure, but a few more questions first. We know you had a maid deported when she got pregnant. Was that because Julian was having an affair with her just like he was with Jennifer Williamson? Except with Jennifer you decided to have her killed?"

"Get out!" she shrieks. "I'm calling my lawyer!"

"I mean, it's understandable, what you did. You had to know about Julian seeing Jennifer, right? The wife always knows."

I don't know what my tell is, but she catches it. Suddenly real-estate Rachel is back with the x-ray eyes on Stun. She looks at my card again and I watch her face as she works it out.

"You didn't know, did you? You're the one in the news, aren't you? You didn't know your husband was screwing Jennifer Williamson, did you? And having kids with her? Who are you to come here and get in my face?"

"At least I didn't hire somebody to kill her."

She takes another look at the address on my card. "Cahuilla Hills, huh? I really admire you. I couldn't live like that. Now get the hell out!"

I've saved the best for last, and now I let her have it.

"Actually, I haven't been completely forthcoming. The fact is, Hale says he never shot Jennifer Williamson."

"Of course he did," Rachel says. "The police say so."

"Here's the problem, though. They haven't found the bullet that went through her throat and killed her yet, and when they do, it won't match the ones from the torso shots."

"How can you know that?"

"Because Smokey Hale conned you. He didn't kill anybody. Jennifer was already dead from the throat shot when he got there. He fired your gun into the sand under a mesquite bush to make you think he used it to shoot Jennifer when he brought it back to you. And, guess what, we found that bullet right where he said it would be."

I reach into my purse, pull out the worst of the torso photos and lay it on the countertop. Again Rachel loses control of her eyes. They lock onto the picture.

"So, when you add it to the five shots you put between Jennifer's legs, that makes six," I say. "And that's all your gun could hold, right?"

I watch as comprehension spreads over her face, followed by something like relief: If Hale didn't kill Jennifer, then she's not guilty of murder.

Suddenly she's all real estate lady again. Her eyes are like calculators. "If this Smokey person didn't kill her, who did?"

"Maybe you. You did go down there and shoot her in the torso not once, not twice, but five times. How did that feel? I mean, shooting a woman there, of all places? So, yeah, I can see you shooting her in the throat."

"But then why would I hire - - get out. Just get the hell out!"

The show's over, so I do. I've told her far more than she's told me. But sometimes you have to seed the clouds to make it rain.

The door slams behind me. I climb into Ike's Beamer and Google the phone number for Julian Bartell's plastic surgery practice. I tap it when it comes up on the screen and ask for a consultation on breast enhancement. When I mention I was referred by a friend of Mrs. Bartell, I get right in the next morning. This time, I'm Becky Sturgis.

I call Ike, sketch my encounter with Rachel Bartell, confirm I can keep the Beamer overnight, and start home.

I take the long way around and come in from the back side of the house, which turns out to be unnecessarily cautious. There's not a reporter in sight. I let myself in, let Duke out, and hit the TV remote for the news. It's just as bad as in the morning, so Netflix it is.

I surf through the listings for a couple minutes, then lose myself in an episode of "Ratched." This one involves an ice pick and a lobotomy. It makes me wish I could hire the psycho Nurse Ratched to pay Rachel Bartell a visit.

CHAPTER SEVENTEEN

— · —

I start my day by printing out a picture of Rachel Bartell off her website, plus my pictures of her Range Rover and the KLOZIT plates.

I pack them into my briefcase and start for the jail.

This time, the guard is a surly Anglo with a beer gut, male pattern baldness, and a nametag that says Brauchen. He marches me down the corridor through the same background din of coughs, mumbles, clangs, bangs, and despair.

Hale's waiting in an interview room, a different one from before but identical except the walls of this one are egg-yolk yellow.

Hale's the worse for the wear today--slumped in the chair, shaggy hair with the jail smell, a few days worth of stubble on his chin. He doesn't speak when I come in.

"Hey," I greet him. This produces a tired wave that says "Just get on with it."

As I pull out the photographs, he finally speaks. "Am I getting out now?"

"Ike's working on it." I lay the photos out on the table. "Based on what you told us, this is the SUV Lady from Gene Autry Trail, and her vehicle."

He picks up the photo of Rachel Bartell. "Yep, that's her. Rachel Bartell, huh?"

"But you were drunk. Maybe you just think she looks like the SUV lady."

"Not that drunk. This is definitely her and that is definitely her rig with the KLOZIT plate. Now can I get out of here?"

"Like I said, we're working on it." I rise and drop the photos into my briefcase. "And now, what are you going to remember?"

"No talking to the cops, not a word, I promise." He points at my briefcase. "And thanks a lot, that was nice work tracking her down. How'd you do it?"

"It's what I do is how. And you're welcome."

I rap on the door and Brauchen ushers me out. I don't even try to keep the big, stupid grin off my face. We now have a witness and a suspect.

I remote-start the Beamer and wait in the shade of the jail as I plug the address for Julian Bartell's plastic surgery practice into the GPS and give the AC a couple of minutes to cool the car down to habitability. The seat is still scorching when I get in and I have to shuffle my butt around to get comfortable. As I back out of the parking spot, I wonder about two things. Why did Ike have to get black leather upholstery, and why do I live here, again?

I pull out and start across town toward the Tall Palm Plastic Surgery Institute on Bob Hope Drive. Bartell's operation consists of the clinic proper, and a small attached pharmacy to the right of the entrance.

A palm tree that must be fifty feet high looms over the front half of the clinic. The entrance canopy is almost hidden by manicured acacias with pale green leaves. Blooming shrubs and cacti fill the strip between the building and the parking lot.

I park at the curb in front and step into the entry. A soothing breeze from the air conditioning bathes me in the scent of something floral and I think how the jail could do with some of this.

A polished Latina receptionist with a plastic face and boobs to match is telling a blond woman she'll have to make an appointment.

"Just for a refill?" the woman says. "Come on."

"Sorry, Mrs. Arthur, that's the rule after three refills," the receptionist tells her. "He can fit you in tomorrow at two."

"Jesus," the woman says. "I can't wait – okay, two o'clock then."

She turns and stalks past me, muttering "This is ridiculous."

The receptionist watches her go, then turns and greets me in a voice like warm oil. "Ms. Sturgis?"

I give her the once-over. From the door, she had the supple honey-brown skin of a twenty-something. From across the counter, the face of a forty-something shows through, but just barely. The boobs look ageless. A nameplate on the counter says she's Ariana Vega.

"That's some nice work," I say. "Dr. Bartell do that?"

"A perk of the job." Ariana glances down at her cleavage. "He's fabulous."

She hands me off to a waiting nurse who ushers me down a quiet hall. Thick, deep blue carpet muffles our footsteps. No banging sounds or distant voices here. The wallpaper is grasscloth in a shade of blue that complements the carpet. I glide along beside the nurse and wish for a moment it was me living this life, not somebody I made up, the somebody who drove here in an electric BMW.

The nurse shows me into a room three times the size of the exam rooms at my doctor's office. It's even quieter than the rest of the place, and is all lavender walls, creamy beige leather furniture, and a chandelier sparkling from the ceiling. Poster-size photos of gorgeous women line the walls. One is Marilyn Monroe, who seems to say I can look like her if I spend enough money here.

"If you could fill this out for us?" The nurse hands me a clipboard and directs me to a plush armchair. "May I bring you something to drink? Sparkling water, coffee, tea? A soft drink?"

I'm tempted to ask for a Corona to see if I can crack her composure, but I have to stay in character as Rebecca Sturgis. "Coffee, please."

"Latte, Frappuccino, macchiato, cappuccino or black?"

"Cappucino, please, French vanilla, if possible."

"Of course." She vanishes and the door closes with a barely audible click. I'm alone with Marilyn, the other beauties, and the whisper of the scented air conditioning.

The nurse is back in less than three minutes with my cappuccino in a tall china cup on a saucer. I'm tempted to curl my pinky as I lift the cup. The cappuccino is perfect, of course.

"Dr. Bartell will be with you in just a moment," she says and vanishes again.

I lay my manila envelope of crime-scene photos on the oak side table, fill out the forms, then glance at a glossy pamphlet beside my envelope. "Discover the New You!" illustrates how I can improve myself with body contouring, skin rejuvenation, fillers, and Botox.

As I finish the form, the smoothest-looking man I've ever seen glides in. A pair of pale blue eyes lock onto mine. His forehead is as unlined as that of a fifteen-year-old boy. It has to have had work, but it's work so good it doesn't show. His hair is dark, perfectly coiffed, and brushed with silver at the temples in the way that makes women call a man distinguished. He's in a crisp white shirt under a black cashmere sweater, with soft leather shoes the color of butter.

"Ms. Sturgis," he greets me. His handshake is as firm and smooth as his forehead.

He invites me into a chair before his desk, seats himself in the one behind it, and spreads out the forms I completed. "I gather you're interested in breast enhancement? We have so many wonderful options - -"

"I want 'em so big they can't close the coffin."

He laughs like he's maybe heard this before, and I steel myself as he studies my chest for a few moments. "We can definitely create a new you in that department. Did you visit our website and take a look at some of our - -"

"I made some printouts from Pornhub." I slide over the manila envelope.

He has the photos spread over the desk before he realizes what he's looking at. Then his eyes widen and wrinkles appear on the expensive forehead. He's still staring when I slip off the Patek Philippe and drop it onto the grisliest of the photos.

"My God." He puts a hand over his eyes. "Who are you? Why are you here?"

"Dana Forsythe, a legal investigator. I work for a criminal defense attorney named Ike Skogel and I'm here to inform you that your wife hired our client, Smokey Hale, to kill Jennifer Williamson." I tap the photo on his desk. "And then she personally put five shots between the victim's legs."

Bartell sinks into his chair with a heavy sigh. "Rachel, Rachel, Rachel. What have you done?"

"What?"

"I got her that watch for our last anniversary. Sterling and Sons let me know an investigator called about it and said it was stolen. But when I asked Rachel about that, she denied it and said it was in the safe at her office. I knew she was lying but - -"

"You didn't call her on it?"

"Not a good idea with Rachel. I decided to wait and see if whoever called Sterling and Sons would contact me. And now here you are." He gestures at the Patek Philippe. "But what makes you think this watch and my wife are connected to the murder? From what I see in the news, the word of your client surely isn't to be trusted. A drifter from Slab City?"

"He's very trustworthy, as it happens. Everything he's told us checks out."

"And that would be what, exactly?"

So I tell him the story, from Hale's fight with Jennifer on Gene Autry Trail right through to Rachel Bartell shooting her corpse in the torso.

Julian thinks it over for a minute or so. Finally he clears his throat.

"Well, if you know this much, you'll probably discover eventually that I was having an affair with Jennifer." His voice catches and he blinks several times. "When I saw the news about her murder that first day, I did wonder whether Rachel might have found out and decided to have her killed. The wife always knows, right?"

A lurch in my gut reminds me of how little I knew about Frank, but I manage a nod. "But having her killed? That's pretty extreme."

He sighs. "I also had an affair with our maid a few years ago. Rachel found out and had the poor woman deported. It was ugly and very difficult for us. I thought maybe she took a different tack this time because Jennifer is...was... a citizen and couldn't be deported." He averts his gaze and swipes at his cheeks. "But then when those two Slabbers were arrested and this Hale fellow was charged and these horrible pictures got on the Internet, I thought 'Well, perhaps it's a random killing after all.'"

"But it isn't."

He sighs. "Was Rachel by any chance drunk when she allegedly hired your client."

"That's what he claims. How did she seem to you in the days after the murder?"

"No different than usual. Moody, drinking a lot. We avoid each other's company for the most part, so I'm not sure I would've noticed if she was...ah...even more troubled than usual. I've tried to get her into rehab or AA, but she won't go."

"She seemed fine when I saw her."

He jerks upright. "You saw Rachel?"

"Yesterday at a listing in La Quinta. She kicked me out when she found out why I was there. She didn't tell you?"

"No, but that would explain last night. Drunk and passed out on the sofa when I got home about six. I helped her upstairs and put her to bed."

"Did she say anything this morning?"

"She was gone when I got up."

"Probably out hiring a lawyer."

"I wouldn't be surprised," he says. "This is my fault for being unfaithful, I know, but sometimes a marriage just goes...you need...you reach out but...and then I met Jennifer at the Chamber office and she was so... I wanted to leave Rachel and marry her."

He seems sincere, like Jennifer got to him the same way she did Frank. I swallow hard. "That's not what Chelsea says."

"You mean Jennifer's ...?"

"Yeah, her best friend. She says you cut off Jennifer's money and threatened to dump her."

He bristles. "You know she's a drug-user and part-time escort, right? I never actually met her but Jennifer told me she even makes dates at the counter of that coffee place where she works."

"Chelsea's not the issue here."

"Okay, okay. Jennifer's spending was out of control and I did want to shock her back to her senses, so, yes, I did cut her off. And, I confess, I thought it would pressure her into marrying me. You don't get many second chances in life. I thought she was mine."

"I hear that a lot. It rarely ends well."

"So I've learned."

"But here's the thing," I tell him. "Smokey Hale says he didn't shoot Jennifer in the throat. And I believe him."

Bartell rocks back in his chair. "Eh?"

Now I tell him the rest of the story, including how Hale went back to warn Jennifer, how he found her dead of a throat shot, how he fired the mesquite bullet so he could con Rachel out of the hit money, and how we tracked the Patek Philippe down in Bamboo Beach. "He even remembered enough of your wife's vanity plate that we were able to find her."

A long pause while I watch the wheels turn. "Then Rachel must have done it."

"Then why hire a hit man?"

His eyebrows gather. "Good point. So Hale must have done it, no matter what he says."

"Except why would he fire the mesquite bullet if he shot her in the throat?"

Bartell gazes off to the right and thinks for a moment. "How would I know? I'm a plastic surgeon, not a criminal psychologist."

"And then there's the math problem," I tell him. "Smokey shoots a mesquite bush with your wife's gun to con her out of the hit money. Then she uses it to fire five shots into Jennifer's crotch. That's six bullets. The throat shot makes seven. There was clearly another shooter."

"Two shooters? My God, poor Jennifer! So it was a random killing after all?"

"Where were you that night?"

Bartell jumps up. His chair bangs into the wall behind him. He slaps his hands down on the desk and leans over it, gaze focused like a movie space laser. "You can't be implying that I...you walk in here with a fake name and now you accuse..."

He sinks into the chair. "You'll have to forgive me, I'm not used to being, well, I've never dealt with anything like this before, but I suppose you have to ask questions like this."

"I do."

"Anyway, I was at a conference in Anaheim that weekend. I gave a presentation on vaginal rejuvenation, which, if you'll pardon my pride, was quite well received."

I don't doubt he's telling the truth. The alibi would be too easy to bust if he's lying. But I push a little, because you never know.

"Anaheim is what, ninety miles? Easy round trip in the middle of the night."

He puts on a smile of martyred patience and pokes the phone on his desk. "Ariana, print out the records of my Anaheim conference, would you? The bill from the car service, the conference schedule, my honorarium, the link to the video of my presentation if they have it up by now. Whatever we have. Ms. Sturgis will collect it all on her way out." He settles back into his chair with a level stare that seems to say "You're up."

"Do you or Rachel own a gun?" I ask.

"I don't, but she has a small revolver, a thirty-eight, I think. She got it because she has so many night showings. I have no idea where she keeps it. Maybe in her car or the safe at her office?"

"Doesn't matter. You and your wife can tell it to the police. "We're going to them with what we have and they can take it from here. Our client never shot anything but a mesquite bush."

"Police? I hate to think... my practice...Rachel's agency, our sons! My God, what will the boys say? I know you have a job to do, but, I don't suppose we could retain you to, ah, assist us in this matter? Do we really need to - -"

"You're trying to buy me off? Seriously?"

"No, of course not, I don't know what I was thinking. I'm just not myself with all this...this..." He buries his face in his hands.

I gather the watch and photos from his desk, and turn at the door for a last look. His face is still buried in his hands. There's no hand-shake now, no polished goodbye.

CHAPTER EIGHTEEN

A s I pull out of the parking lot at Julian Bartell's clinic, I get Ike on the phone and suggest an update and strategy session. He's free and hungry, so we agree on a late lunch at the Sand Trap.

I'm still in his Beamer, which is telling me it's up to 108 now. It's the usual exit drill when I park at the Trap: crack the windows half an inch, spread heat deflectors over the dash, and race across the asphalt to the air-conditioned haven of my favorite dive.

It's past lunch time and the Trap is quiet. Ike is just being seated when I come in. I join him and we order iced tea from Rusty in her trademark cutoffs and Cowboy boots, plus a taco salad for me and a Reuben sandwich and fries for him.

As Rusty returns to the kitchen, I fill Ike in on my encounters with Rachel and Julian Bartell.

"So big they can't close the coffin," he chuckles when I finish. "I like that. You are one weird lady."

"I guess I've got a few moves. So what now? Keep digging or talk to the cops?"

Ike takes a big bite of his sandwich. Too big a bite. A shred of sauerkraut dangles from the corner of his mouth. I look away, steal two fries off his plate, and wolf them down.

"Back to the cops, I think," he says. "Seems like we've taken it as far as we can."

"Pretty much. Smokey's story seems to be true, Rachel Bartell is fairly well cornered as the torso shooter, and Julian Bartell has what looks like solid alibi for the night in question."

"Which leaves the throat shooter," Ike says. "Any ideas there?"

"None so far. You?"

"Same," he says past a mouthful of Reuben. "But if Smokey's in the clear it's not our problem."

"Nope."

"Then, yeah, I'll see if we can spring him, or at least get his bail lowered enough that Grandpa will pay. You wanna call your buddy St. Clair about meeting with him and somebody from the prosecutor's office?"

"Hold on a minute, he's in my phone." I pull up the contact, tap it, and the phone starts ringing.

When St. Clair answers, I put the phone on speaker and tell him enough to get him interested. He puts us on hold for a couple minutes. When he comes back, he says we can come in at eleven o'clock tomorrow, but he'll be tied up. It'll be just Ike and me, Gary Avila, and Susan Jung, the prosecutor on the case. Ike nods and I confirm the meeting.

I reach for my purse, but Ike holds up a finger. "I almost forgot. We heard yesterday, the adoption will finalize in four months, plus or minus."

"That soon?"

"Yeah, exactly, it's normally more like six. But Chip Hanover, he's like this adoption whisperer. Plus, with Yolanda and her husband having such a stellar record in the foster care system, that helps."

"Thanks, nice work all around. You need anything from me?"

"Not at the moment," Ike says. "There'll be some documents to sign later, that's about it."

"So where are we on Jennifer's condo and her car?"

"They're both listed," he says. "Won't take long to sell them in this market, I'm thinking. What do you want to do with the money?"

"I want to set up a trust for the twins. Provide monthly mainte-nance payments to Yolanda, and add to the college fund Frank set up with the union. That doable?"

"Sure, I can get it moving. I gotta say, it seems like Frank did all right by his kids and their mom."

"He sure did. The bastard."

"Oh, God," Ike says, "What was I - -"

I wave it off. "That's my life these days."

We slap down twenties, exchange Ike's Beamer for my Vic, and I start back up to the Cahuilla Hills.

Once home, I settle in for my daily news cruise, which I didn't have time for this morning.

There's nothing new on the Jennifer Williamson case, thank God, just a small item in the *Herald* saying exactly that, so I relax into some recreational reading.

Marilyn Monroe has been dead over half a century, but she's big news in Palm Springs. That's because the city is bringing back the Forever Marilyn statue. It's twenty-six feet tall and shows Marilyn's white skirt billowing up over a subway grate in the famous scene from *The Seven Year Itch*.

Forever Marilyn was a big tourist attraction here for years, but what the tourists mainly did was take pictures of themselves looking up her skirt. Eventually the pearl-clutchers prevailed and Marilyn got run out of town.

But the past is never past, not in Palm Springs. The city now plans to install Marilyn downtown in front of the local museum.

A museum board member complains the statue will encourage unhealthy behavior by women. A college professor faults it for pandering to the male gaze. The Coachella Knitting Club is making leg warmers to protect Marilyn from the updraft out of that subway grate.

Out in Slab City, Cassandra is wondering on Facebook if anybody has seen "my truck, my dog, or my boyfriend Maverick." Morlock asks in a comment if she's writing a country song.

A would-be Slabber from back east asks how people make money there. Pokeman explains the main hustle is "spanging"—going into El Centro to panhandle for spare change in front of the Wal-Mart. Pro tip from Pokeman: You'll make more if you take a woman or a dog, ideally both.

And so it goes. Another beautiful day in the desert.

I spend a few hours on laundry and other household chores, pay the bills, and go out back to throw sticks for Duke in the waning afternoon. But only a few sticks, because it's still in the upper nineties. In less than ten minutes, Duke--panting and dripping sweat off his tongue--heads back to the patio.

As I let him into the house, my phone lights up and the caller ID says it's Liz Hernandez. "Hey, girl," she says when I answer. "Isn't it about time we hit the Outrigger?"

I respond with an extended silence.

"No questions about the case, I swear. I'm leaving my notebook at home."

"About time."

"Yeah," she says. "Again, I am really sorry about that story I did, but, you know, these things take on a life of their own, my editor was on my ass. And if I handed it off to another reporter, it would have been even worse."

"Forget it. We're both pros. If I still had a badge, I'd have to bust you if the situation called for it."

"Whew," she says. "Thanks. So...some girl time?"

I spool back through the past few days and conclude she has a point. The Outrigger is a tiki bar in north Palm Springs, complete with torches on the walls and servers in lava-lavas bearing cocktails with tiny umbrellas. It's mostly a gay hangout, but they do let straights in, they do make a decent Moscow mule, and it's where Liz and I go for girl time. And if I ever needed some of that, it's now.

"Absolutely," I tell her. "Give me an hour to rinse off the grime and I'll meet you there."

It's a week night and a little before the dinner rush, so the Outrigger is pretty quiet when we walk in. But not so quiet that Liz can resist saying what she always does when we hit the Outrigger: "Why are the cute ones always gay?"

"Because God hates women, duh. The snake and apple thing?"

Surname notwithstanding, Liz is blond with green eyes. She's six feet tall. She calls short men "chin rests," but says it doesn't matter when you're horizontal. She's lean and rangy with antelope legs and a clear, smiling face that says 'fun.'

We ask the hostess for our customary table in the corner—we're more audience than participants at the Outrigger—and she takes our drink order before she goes. A Hawaiian margarita for Liz, a mule for me. "And keep 'em coming," I add.

Liz chuckles. "One of those days, huh?"

"More like ten in a row."

"Yeah," she says. "And I promised not to ask you any questions about the case and I won't. Unless you need to talk about it, of course."

"Definitely not," I say. "What I need is to kick back and not think about anything. And quite possibly consume enough mules that you'll have to drive me home."

"You got it," she says. "We'll worry about your car tomorrow."

We watch the couples on the little dance floor camping it up to retro disco music until our favorite waiter, Darwin, shows up with the drinks. "Hey, ladies! We've missed you. Whereya been?"

Liz waves a hand. "Oh, you know. Busy."

"Lucky you!" Darwin says. "Are we wanting food tonight to soak up the alcohol, or do I just need to keep those glasses filled?"

"Both." Liz looks at me. "Large pupu platter?"

"I'm in."

Darwin marches off in his lava-lava, more adorable than hot. Liz sighs. "If I ever have a kid, I hope he grows up to be Darwin."

I smile and sip from my Moscow mule. It slides down my throat with the familiar cool, green tang.

Liz plucks the mini umbrella out of her Margarita and takes a drink. "So, again, I know you don't want to talk about the case and I won't try to make you, but I feel like I need to know one thing and that is, what's going on with the twins that, ah, Frank and, ah, that woman, well, you know. The twins? Not the case, but the twins?"

The twins, I discover to my surprise, are something I can talk about a little. I sketch the adoption situation for her.

"And so you'll be in their lives, I guess, or...?"

"I'm *Tía* Dana till the time comes to tell them the rest of it."

"That'll be quite a day."

"I don't want to think about that. Or talk about it any more. Let's change the subject."

"Right, right, yeah." Liz takes a drink from her margarita. "So, ah, let's see, okay, yeah, what's it been, eight months? You ever think about getting out there again?"

"Don't start."

"I mean, eight months."

"Nine now."

"So you're keeping track."

"Doesn't matter, it's still too soon," I say. But I'm lying to both of us. "At least, it was till I found out about Frank and that woman."

"You know what they say—the way to get over one man is to get under another one."

Old as it is, the joke makes us laugh, which I've not heard myself do in a while. "But I'm not like you."

"Meaning what?"

"You're like, I don't know, a female version of Ike. Unfiltered and ever-ready."

"That's an overstatement," she says with a grin. "But not totally wrong."

"I actually admire that but it's not me," I tell her with a grin of my own. "Over-thinking everything, that takes time."

"Your specialty, girl." She laughs and we let it rest for a moment while we watch the dancers and finish the pupus.

Then I pick it up again despite myself. "I don't know. I mean, our asshole client says I need work on my neck and forehead and, you know, the competition around here - -"

"Smokey Hale?" Liz interrupts. "Screw him, natural is in now. You look fine. You still hitting the Peloton? Because I never saw you in better shape."

"God bless you, Liz Hernandez, even if it is best-friend BS. But, seriously, how would I get out there even if I wanted to?"

"They have phone apps for that now," she says. "And web sites. And Facebook groups. Anything from a soulmate to a hit-and-run."

"No, no, I mean the minute a guy Googles me, he's leaving skid marks to get away, right?"

Liz studies my face and spots something I haven't admitted to myself. "Somebody's on your mind."

"Not really, it's just..."

"Give."

And suddenly I'm telling her about the Chaplain, including things that surprise even me, like how he smells.

"Holy shit," she says again when I finish. "What are you waiting for?"

"I don't know if he...it's just...I can't, not yet."

"Let me see if I have this straight. A shadow man on a motorcycle who only comes at night, his scent is leather and man-sweat, you don't know his name, and you're still not sure?"

"Right."

"Can you give him my number?"

CHAPTER NINETEEN

—·—

The next morning, Ike and I rendezvous at police headquarters five minutes early and are shown into a conference room. At eleven o'clock, Gary Avila steps in, followed by Susan Jung.

She's impeccable: red blazer with bold gold buttons and a standup collar, slim black skirt, and matching three-inch block heels that say, "Professional woman here, don't waste my time." I slide my Birkenstocks further under the table as we exchange cards.

Jung was the prosecutor we cops always wanted in the courtroom on our cases. She handled three of mine and she was direct, confident, and ruthless. The only one she lost was when Ike was at the defense table.

Avila is in a white shirt that's tight across the belly and a paisley tie that's loose at the throat. His expression says he'd rather be getting a prostate exam.

Jung takes the chair beside him. "Gary, why don't you bring us up to date."

Avila rattles off a case summary in a bored monotone. He discloses the absolute minimum, but it's clear they have nothing new. In particular, they do not have the bullet from the throat shot.

Jung appears to tune out as Avila speaks. Her eyes are on her phone, and she thumbs the screen now and again, presumably working through emails and texts. A couple of times she frowns at the screen, once she smiles.

Avila finishes and she looks up. "So, Ike and Dana. What can we do for you this morning?"

"It's what we can do for you," Ike says. "I'm happy to report that Dana here has worked a couple of her miracles. She's dug up some information that we think will be valuable to your investigation." He gazes around the table.

Jung raises her eyes from the phone and looks interested. Avila looks alarmed. They both know Ike. And me.

"Bullshit," Avila says.

"Exactly how valuable?" Jung asks.

"Extremely. Enough so that we'll be moving to get Hale released on his own recognizance, or at least a bail reduction to something his grandfather will put up. We think you'll go along once you see what we've got."

Avila grunts. "Come on, Susan, you're not - -" She raises a hand and he stops.

"Ike," she says. "You're always full of shit, but in my experience you're not an actual bullshitter. So we'll listen. Won't we, Gary?"

Avila sighs and pulls out a pen and a notebook.

I take them through what really happened the night Jennifer Williamson was killed, from Hale dumping her by the road up through the SUV lady's no-show the following day at the Westgate Mall.

"So," I conclude. "It's obvious. Somebody shot Jennifer in the throat, the SUV lady shot her in the torso, and Smokey Hale didn't shoot anything but a mesquite bush."

Avila comes to life. "What a load of crap! We have a body, five of the six bullets, and phone tracking that shows Hale was in the area at the time of the shooting. It's open and shut. He did it." He shoots me a challenging glare.

"But you don't have the murder weapon, right?" Ike says. "Or the bullet from the throat shot. Did you check the traffic camera footage from Gene Autry north and south of the scene that night? Maybe there's a fancy SUV with custom plates in that video?"

Jung peers over her phone at Avila's face.

"We're on it," Avila snorts. "It's just a lot of fucking donkey work. We'll find the bullet from the throat shot. We'll run down any vehicle where we can get a plate number off the video. But what we're gonna find is that your guy in his cousin's pickup is the only person of interest who was there. No mystery lady in an SUV, no throat shooter in another vehicle, just Smokey Hale."

I don't speak.

"Look, Dana," Avila says. "I admired your husband, may he rest in peace. Frank was a cop's cop, and I used to think you were a pretty good one yourself, at least for a female officer. And I know you've had a lot to work through since...well, since what happened and, you know, with Frank's, ah, personal connection to this case. But Hale admits he kicked Jennifer out of the pickup right where the body was found. He's the last person known to be with her. His DNA showed up inside her. He straightened her out, isn't that what he said? Maybe he knocked her down and raped her, she laughed at his little baby dick, and he corrected her six times with that thirty-eight. Started at the throat, worked his way down. "

I swallow back the bile in my throat. "Hale says they had consensual sex in a bathroom at the Chapel City party. He says she called out Frank's name when she came."

The room fills with a thick, stunned silence. And pity. Ike clears his throat. Jung looks at her phone.

"How would Smokey Hale know my husband's name if he's not telling the truth?"

"From the news or jailhouse gossip?" Avila says. "Who knows? The point is, this lowlife is blowing sunshine up your skirt and you just can't see it."

So Avila thinks I lost my mojo because of grief? Excellent. I give him my sweetest smile. "That's what we thought at first."

"Yeah," Ike says, "Too crazy to be true, right? But then we were like, 'Wait a minute, who would make up a story this crazy?'"

"And Hale," I say, "he just read like a guy who was telling the truth. So I poked around."

Jung now looks like she's enjoying this. She grins at Avila. "Did you hear that, Gary? She poked around. I hear it's what cops do."

Avila's face reddens, but he keeps his mouth shut.

I reach into my briefcase and pull out the Patek Philippe and drop it on the table.

Jung lowers her phone, studies it for a moment, and murmurs, "Huh."

Avila stares at it like he would a scorpion in his sock drawer. "What's that?"

"The SUV lady's watch," I answer. "I got it from that artist woman Hale was shacked up with in Bamboo Beach. In fact, she was with him when he got arrested for the bar fight, and the watch was right there on her wrist the whole time. Ironic, huh?"

Silence from across the table.

Ike chimes in. "And security video will prove Hale was at the Westgate Mall the next day to swap the watch for the hit money, but the SUV lady never showed up."

I flop down a car registration beside the Patek Philippe. "Not to worry, though. I tracked her down for you."

Jung's phone is now face down on the table. She whispers something that sounds like, "Of course you did."

"This is the registration for a dark blue Range Rover SUV with vanity plates that say 'K-L-O-Z-I-T,'" I tell them. "KLOZIT. Like when a real-estate lady closes a sale? Hale thought he remembered 'CLOSE-UP' on the SUV's plates. KLOZIT, CLOSEUP, close enough, don't you think?"

"Fuck," Avila breathes.

Ike fills in the rest. "The vehicle belongs to Rachel Bartell, owner of RaBar Luxury Properties, chair of the real estate committee of the Desert Chamber of Commerce, and wife of plastic surgeon Julian Bartell. Hale will swear she hired him to shoot Jennifer that night. And I'll note for the record that Jennifer worked at the Chamber office. Also pretty close, don't you think?"

Ike picks up the watch, dangles it. "And this? Julian Bartell says he gave it to his wife for their anniversary."

"He also volunteered the information he was having an affair with Jennifer," I add. "He assumes that was his wife's motive for wanting her dead."

Avila's brow is beaded with sweat.

"Julian Bartell, Julian Bartell," Jung says. "Wait, the plastic surgeon with the billboards? Specializes in vaginal rejuvenation?"

"That's him," I say.

I dig into my briefcase, pull out a baggie holding the bullet Edgar found, drop it beside the watch and the registration papers.

Avila stares at it. "That better not be the friggin' bullet from the throat shot. That would be evidence tampering, right, Susan?"

He looks at Jung for agreement. She stares him down, remains silent.

"Again, not to worry," I tell Avila. "We believe it's the sixth round from the gun that fired the five shots into Jennifer's torso. Rachel Bartell's gun. Our metal detectorist found it right where Hale said it would be: under a mesquite bush a few yards south of the crime scene. Hale says he shot it into the sand there to make the SUV lady think her gun had fired the shot into Jennifer's throat so she would pay him what they agreed on. How much you want to bet forensics will confirm it came from the same gun as the torso shots?"

Jung is laser-focused on the proceedings now.

"So," I say, "That would make six bullets from Rachel Bartell's gun. The throat shot would make seven, strongly suggesting the work of a second shooter with a second gun. All of which would seem to prove Mr. Hale is telling the truth when he says that Jennifer was already shot through the throat when he got there to warn her that a crazy lady in a fancy SUV was trying to have her killed."

"He could have had seven bullets, or maybe..." Avila mutters. Jung scowls. Avila lowers his head.

The room is quiet except for the hum of the air conditioning and the distant trill of a desk phone.

Jung drops her phone into her briefcase and shuts it with a loud snap. "Any theories on the throat shooter, Ms. Forsythe?"

"No."

"How about Julian Bartell if this whole business was about his affair with the victim?"

"Reasonable question, but why would he? He did volunteer the information about his affair with Jennifer and he seems to have a rock-solid alibi. He was out of town at a conference." I pull a folder from my briefcase. "Here's a copy of his travel arrangements and proof of conference attendance."

Jung pulls it across the table, glances through it, shoves it toward Avila.

"In any case," I tell him. "We're not here to do your job. We're here to get our client out of jail. We're happy to have helped, but the Bartells are not our problem. They're all yours."

When Jung speaks, her voice is cold. "Gary, you need to talk to the Bartells. And you need to draw up search warrants for their home and businesses, so I can see if the court will agree that Ms. Forsythe here has furnished us with sufficient evidence to justify the warrants."

Ike interrupts. "We've been scrupulous about the chain of custody and everybody involved is ready to testify."

"Least surprising thing I've heard all day," Jung says.

She turns her attention to Avila. "You need to find that bullet from the throat shot, Gary. I don't care if you have to put an army of metal detectorists out there."

She gathers her things, nods at me, then Ike, glares at Avila, and stalks out. Her block heels rattle like small-arms fire, and the slamming door booms like a cannon.

"How did you do this?" Avila says.

"I had an unfair advantage," I answer. "I believed Smokey Hale."

CHAPTER TWENTY

The clouds are seeded. There's nothing to do now but wait for rain. A hot desert afternoon stretches out ahead, empty as a plastic bag snagged on a mesquite bush. It's my first such afternoon in a while—in fact, since the Chaplain dropped off the twins ten days ago.

Ten days? It seems like a lifetime.

I dream up things to do. First a walk with Duke, a short one because of the heat. The neighborhood roadrunner shows himself briefly, but Duke's not interested. It's even too hot to chase roadrunners, apparently.

Back inside, I try "Ratched" on Netflix, and land on an episode where a client hires a PI to track somebody down, then the client hires him to murder the somebody, then Ratched has sex with him in a hotel room. That's "Ratched," all right, at least one murder and one sex scene in every episode, and plausibility be damned.

Normally, that's all good. But not today. Today, I've got too much of the murder part in my life and too little of the sex part, at least according to Liz.

I flick off the TV, do the laundry, scrub out the bathtub, lie down for a nap, and offer a prayer of thanks when my phone wakes me and the screen lights up with Lita's face.

"I found Bill Davis," she says.

Bill Davis. It rings a bell in my sleep-fuzzed brain, but not a loud one. "Who?"

"Our car-crash witness. Remember?

"Oh, yeah. The lady got paralyzed, but the cops on the scene only got his name."

"Well, I found him. Actually had to go knock on his door all the way out in Thermal. Talk about hot, but it was the right Bill Davis and he's ready to talk. I sent his info to the lady's lawyer already."

"Nice work as usual. And how are the twins today?"

"Missing their *tía* is how they are."

"Tell them *Tía* Dana is taking them out for ice cream, how's that?"

"Kids' Corner, then?"

"Meet you there in thirty minutes."

Kids' Korner is in a ritzy mall in Rancho Mirage. It has not only ice cream, but also a play area for the littles called Toddler Heaven. It's all bright reds, greens, blues and yellows, with big stuffed animals to ride on. It has plastic tunnels to crawl through, a ball pit to dive in, and a miniature school bus that doesn't go anywhere but does have a steering wheel that turns. Best of all, there's a coffee area for us bigs that's within eyeshot and easy grabbing range of Toddler Heaven.

Half an hour later, Lita and I are settled there, each with a kid on one knee industriously smearing the contents of ice cream cones over their faces and hair while we down caffeine. The idea of giving them ice cream before turning them loose to play came from Lita, veteran kid wrangler that she is. They'll burn off the sugar in Toddler Heaven, then crash in the car on the way home.

My knee is occupied by Sonny, who looks up from his cone, gives me a chocolate-smeared grin, and says, "Eye keem." Then he holds the cone up for a lick.

I take one and say, "Mmmm, good."

He says, "Dukie here?"

"No, Dukie's at home. We'll see him next time."

"Watch *Fwozen*?" Rose asks from Lita's knee.

"Oh, sure," I say. "We'll watch *Frozen* again, too."

The kids look at each other and Sonny says, "*Tía* Dana." Rose pokes her cone at me and I lean over for a lick of strawberry.

"You're a good *tía*," Lita says.

"It's kind of growing on me."

The kids finish their cones and we clean up their faces and escort them over to Toddler Heaven. Sonny climbs into the little school bus and takes the wheel. Rose, in her princess dress again, insists that Lita help her onto the stuffed unicorn.

"What else do we need to catch up on?" I ask when we're back in the coffee area. "Anything I should know about Jennifer's friend Chelsea Miller?"

"Poor thing, divorced, husband got the kids, not qualified for anything but minimum wage jobs like a barista. She got arrested in Nebraska for soliciting prostitution and again last year for soliciting and possession of OxyContin at a motel in Desert Hot Springs."

"The fun never stops up there. How'd it turn out?"

"I'll email you, but it seems like the possession charge was dropped and she pleaded on the soliciting and, let's see, got a two-hundred-and-fifty dollar fine and a year on probation, which I think she's still on. Isn't that kind of light for, you know, drugs and prostitution?"

"We called it not worth the paperwork when I was with the sheriff's office. It costs money to put somebody in jail for a year and the prosecutors figure what's the point when it's this kind of stuff?"

"*Que lastima*," Lita says. "A life such as no woman should have to live."

Back home, I'm surfing for a suitable episode of "Ratched" when my phone pings. It's not a text but my ISS app. It tells me the International Space Station will pass over Palm Springs tonight at a height of forty-nine degrees above the southwest horizon a little before three a.m.

ISS-watching is a huge thing out here. By rumor, several Palm Springs babies have been conceived during ISS crossings, but I have my doubts. It's never visible more than five minutes, and whose timing is that good? There are a couple of official Dark Sky Parks within an hour's drive where the viewing is prime, but you don't need to bother. Any desert spot away from the city will do.

I take a shot down Cahuilla Canyon with my phone and post it on Facebook with the usual "beautiful day" caption.

Twelve minutes later, a strange number shows up on my screen, meaning the Chaplain has changed burners again. I tell him about the ISS and ask if he'd like to watch the show with me from the wind farm on North Indian Canyon.

"Let me think," he says. I hear him cover the phone and talk with someone in the background.

"I could do that," he says when he comes back on.

"Meet you at one-thirty?"

"Two o'clock is the soonest I can get there."

"From where?"

"San Diego."

"What are you doing in - -"

"Delivering something."

"I probably don't want to know what, right?"

"Not guns or drugs. Ashes."

"Ashes? You mean like from a cremation? Who - -"

"Please, Dana," he says, and then he's gone.

At least he told me something. "Ashes" isn't much, but it's something.

I collect a big beach blanket and two bottles of wine—one of each color because I don't know what he likes, or if he even drinks wine. After that, corkscrew, napkins and plastic cups, and I'm packed.

I watch some "Ratched," then comes the hard stuff, all of the things a woman does before a first date, especially if the guy may not know that's what it is.

A long bath is taken, things are plucked and shaved that have been allowed to go feral since Frank's funeral, hair and makeup are given detailed attention.

And what to wear? Something cool, of course. Even at two in the morning, it'll be ninety degrees in the desert.

I pick the lightest and most translucent shorts and top I own, and try them on without underwear. "Nope," says my reflection in the bedroom mirror. "You cannot carry that off and you know it."

I compromise on my best bra and a lacy pink thong that shows through the shorts a little. My reflection winks and says, "This I think you can do."

Then comes footwear and reality elbows its way in. The desert harbors too many things that bite and sting for anything but high-top sneakers. At least they're white like the rest of my outfit.

CHAPTER TWENTY-ONE

I'm almost to the wind farm when the Vic's headlights pick out a Harley parked on the shoulder at one of those roadside shrines people put up for a loved one killed in a crash. They're called *descansos* around here, meaning "rest." A tall, bearded figure in a biker vest is kneeling in front of the *descanso*, head bowed.

I pull over a few yards past the *descanso* and walk back. Without looking up, the Chaplain raises a hand in a way that says both "hi" and "don't speak."

So I wait in the bright moonlight and study the shrine in the glare of the idling Harley's headlight. There's a white cross draped with a Moguls vest, a crucifix on a leather thong, and a wreath of mesquite. On one arm of the cross, "Tuco" is lettered in black; on the other, "RIP." At the foot of the cross is a Moguls helmet bearing the club's death's head logo with "Tuco" underneath. The whole thing is surrounded by a low green plastic fence with artificial flowers inside. In the middle of the flowers, a small American flag is stuck into the sand.

Finally the Chaplain rises and looks at me. "He drove his bike head-on into a semi on this spot."

"Suicide?"

"Maybe tweaking. Who knows? My half-brother. I couldn't save him."

He pulls a leather pouch from his vest and pours what looks like powdered concrete over the cross and the plastic flower bed. "That's why I was in Mexico. His funeral."

Suddenly a glimpse of the Chaplain's life is laid out in front of me. "So it was his ashes you took to San Diego?"

"To his wife and kid." The Chaplain studies the *descanso.*

I study him, and think if there's a way to lighten the mood without disrespecting the dead. "Tuco, huh? So he was ugly?"

"Ugly-beautiful. Like a warthog. And kind. Women loved him."

"That can happen," I say. "I'll wait in the car."

I return to the Vic and watch in the rear-view mirror as the Chaplain drops to his knees again. Finally he rises, mounts the Harley and pulls out. I follow him to the wind farm and park at the No Trespassing sign, then I swing up behind him and he steers the Harley a couple hundred yards out into the desert. We get off, lean on the bike, he lights a joint, we pass it back and forth under the star-draped sky and watch for the ISS over the silhouetted ridges to the southwest. The desert is silent except for the soft thrum of the windmills and the sigh of a southeast breeze through the mesquite.

I see the ISS first as it pops into view a couple of hand-widths above the mountains. I touch the Chaplain's forearm, and point.

He grunts and we watch it arc over the southern horizon against the black velvet backdrop of space. The ISS is the biggest, brightest star up there, and by far the fastest. It's like Venus on steroids.

"You think they have sex up there?" I giggle from the weed at the thought.

"They human?" he says.

"But how? There's no gravity. They'd bounce off of each other."

"Maybe wrestling holds."

"Wait, I got it," I say. "Bungee cords."

"They strap themselves together?"

I try to say "Absolutely," but we both collapse in laughter before I can get it out.

The laughter passes and we're silent until the station completes its transit and winks out at about the same altitude as when it appeared. The fact that it appears so abruptly from nowhere, then vanishes, rather than rising or setting like the moon or regular stars, has to do with how its track takes it through the light of the sun, then through the shadow of the earth, then back into the sunlight. Basic orbital physics if you're an astronomer, pure magic if you're leaning on a Harley and sharing a joint with the Chaplain in the dark.

"Want to hear a story?" I ask.

"Always," he says.

So I tell him about Sylvia, Ike's shattered client in the lesbian divorce case, about Mee-Maw, and about the stolen recipe box.

"Something bad should happen to somebody over this."

"No, no--no hammer, please. But it'll be months before the court rules, and we could even lose."

"Any idea where it is?"

"Maybe." I explain about the couple's homes here and in Malibu, and about Miranda's new chalet at Tahoe. "Sylvia's in the house here and it's not there. She went down and checked the Malibu house and it's not there either. So..."

"Tahoe."

"My guess."

"I could take a run up there."

"That's a long run for a long shot."

"I need to check in with our Reno charter anyway." He pulls on the joint, passes it over.

"I'll text you the address."

We share the joint and the desert night in silence for a few minutes, then I ask, "Were you gonna tell me the rest of your Afghanistan story?"

The silence stretches on for a few more minutes and I give up on hearing it tonight. Then he sighs.

"I never told anybody. Maybe it's time." he says. "One of our Humvees got blown up by an IED. It killed two of our people. One of them was this girl Renata. I was mentoring her. Sort of a kid sister thing."

"I'm so sorry."

"It was war. That happens. But we caught the guy we thought planted the device. I couldn't stop thinking about how scared Renata's eyes were when the medics were trying to save her. I slipped into the hut where we were holding the guy. I..."

I wait.

He coughs. "I cut his throat."

I pass him the joint and he takes a hit.

"Then a couple days later, they were water-boarding a guy. He unexpectedly confessed to planting the IED. He looked exactly like the guy I killed. They were brothers, a couple years apart. Almost as identical as twins."

"Wow."

"Yeah. I killed the wrong guy. I started using heroin. It was as easy to get as chewing gum over there."

"And that worked?"

"Not really. So I decided to kill myself with it as soon as I could work up the nerve." He stops, draws on the joint, and passes it over.

I take a hit and let it out slow.

"Frank caught on and pulled me back. He told me about moral injury. He said something that stuck with me. 'You have to learn to forgive yourself. Especially in war.'"

The Chaplain stops and gazes across the desert at the windmills and the mountains on the far side of the valley.

I don't know if he's waiting for me to speak, but I finally do. "It's easier said than done."

"But somehow it worked," he says. "What Frank said saved my life. I quit killing people. That helped too. I got my own kind of religion. That also helped. I quit security work and came home. I got the bike here." He pats the Harley's gas tank. "I got into the Moguls. Most of them were as broken as me. That's how I ended up becoming their chaplain."

"Bikers have spiritual needs?"

"Everybody does. They're mostly ex-military. Iraq, Afghanistan. Even a couple geezers from Vietnam."

"That thing in Afghanistan. Is that why you're wanted?"

Against the starry sky, I see him nod.

I put my hand on his bare arm, feel the heat of his skin, the packed muscle underneath. "If you could wish on the ISS, I'd wish we both could find a way to put ourselves back together."

He pats my thigh and says, "Not likely. But thanks. At least I accept myself now."

We smoke in silence for a while. My skin burns where he touched me. Finally I work up the nerve. "I've got a blanket and some wine in the Vic."

He gives me a look and my heart hammers as his eyes widen and he smiles in what could be affection, or regret. "For me, you're still Frank's woman."

"Can we go back to the Vic now?"

He starts the Harley, I swing on and wrap my arms around his middle, and we trundle back across the sand to the car. I open the passenger door, get my purse off the seat, pull out the pink Glock I call Miss Kitty, and rack a shell into the chamber.

"Whoa, whoa, whoa," he says. "You don't wanna be - -"

"Don't worry, it's not for me." I fire a round into the Vic's front fender. I walk along the side of the car, putting in another round every few feet. By the end, I'm at the Vic's filler neck and gasoline trickles onto the sand after I shoot. The smell of it fills the air.

I look at the Chaplain. He's smiling in comprehension and what looks like approval.

"Help me get the plates and VIN tags off?" I ask.

He digs a big flathead screwdriver out of a saddlebag and we strip the car of identifying information by the flashlight on my phone.

"Got another clip?" he asks as I take my purse out of the Vic, plus the wine and the beach blanket.

"Duh." I pull out my spare clip, reload, and put Miss Kitty in his hand.

He walks around the rear of the car, emptying the Glock into the Vic's gas tank. The smell gets stronger and the patch of wet sand under the trunk gets bigger as I load my stuff into the Harley's saddlebags.

He pulls out a match, lights it with his thumbnail, and tosses it under the Vic.

We watch the gas blaze up.

"I was Frank's woman," I say.

He ponders that as light from the flames flickers across his face. "Luther."

Now I ponder, but come up dry. "What?"

"My government name is Luther."

"First or last?"

"Please, Dana."

"With 'Luther' and that traffic fatal Tuco was in, you know I could figure it out."

"Will you?"

"Of course not," I say. "Same as I never ran the plates on your bike."

"They're undercover plates," he says. "A lady from Crescent City would come up if you did." He swings onto the Harley. "But thanks for not trying."

I swing on behind him, and we pull away.

I watch over my shoulder as the fire under the car gets brighter. We're a quarter mile down Indian Canyon when the gas tank blows and Frank's Vic lights up like a torch.

CHAPTER TWENTY-TWO

— · —

The next morning I sleep in.

And in.

And in.

When Duke woofs dog breath in my face about going out, I open one eye to see 11:48 on the clock radio. I slide into my flip-flops and open the back door. Duke trots out, sniffs the blow-dryer breeze off the desert, and disappears into the brush. The thermometer on the patio says it's ninety-nine degrees, and my phone calls for a high around 110 before the day is out.

As I survey the prospect from the patio, I sense something is missing. There's my Jeep in the carport, but where's the Vic? Was I so stoned last night I left it at the wind farm? Do I need to call an Uber and retrieve it?

Then I remember the Vic going up in flames under the windmills and the Chaplain dropping me off here. He didn't spend the night but he did help me destroy Frank's car. And he told me one of his names. That's progress, I guess.

Duke returns from his foray into the desert and looks at me as I look at the empty space in the carport.

"You're right," I tell him. "We need to finish the job."

I march into what was our bedroom till Frank got shot. Since that day, I've never slept in it. I use the guest bedroom instead. In fact, I've barely even entered it since his death.

Other than smelling like a room does when it's been closed up too long, it's just as it was that morning when he left for work. I was on a graveyard shift, so I was gone when he got up around seven. As usual, he left the bed unmade, and after his shower he tossed the bathrobe I got him three Christmases back onto the jumble of covers. It's still there.

I pick it up and sniff it. It's burgundy, and made of lightweight cotton because this is the desert. Frank's scent—a mixture of his after-shave, cigar smoke, and male sweat—is barely detectable now. I hold the robe out to Duke and he sniffs, too. He mouths the cuff of one sleeve and looks at me like he doesn't want to let go.

"You want it for your dog bed? Sorry, buddy, not gonna happen."

I take back the robe, return to the patio, throw it on the grill, and light the gas. The cotton goes up fast and smells like a campfire. It leaves a feathery gray ash as the fire eats it away.

It's nearly gone when I remember Frank's iPhone. I call it on my phone, it warbles from the kitchen drawer, and I leave him a voicemail saying, "So long, asshole."

I retrieve the iPhone from its drawer, toss it onto what's left of the bathrobe and turn the gas on high.

Whatever an iPhone's made of, it's tougher than a cotton bathrobe. For a while, nothing happens. Flames lick up from underneath and curl over the edges of the screen, but it stays as black and shiny as ever.

Then the screen starts to scorch, the phone swells, and the smell of burning plastic comes up with the smoke. Finally the seams let go and black goo bubbles from inside the phone. I close the cover on the barbecue, let it burn for another five minutes, then turn it off and walk away. One day I'll clean it up or get a new barbecue. But not today.

I go back inside, shut the door against everything outside, make a dark roast, and sip it between sobs. Apparently hating somebody doesn't mean you stop loving them.

"No way, baby. Love is a condition, not a choice."

I raise my head and there he is on the stool beside me at the kitchen island. Imaginary Frank is in his off-duty uniform--t-shirt, shorts, and sandals—and drinking coffee from a mug with the Vic owners club logo. The same mug that I can see hanging from a pewter cup tree beside the Keurig.

"A lot you know about love, asshole."

"Guilty as charged. But who does know anything about it?"

"Not me," I tell him. "I thought I did, then your kids showed up on the patio."

He pauses for a puff on the Partagas. "You burned my phone."

"And your bathrobe."

"And the Vic," he says. "That was quite a show."

"That was the idea."

"How'd it feel?"

"Not as good as I hoped. Same with the robe and phone."

"Speaking of feelings."

"I don't want to talk about that."

"Of course you do."

I don't answer.

"Remember," he says. "I know what's in your head."

"Unfortunately."

"The Chaplin's a good man. I hope that happens."

I look at him in surprise. "You mean it?"

"You know me pretty well. Do I say things I don't mean?"

"How do I know I can trust him? Look who's giving him a character reference."

"Touché. But you did tell him I'm in the rearview. 'I was Frank's woman,' you said."

"I did."

"Did you mean it?"

"I think so. I'm trying to."

"Good to hear."

"Really?"

"Uh-huh. In the rearview is where I belong now. We both know it."

"I'm not sure that's where I want you. How do I break off that big a chunk of my life?"

He grins that grin of his. "You don't have to. You just need to organize it into its proper place."

He heaves off the stool, moves behind me, and puts his hands on my shoulders. He kisses the top of my head and I catch a whiff of his personal scent—Partagas, sweat, aftershave and...just Frank.

"You're leaving?"

"Apparently."

He walks to the front door and opens it. The Vic is idling in the driveway. He turns and we lock eyes. "You and the Chaplain, you can save each other."

He goes out and climbs into the car, puts on sunglasses. I watch from the stoop as his window whirs down.

"Will you be back?" I shout.

He puts his head out. "How would I know?"

He gets a few yards down the canyon, then reverses and backs into the driveway. The window whirs down again and the left hand comes out holding the Partagas.

It's still wearing a wedding ring, I notice. Frank waves it and shouts, "Love ya, baby."

Then the Vic rolls away and disappears around the first turn.

It's a half hour before I can force myself to start my day. My phone shows two voicemails from Ike. The most recent is forty-five minutes old. I punch it up and hear him say, "Check the news and call me, but try not to get mad."

I open my laptop to the *Palm Springs Herald* website and there it is: *Cops: Accused Torso Shooter was hired hitman.*

The reporter is Liz yet again. The story, based on confidential sources, names Hale as the alleged hitman.

Who hired the hitman? Not disclosed and Liz would disclose it if she had it. I guess there are things even she can't coax out of a cop. Rachel Bartell has gotten a pass.

Hale's situation is getting worse instead of better. And that's because of our visit with Jung and Avila, and Ike's agreement to let them question him about his story of Jennifer's murder.

Now I'm plugged in again. The cremains of my former life are forgotten in the barbecue. The Jennifer Williamson case has started my day for me.

I return Ike's call, but Glenn the pony-tailed secretary says Ike's with a client and he'll call me back.

Ninety minutes later, I've sweated out my half hour on the Peloton and I've tried Ike again. I've had grapefruit and a bowl of granola and tried Ike yet again. I've showered and dressed and tried Ike one more time, still to no avail.

So I stomp out to the Jeep, take off down Cahuilla Canyon, push the speed limits and shoot the lights all the way to Ike's office.

Glenn and his ponytail are at the copier when I arrive. I brush past him and bang open Ike's door, which interrupts his conversation with a well maintained forty-something brunette.

He looks up in alarm and says, "Now, Dana."

"Don't now-Dana, me, Ike Skogel. How is Smokey Hale in even worse trouble than before?"

"One client at a time, okay?" He nods at the woman in front of his desk. "This is Dr. Sylvia Webster, our client in the divorce case?"

Oh, yeah. The dueling lesbians with the stolen recipe box. That takes away some of my fire. Clients aren't just case numbers and billable hours. They hurt like the rest of us.

"Good to meet you, Dr. Webster. I'm Dana Forsythe, Ike's legal investigator."

"My pleasure," she says with a bitter little smile as we shake hands. "Other than the circumstances that bring us together, of course. And call me Sylvia."

"Did Ike tell you—Ike, did you tell her we - -"

"Yep," Ike says. "She knows you found the chalet in Tahoe."

"Thanks," she says. "Thank you so much, Dana. Is my...did you...can you find...?"

"Your recipe box? We're checking."

Her eyes brim with quicksilver but don't spill over. "Checking? How?"

Ike clears his throat. "Sylvia, Dana sometimes employs, ah, means and methods that she prefers not to discuss. Even with me. Which I also prefer."

He turns to me. "We were just wrapping up. Couple minutes, okay?"

I step out to the reception area, but it's eight minutes, not a couple, before Sylvia emerges from the office. Ike is close behind with his fingers brushing the small of her back. He shows her out, and takes me into his office.

"You're hitting on her, Ike? You do know which team she bats for, right?"

He lights up with a smile that turns his shipwreck of a face into something almost beautiful. "As I think I mentioned, we deny sleeping with our ex-husband. Underscore *husband*."

"Ah."

"It's called erotic plasticity. You girls have more of it than us boys, apparently."

"It's women. And we have more of everything than you, except money and power."

"What can I say?" He turns up his palms with a look of injured innocence as fake as Rachel Bartell's boobs.

"You can say how Smokey Hale ended up worse off than before we talked to Jung and Avila," I tell him. "He's a hit man now?"

"Don't panic, Hale's not really worse off, not yet. That story in the *Herald* this morning, it didn't actually say he's charged with anything new, just that the cops think he was hired as a hit man. Underscore *think*."

"Uh-huh."

"So your friend Liz," Ike says. "She's working her magic and getting the cops to tell her more than they should."

"She bats her eyes and flips her hair and they turn into idiots. But what's really going on?"

"It's true Jung is dangling new charges, but that's just to back us off while they look for the throat shot bullet. Have you been up to the murder scene today?"

I shake my head.

"Well, I drove by before I came in this morning. This was like, seven a.m., and they already had at least five cops at work with metal detectors, plus some kind of sifter thing with guys shoveling sand into it, and two K-9 units sniffing around. You were a K-9 officer, right? Can a police dog smell a bullet in the sand?"

"Maybe if it has gunshot residue on it."

"Whatever," Ike says. "Point is, this is just part of the dance. I'm not worried about Hale's story falling apart."

"But you've got that look . What else is going on?"

"Hale's grandfather called just before Sylvia came in. He saw the *Herald* story online, and he's pissed because Hale is not only still in jail, but now also a hitman. He's sending the family lawyer out here to review our work and hire a real criminal defense attorney. Underscore *real*."

"Well, screw him. Let's keep- -" I stop at the look in Ike's eyes.

"Look, this case is a pain in the ass, like anything with rich people and Slabbers. It just goes on and on. And we've got it to a point where there's no way they can get Hale for anything serious."

"So?"

"So, maybe we should let Grandpa turn it over to somebody else. We've had our fun, we've done our job, maybe it's time to move on. There's an extremely rich lesbian who will pay us handsomely to grind her wife to powder."

I can see Ike's point. Sylvia's divorce case is easy money, and lots of it, plus she appears to be that rarest of birds in legal work, a truly innocent victim. I should jump at the chance to be rid of this dumpster fire of a case and the drunken lunatic who tried to hire our drunken client to kill the drunken mother of my husband's outside kids.

But I can't.

Which Ike figures out from the expression on my face. "Now, Dana."

"No way I'm letting some East Coast three-piece in wingtips yank this out from under me. I'm in too deep."

"Just what I was afraid of," Ike says. "But I'm under orders from Grandpa to park the case till his guy gets here. You're on your own. Do not tell me what you're doing, and do not send me a bill when it's done."

"I won't."

"And do not call me about it unless you're in jail and need representation."

"Nope."

"In which case, what's the rule?"

"Don't talk to the cops."

"Very good. Now - -

"When is this guy coming?"

"Flying in on the family Gulfstream Sunday night," he says. We're meeting first thing Monday."

"So I've got three days?"

"You didn't hear this from me, but good luck."

The Chamber of Commerce headquarters where Jennifer worked and the Coffi next door where Chelsea works are due east of Ike's office on Tahquitz Canyon Way. But somehow the Jeep turns west instead. I have to see the metal-detector army for myself.

Ten minutes later I'm on Gene Autry Trail, a mile south of the 10, the spot where Jennifer died, and there's no army to be seen. Just crime-scene tape and a patch of plowed-up desert.

A couple hundred yards past, I pull over and call Avila's number. When he answers, I tell him what I've seen and ask if it means they found the throat-shot bullet.

"Drop dead," he says. "I'm not telling you shit about what we found or didn't find out there. Direct orders from Jung's office so don't bother calling her or your friend St. Clair either. Nobody's talking."

I want to ask if that applies to Liz, but for once I bite my tongue. "Was it good news or bad news for Smokey Hale?"

"Sorry, not playing today." He taps off.

I drum my fingers on the Jeep's console for a few seconds, then tap Liz's number on my phone. I'm still telling myself to hang up when she answers.

"Hey, girl! What's up? Time for another Moscow mule?"

"Not today. I have information to trade."

"Yeah? Like what?"

"I know who hired the hitman, who by the way is no hitman. He's a con man."

"Seriously? Please proceed."

"As if."

Liz chuckles. "Of course you're not giving it away. No girl ever should. What's it gonna cost me?"

"I think our friends in blue found another bullet up at the murder scene today, the one that went through Jennifer Williamson's throat. I want to know if it matches the bullets from the torso shots."

"Of course it will," she says. "Because why wouldn't it - - never mind, you wouldn't ask unless you knew it won't, right?"

"I just need to be sure."

"I'll see what I can do. But it'll probably take them a while to analyze it."

"Duh."

Fifteen minutes later, I pull into the Coffi where I found Chelsea before. Patrick of the "Manager" nametag is at the cash register this time, too.

He frowns when I reintroduce myself and ask for Chelsea. "Not today," he says. "No call, no nothing, she just didn't show."

"Is that unusual for her?"

"One day of no-show without calling, no. She's not that reliable."

Patrick pauses to ring up two skinny lattes for a gym-buffed guy in a black mesh t-shirt, very short shorts, and neon-blue sunglasses with huge mirror lenses.

Then he turns back to me. "So with Chelsea, no, one no-show would not be a surprise. But two in a row, yeah, that is unusual."

"I hear it's tough to find good help."

"Tell me about it."

"So, look, I really need to talk to her, and I know this is probably against the rules or something, but is there any chance you could give me her number? It would really help me out."

If you haven't tried it, you'd be surprised how often this works—telling somebody you know they probably can't help you, then throw yourself on their mercy and ask them to do exactly that. I don't understand the psychology, I just use it.

"Sure, I guess." Patrick clicks on his computer screen, copies her number onto the back of a Coffi punch card and hands it over.

"Don't bother," he says as I tap the number into my phone. "I tried her three times already."

Chelsea's number rings four times, then goes to voicemail—not her voice, but a metallic robot saying the party is unavailable.

I tap off. "I should probably run by her place, then. Can you put the address on there?"

I hand Patrick the card. He hesitates barely a second, then glances at his screen and scrawls down an address in Chapel City—35220B Fan Palm Drive.

Coffi is filling up. Patrick now has a line of three people at the register, led by a woman with a wailing baby in a front pack. He leans in close and mutters in my ear. "If she's home, tell her that her sorry ass is fired. I've had enough of her shit."

He turns and smiles at the woman with the baby. "And how can I help you two this lovely afternoon?"

Soon I'm parked in front of 35220 Fan Palm. It's a white bungalow, mid-century but definitely not modern. More of a mid-century original.

Problem is, there's no "B" in sight. Just the little white house with faded blue trim and 35220 in gold letters beside the front door. No vehicles in sight, no plants on the stoop.

I knock and wait in the blasting sun, without result, then repeat the process. Still nothing. A peep through a gap in the drapes reveals a cheaply furnished interior with a look of empty sterility about it—no coffee cups on the end tables, no mail on the counter, not a house plant in sight.

This tells me 35220 is one of two things.

It could be a short-term rental for snowbirds, of whom there are zero in the Coachella Valley just now because we are in the middle of the nuclear furnace known locally as the months of July and August.

Or the owners could be reverse snowbirds—Palm Springs residents who flee north in the summer to hole up in the mountains of Montana or Wyoming.

But what about the "B"?

A gravel driveway runs along the side of the house and disappears around the back corner. I follow it and find a detached garage that's been converted into a rental unit with "B" on the door and an Amazon box on the stoop. Next to it is a green Kia sedan that I judge to be eight or so years old. A cracked taillight wears a patch of translucent red tape. A black Coffi polo lies crumpled on the passenger seat beside a McDonald's bag, and there's a paper Coffi cup in the console.

Prolonged knocking at the door produces no more result than it did at the main house. The front window is blocked by a white honeycomb blind, as are the two windows on the right side of the house.

The lone window on the left side isn't covered. It shows a kitchen, with a glimpse of the living room. A door in the rear wall of the living room wall no doubt leads to the bedroom.

Nobody's in sight, but the place is obviously inhabited. A ceramic "Coffi" mug is visible in a dish rack under the kitchen window, and a half-bottle of cabernet with a screw-on top sits on the counter beside an old green refrigerator. Next to it is an empty wineglass with a puddle of red at the bottom. In the living room, a wooden coffee table supports a green glass bong and an unopened Amazon box. A calico cat sleeps in front of the bedroom door.

It's also obvious the inhabitant is about to hit the road. Cardboard moving boxes take up most of the living room floor, half of the kitchen table, and two of the seats on the sofa. Some are taped shut. Some are still open. Clothes spill over the sides and household goods stick out the tops.

My neck hair bristles and tells me I should go in, so I return to the Jeep for a tire iron. That turns out to be wasted effort. When I try the knob, the door swings open. The cat streaks for the kitchen and vanishes from sight.

A knock on the bedroom door produces only silence, so I ease it open.

Chelsea is on her back on the bed, coverlet pulled up to her waist, right hand flung out with a small revolver on the floor beneath it. There's a small dark hole in her right temple with a trickle of blood below.

Her head is turned to the left, so the exit wound isn't visible. But a big black stain on the pillow tells the story.

Sometimes, a suicide bullet doesn't make it out the far side of the skull and there's no exit wound. Sometimes it does get out, but doesn't expand in its passage through the head, so the exit wound is small. And sometimes it expands a lot, and the exit wound is big and bloody. That appears to be the case with Chelsea Miller.

She's naked, at least the part of her that's uncovered. That's not common, in my experience, but it seems to mean the victim was serious about it. I've never seen a failed suicide attempt by someone naked. If they're dressed and they survive, it's generally a cry for help.

She doesn't smell yet, so she probably hasn't been dead long. But with air conditioning, it's hard to tell. That's the medical examiner's problem, not mine.

I pull out my phone and tap in nine-one-one as I squat beside the gun on the floor. It's a nine-millimeter Ruger LCR, a revolver so little it holds only five rounds rather than the usual six. A perfect lady gun, a small weapon for small hands and big decisions.

My neck hair is mostly relaxed now.

Chapter Twenty-Three

I t's midmorning a day later. Duke's out for a game of tag with the neighborhood roadrunner and I'm halfway through my first dark roast. My phone warbles and Liz's name comes up.

"You called it," she says before I can say hello.

"Called what - - wait, they found the bullet from the throat shot, right? Give!"

"Not on the phone, this is too hot. Susan Jung is on a tear and Homicide is upside down."

"Excellent," I say. "The Sand Trap in an hour?"

She's silent for a few moments.

"*Problema?*"

"Cops tend to come in there for lunch."

"So now you can't even be seen talking to me?"

She's silent again, then, "Ah, the hell with 'em. As long as we can get that booth in the back corner."

"I'll show up a few minutes early to scope it out. You don't hear from me, it's cop-free."

She rings off, I call Duke back in, run through the rest of my morning routine, and start downhill in the Jeep.

An hour later, we're sipping iced tea and waiting for our food to arrive—for Liz a jalapeno burger and fries, for me a chef salad and the attendant eye roll from the waitress Rusty.

"So, yeah," she's saying. "They did indeed find the throat shot bullet—it managed to land in a junked refrigerator."

"Like it went through the door and landed in the freezer compartment or something?"

She laughs and drinks from the iced tea. "Not even. It landed in the part underneath. You know, where the pumps and cooling coils and stuff are? Apparently whoever dumped it had pulled off the back panel and the bullet just petered out and fell in there. Then that windstorm we had the other day filled it up with sand."

Now I have to laugh. "So they didn't need metal detectors or gravel sifters or any of that?"

"No, just a dog. A firearms dog named Ladybird sniffed it out."

We're both still chuckling as Rusty shows up with our order. She sets down my salad with another eye roll.

"Sure you don't want some real food, ma'am?" Before I can say she should stop calling me "ma'am" and start worrying about her muffin-top instead of my diet, she winks and hustles off to a table full of guys demanding another round of Dos Equis.

"And this bullet, it doesn't match the ones from the torso shots?"

"Absolutely not," Liz says as we dig in. "It's a nine-millimeter, not a thirty-eight."

"But they think it killed Jennifer?"

"They do. The preliminary lab work turned up traces of her blood on it. They have to finalize it, but my guy says there's not much doubt."

"So they've got two shooters?"

"That's the working theory, yeah."

"They getting anywhere on the throat shooter?"

"Not yet," she says.

"I owe you."

"You certainly do. Now, spill. What have you got?"

I pause for a mental inventory. If I tell Liz what we know about the case, will it reveal anything we didn't tell the police? The answer comes up 'no.' The police already know what we know.

"We're off the record, right? You can use the information, just don't say where you got it?"

"How about you're a source close to the case?"

"Perfect. Jung will blame it on the cops."

"That's my thinking. So?"

"So you don't know half of what happened up on Gene Autry that night," I tell her. And I lay out the whole saga: Smokey Hale, the SUV lady with the cheating husband, the ten-thousand-dollar con, the Patek Philippe, the bullet under the mesquite bush, Cara the artist in Bamboo Beach, all of it.

All of it, except for two things. One of the things I don't tell Liz is the identity of the SUV lady, which she pounces on the moment I finish.

"This woman who hired Smokey, she have a name?"

"Of course she does."

"Dana, do not eff with me."

"This bit will definitely cost you a Moscow mule at a date to be named later."

"Dana."

"Rachel Bartell."

"Huh, that name is familiar but I can't - - who is that, exactly?"

"Ever hear of RaBar Luxury Properties? Or a plastic surgeon named Julian Bartell, the one with the billboards?"

"Those Bartells? Oh, my God!"

"Exactly."

"So he was cheating on her and she hired your guy to kill the girlfriend?"

"Tried to hire him. Like I said, Smokey was conning her. He was never gonna kill Jennifer Williamson or anybody else. Far more likely he'll get himself killed one of these days."

"Right, right," Liz says. "And Rachel Bartell is the one who fired the shots into Jennifer's, ah, torso?"

"She is."

"Wow. Talk about a woman scorned."

"There's a lot of it going around."

"Let me see if I have this straight." She runs back through the story and gets it right except for a couple of minor details that we fix on the spot. "That's it, then? You got anything else for me?"

"Not today."

"Well, thanks. Seriously." She reaches for her purse, but I tell her this one's on me. She finishes her iced tea and slips out the back door, the same way she came in.

And the second thing I didn't tell her? I only made the connection when my neck hair bristled in the middle of our conversation: Jennifer Williamson died from a nine-millimeter slug.

So did her best friend Chelsea Miller, the wannabe to the Queen Bee.

The question is, does Palm Springs homicide know about this?

Probably not, I'm guessing. Like a lot of the smaller communities patchworked around Palm Springs, Chapel City doesn't have its own police force. Instead, it contracts the work out to the county sheriff's office, my old employer.

It's not that the Palm Springs police and the sheriff's office don't communicate with each other. They do. It's that there's no particular reason they would do it for a routine suicide like Chelsea Miller's.

Gary Avila is not easy to get hold of. His number rings twice, then goes to voicemail. I take that to mean he looked at his caller ID, recognized my number, and bumped it to voicemail with malice aforethought. I'm drumming my fingernails on the table and trying to figure out what to do about it when the man himself walks into the Sand Trap. He mounts a stool at the bar, eyes on his phone.

I could go ahead and leave my voicemail and ease out the back like Liz did, but this feels like a message from the universe. I tap off the call and start for the bar. Gary's giving Rusty his order for a half-rack of ribs and a Corona when I slide onto the next stool and say, "Hey, sailor, looking for a good time?"

He looks at me, recoils, and gives a what-now sigh. "Jesus fuck," he says. "You here to gloat?"

Rusty arrives with his Corona and he takes a swallow.

"Indeed not, Lieutenant. I'm here to help. Yet again."

He squeezes his eyes shut and pinches the bridge of his nose as if he just got a migraine like a skull full of fire ants. "Yeah?"

"You guys plugged into that suicide that was found yesterday in Chapel City?"

He opens his eyes and gives me a wary stare. "Why would we?"

"I've been poking around some and what I'm hearing is, the victim, a woman named Chelsea Miller, was Jennifer Williamson's best friend."

"Huh."

"You know the name?"

"Yeah, one of our people talked to her early on," he says. "I saw the interview notes, didn't look like we got much. Why?"

I give him the short version of the Chelsea Miller-Jennifer Williamson story, up to and including when I paid a visit to Chelsea's rental in Chapel City and found her dead of a nine-millimeter round to the head from a five-shot Ruger.

He stares into his Corona for a long time. Then, "A nine-millimeter. Just like Jennifer Williamson."

"Yep."

"Jesus fuck."

"You said that already."

"How the hell did you...no, I'm not gonna ask. Point is, they were both killed by a nine-millimeter, and you think it was the same gun."

"Yep."

"A lot of people have nine-millimeters," he says.

"Yep."

"So why would this Chelsea Miller kill her best friend?"

"Because she wanted to *be* Jennifer Williamson and she finally figured out it wasn't gonna happen. You wanna be a Jennifer Williamson, you gotta win the genetic lottery."

"You got that right," Avila says. "That face, that body, she - -"

"I know, Gary. You realize who you're talking to, right?"

"Oh, shit, I'm sorry and...well, I - -"

"Let's move on."

"Right, right. So, we'll get the Ruger and the bullet from the sheriff's office in Chap City and run the ballistics and - -"

"And if you get a match we're done here? Smokey Hale gets out of jail?"

Avila sighs. "Yeah, basically. But that scumbag, we gotta pop him for something, I mean - -"

"How about leaving the scene of an accident?"

"Accident? What accident?"

"A no-injury accident. He knocked over a speed limit sign, remember?"

Avila chuckles. It's the first time I ever heard him do that.

"God help me, Dana, I'm starting to like you. Drinks and dinner sometime?"

"Second Tuesday of next week work forya?"

He chuckles. Again. "Go fuck yourself."

"Love you, too, Gary."

My next stop is Ike's office. He's about to leave for a hearing, his secretary Glenn tells me. He'll want to hear this, I tell Glenn. Glenn says he'll see if Ike has a minute.

Ike does. "Make it quick, okay?" he says as he packs his briefcase.

There's no quick version of the Jennifer-Chelsea saga, but I do my best and bring it across the finish line in under two minutes.

"The Queen Bee and the wannabe, you say?"

"Oldest story in girl world."

"Jesus Christ, you're Batgirl, you know that?"

"Wonder Woman, if you please."

"Absolutely," Ike says. "But seriously. Assuming the ballistics check out, I can have Hale out of jail before his Grandpa's asshole of a lawyer gets here."

"I thought the case was officially parked."

"Act now, apologize later, Dana."

Chapter Twenty-Four

—·—

The top story in the *Palm Springs Herald* this morning is about a Maltese named Jasmine who is the latest local dog to become coyote cuisine. Jasmine had big love-me eyes, long white silky hair, and, until yesterday, a comfortable life in a gated condo complex not far from my perch in the Cahuilla Hills.

Today, she's just a memory for her owner, an eighty-three-year-old Minnesota snowbird named Edith Hemmelgarn. The story on the *Herald* website links to a doorbell video of the coyote sneaking up on Jasmine, pouncing, and carrying her off as she howls in terror.

"They're jumping fences and grabbing dogs now?" Edith tells the *Herald*. "The city should poison them!"

The online comments run three to one in favor of the coyote. Two commenters say the coyote should have grabbed Edith. Welcome to Palm Springs, Edith.

The coyote story has pushed the latest developments in the Jennifer Williamson case to second position on the *Herald* website.

Cops believe Chap City suicide killed Jennifer Williamson is the headline on Liz's story. The subhead reads, *But real estate queen was Torso Shooter!*

The story lays out the events on Gene Autry Trail in detail and goes on to report that Rachel Bartell is negotiating a plea deal after leading police to the gun that she used for the torso shots and Hale used to shoot the mesquite bush.

She'd hidden the weapon—a Smith and Wesson Bodyguard thirty-eight--under a Burbank Spineless cactus in one of her real estate listings in La Quinta. There's a photo of the property from the street. I recognize it as the one where I visited Rachel and showed her the crime-scene photos of her handiwork.

I'm halfway through my half hour on the Peloton when my phone lights up with Gary Avila's caller ID.

"I figured I should share and share alike," he tells me. "Since you passed along the tip about the Chap City suicide and the nine-millimeter thing and all."

The bullets did match, he reports, and the only fingerprints on the Ruger were Chelsea's, meaning she has to be the throat shooter. Plus, there was gunshot residue on the frame of her Kia's passenger window. So, they're closing the case.

"What was her story anyway?" I ask him.

"The gun was registered to her ex-husband back in Nebraska," Avila says, "so we got in touch with him."

Chelsea, it seems, got the gun in the divorce but nobody bothered to change the registration. The husband was shocked but not surprised to hear of the suicide. He said it was her drug use and infidelity that led to the breakup, and to him getting the kids. She moved to California for a new start and it turned out like most of her dreams.

"So Chelsea Miller and Rachel Bartell were both trying to kill Jennifer Williamson on the same night," he says. "What a coincidence, huh?"

"Maybe not. Rachel could have been waiting until her husband left town for his conference in Anaheim to make her move on Jennifer. And Jennifer could have gone to the party in Chapel City to play while her sugar daddy was away. She didn't invite Chelsea along and maybe that was the last straw."

"Could make sense," Avila says. "Her phone did show she got a call from Jennifer around midnight that night. Probably for a ride after Hale dumped her off."

"Yeah," I say, "Chelsea told me about that. She said she had been drinking too much to drive, so she told Jennifer to call a Lyft."

"Except she took off up there and killed her before the guy arrived," Avila says. "So besides being a druggie and part-time hooker, now she's a murderer. She sees her life is a pile of dog shit that can only get deeper and she's tired of it so her exit strategy is the same nine-millimeter she used on Jennifer."

"Listen, thanks," I tell him. "I owe you."

"That dinner offer is still open," he says. "And not at the Sand Trap. Some place with cloth napkins. Like Marvyn's?"

This is the heavy artillery. Marvyn's is a classic mid-century beef-and-bourbon steakhouse, a Palm Springs legend once frequented by Frank Sinatra and the Rat Pack, even Frank's mom. It features nosebleed prices, a snooty maitre' d' named Byron, and waiters who set your food on fire at the table.

"Rain check, okay?"

"Yeah," he says, "I guess you're not ready to date yet."

"Exactly," I tell him. "Thanks for understanding."

It's not dating I'm not ready for. It's Gary. But what he doesn't know won't hurt him, and it keeps the channel open. I might need him again sometime.

By the next morning the murder charges against Smokey Hale and Rachel Bartell have been dropped, according to the *Herald*. Both have bailed out of jail.

Rachel's charges are now down to mutilation of a corpse and attempted murder for hire. A deal is being cut that will give her six months of rehab and a year's probation rather than jail time.

Hale, true to form, has all but skated. He's charged with drunk driving and leaving the scene of an accident. Avila is quoted as saying he's been a cooperative witness, very cooperative. "He's not a killer, just a con man," Avila tells the *Herald*.

In a separate story, Liz sketches Chelsea Miller's sad little life, culminating in murder and suicide. It seems she has an Aunt Vivian, who's shown standing beside a green minivan in front of Chelsea's place in Chapel City. She tells the *Herald*, "I'm not surprised by any of it, poor thing. Back home, she cut off a boyfriend's ear with hedge clippers. Served him right for passing out in the yard, if you ask me."

I close my laptop and check in with Ike, who confirms it all. We agree it's about time for our traditional postmortem at the Sand Trap, now that the case is wrapping up. . He says he'll call me when he gets back to the office on Monday, and we'll set something up.

Wow. A whole weekend with nothing but time on my hands. I decide to take Duke for a walk, then go see the twins at Yolanda's place.

It won't be much of a walk because it's already 102 degrees in the shade of the patio. But it's a chance to get out of the house by choice rather than necessity.

I put on my high tops, since summer is peak scorpion season, along with a huge sun hat and dark glasses that make me look like somebody's Aunt Gladys. Better that than skin cancer, and Duke doesn't judge.

As we start down the trail behind the house, he ranges off into the brush, no doubt in search of his roadrunner buddy. Or maybe he's scented the lady coyote who a couple of years ago produced four pups too big to be pure coyote but about the right size to be half German Shepherd. Plus, there was a strong family resemblance.

If Duke does find her, it'll be purely platonic because those pups put an end to Duke's sex life. Over Frank's objections, I had him fixed and now there'll be no more coyote hybrids in the Cahuilla Hills. Duke is strictly platonic now.

He soon returns with a deflated look, which I take to mean neither roadrunner nor ex-girlfriend was to be found. We make our way down the trail for a half-mile, then turn back so as not to overdose on the heat.

As we approach the last turn before the house, Duke alerts. His hackles rise, and he rumbles low in his throat. I peer around the outcrop and through a creosote bush I spot in my driveway a Range Rover SUV with KLOZIT on the rear plate and Rachel Bartell at the wheel.

"*Sitz!*" I hiss—German for "Sit!"

Duke drops to his haunches, ears up, nose testing the air.

Now what? Considering how crazy Rachel Bartell is and what she's confessed to, she could be here for payback. If I hadn't meddled, she'd still be selling overpriced real estate to clueless snowbirds.

I slap the back of my jeans and discover I've left Miss Kitty in the house, which proves just how retired from police work I am. What I do find in a hip pocket, though, is my phone. I don't recall picking it up when I got out of bed, nor putting it in my jeans when I dressed. But there it is, like some ubiquitous but unseen but ever-present family retainer.

Rachel Bartell has no way of knowing if I'm armed or not, so I hit the website for RaBar Luxury Properties. Just as I expected, Rachel has listed her cell as well as her office number.

I make the call, then watch as she brings up her phone and stares at the screen.

There's no reason she should recognize my number and she apparently doesn't. "RaBar Luxury Properties," she answers in a bright, professional tone. "Rachel Bartell speaking."

"Step out of the vehicle," I tell her. "Put your hands on the roof and don't move."

"What? Who is this?"

"Who do you think? Now exit the vehicle and put your hands on the roof."

Her head swivels but she doesn't spot me behind the creosote bush.

"Dana?" she says. "Mrs. Forsythe? I just need to talk to you. I mean you no harm."

"Then do as I say or I call nine-one-one."

She throws open her door, steps out, lays her phone on the roof, and puts her hands on either side of it. Then she jerks them back. "It's too damn hot," she shouts into the phone.

"*Voraus!*" I tell Duke. That's German for "Forward!" and Duke is happy to oblige. He races ahead and stations himself a few feet to Rachel's left. She turns her head to look at him. He growls. She whips her eyes back to straight ahead and hovers her hands an inch off the navy blue metal of the Range Rover.

"Don't move or I tell him to attack," I say.

She's like a statue as I ease up behind her and pat her down. She's clean.

"Stay there," I say, then search her car, purse, and briefcase for a gun. They're all clean, too.

"*Aus!*" I tell Duke, and he relaxes. No longer on guard, but eyes fixed on Rachel.

"All right," I tell her. "Come inside and explain yourself."

"I'll need my briefcase."

I nod and she brings it along as we go into the house and take seats at the dining table. Duke drops to the floor near her bare ankles. Rachel glances down and moves her feet away.

"Your dog scares me."

"That's his job. What do you want?"

"Perhaps a glass of wine?"

"Not a good idea," I tell her. I start a dark roast for me, bring her a glass of water, and watch as she sips from it. She's in skinny jeans, a white top that displays a strategic amount of cleavage, and a pale blue jacket. The water seems to put her back together. Real-estate Rachel re-emerges..

"May I open my briefcase?"

"Carefully."

She pulls out a folder with "Coachella Security" printed on the cover. She lays it on the table and looks up at me.

"You already know most of my story."

"Except whatever possessed you to hire the likes of Smokey Hale."

"I married the wrong man is what."

"Copy that."

"I know your story, too," she says. "The news people have had quite a time with it."

"We're not here to talk about me."

"So you know I never showed up at the Westgate Mall to pay Smokey his ten thousand for killing that woman, as I thought he had done."

"We figured you stiffed him because you knew he wouldn't go to the police."

"Not at all" she says. "I was perfectly willing to pay him. I wanted to get my watch back to cover my trail."

"But?"

"I was going to take it out of this emergency fund we keep in the bedroom safe. Twenty thousand in case, well, in case of an emergency. Two packets of hundred-dollar bills, one in a blue rubber band, the other in a green one."

"Okay."

Rachel sips at the water and studies the glass with a look of distaste. "I'd really prefer wine."

"I thought you were in rehab."

"It didn't start yet."

"I'm not helping you relapse. So you had twenty thousand dollars in your safe. And?"

"When I was going down to the Westgate Mall to buy my watch back, I opened the safe to get the ten thousand I owed Smokey but the money was gone."

"Gone where?"

"I didn't put it together till I saw that woman's picture on television."

"You mean Jennifer Williamson? What - -"

"Not her. The woman who shot her."

"Chelsea Miller?"

"Yes. When I hired these people"—she taps the folder from Coachella Security—"to find out if Julian was cheating again, it took them a couple of weeks to establish that he was having an affair with Jennifer."

"So?"

"So they're very good at what they do. They photographed him with several women. The circumstances were normal, with two exceptions. One was Jennifer Williamson. This was the other one."

She pulls a print from the folder and lays it on the table. It shows Julian Bartell and Chelsea Miller huddled over drinks in a booth in a bar. They're engaged in intense conversation. Intense like you just got a cancer diagnosis or found a meth pipe in your kid's bedroom.

I pick up the photograph, study it and copy it onto my phone. "They both told me they didn't know each other."

She arches her eyebrows and waits.

"So you think - -"

"I think he hired Chelsea to kill Jennifer while he was at his conference in Anaheim, which is why the money was missing when I went to get it to pay Smokey off and recover my watch. Then you figured out Smokey didn't shoot Jennifer and confronted Julian about it and he realized the walls were closing in. So he killed Chelsea and made it look like suicide to cover his tracks."

"You didn't recognize Chelsea when Coachella Security brought you this photo? She worked at the Coffi next door to the Chamber of Commerce. You were in and out of the Chamber all the time. You never went over for a latte?"

She shudders. "I only drink tea. And wine. Drank wine, I mean."

"There must have been other things your husband could have done with the money. Maybe he has a gambling problem? Or a new woman since the old one got herself killed?"

"One gun, two dead women," Rachel says. "It speaks for itself."

I study Rachel over the rim of my cup. "Let's back up. You're ready to pay Smokey his ten thousand, but you find the money's missing. Then what?"

"Then nothing. Like you said, I knew there was no way Smokey would go to the police about not getting paid, since he had killed Jennifer, at least that's what I thought at the time. So I decided the smart thing was to let him keep my Patek Philippe and tell Julian that I must have lost it somewhere and file an insurance claim if he even noticed. Which he didn't, the son of a bitch."

"Did you ask him what happened to the money?"

"Of course not. I couldn't tell him I knew it was gone. He would have asked too many questions."

"Why would he have Jennifer killed? What was the worst that could happen if you found out about Jennifer? Another divorce in Palm Springs? Who would notice? Or care?"

"I'd cut his balls off is what would happen. I warned him about it after he raped that maid and got her pregnant and we had to deport her. I come from money, and I make more from RaBar Properties than he does from that stupid clinic, which by the way I own. He's just a hired hand. And a lousy doctor to boot."

"Really? He didn't do your...you don't use him yourself?"

"You kidding? Two years ago he botched a labiaplasty. There was nerve damage, loss of sexual function." She shudders. "It cost me double commas to settle it."

"Why come to me with this? Why not the police?"

"I did. But by the time they talked to Julian he'd replaced the money somehow and that was the end of it."

"How would he do that?"

"Through that pill mill of a pharmacy next to the clinic, I assume. That, he actually owns himself."

"And the police didn't find any evidence he was at Chelsea's place the night she died?"

"Apparently not. They weren't very forthcoming."

"They usually aren't with civilians." I hold up the photo of Julian and Chelsea having a drink. "How did the police explain this?'

"They didn't. They told me to ask Julian. As if."

"Who was the detective you talked to?"

"This guy." She pulls a business card from her folder and slides it across the table. It has Gary Avila's name on it.

"Ah. So let me ask you this. Why worry about Julian? Your life is already a dumpster fire. You're looking at a year and a half of rehab and probation, and you've got your boys to worry about. Why finish blowing up their lives by having your husband tried on a murder charge he's likely to beat?"

"He has to pay for what he did! It's all over Palm Springs that I tried to have somebody killed and now they're calling me—I can hardly make myself say this—the torso shooter. Julian is by God not going to be walking around scot-free, the lying cheating, murdering bastard!"

I hold Avila's card up for Rachel to see. "How about we have a chat with the good lieutenant?"

"What for? He won't talk to me."

"He will to me."

"Why would he?"

"I have something he wants."

I punch up Avila's contact on my phone. I hold a finger to my lips and tell her "Shh!" as I put it on speaker.

Avila comes through like a champ. "Dana!" he booms. "Ready to cash that rain check?"

"We're in the desert, Gary. It won't rain till December."

He sighs in a way that says he'll wait. "What can I do you for today?"

"I hear you guys had a chat with Julian Bartell."

"You heard that, huh? Where?"

"A walk-in, what can I say? My question is, what did he tell you?"

"So the wife talked to you, too."

"I talk to a lot of people."

"Don't remind me. But, yeah, she thinks he hired the Miller woman to kill Jennifer Williamson, then killed the woman to cover it up. But there's just no evidence for it. He denies it and there's no sign of him ever being at the woman's place or touching that nine-millimeter. No fingerprints, no nothing."

"Was there something about a missing twenty thousand?"

"All part of the wife's conspiracy theory. The money was missing, then it wasn't, and somehow that proves he did it. He says it was never gone and she's a scorned woman making it all up. Not to mention a crazy drunk."

"What do you say?"

"I say we've got no case against him. If he did it, which he didn't, he did it right and he's gonna get away with it. Which he should, because he didn't do it."

"What about the picture of him and Chelsea Miller plotting murder in a bar?"

Another sigh, heavier than the first one. "Guy will screw anything in a skirt and it proves something that he was talking to a hooker? He says he was making a date."

"With a dead hooker that he lied to me about knowing at all."

"If you were married to that woman, would you lie about knowing a hooker?"

I can see Rachel is about to blow, so I end the call with a quick "I owe ya, Gary!"

"'Scorned woman!'" she exclaims. "My husband kills two women and rapes a maid and I'm a scorned woman!"

She clenches her jaw and fights it, but her mouth stretches into a hideous grimace and she ugly-cries like a prom queen just dumped by the quarterback. Tears carve channels through her makeup and the Botox forehead crumples into deep furrows.

"I need wine," she sobs.

"No, you don't. Rehab, remember? I'll make you some tea."

I rise and start for the kitchen. She tells my back, "Put some wine in it."

I don't, and in a few minutes she's regained some of her composure. She's made emergency repairs to her face and is sipping from a mug of chamomile.

"That bastard," she says.

"Avila or your husband?"

"Both of them. All of them. All men. They're all bastards."

"Copy that."

She fumbles in her briefcase and brings out a checkbook. "I want to hire you to get my husband."

"What can I do that the police didn't?"

"I don't know what, but I know you can do it. You did it before."

"No, thanks." I push with my hands in the international symbol for "Not my circus, not my monkeys."

Rachel's forehead is furrowing up again and her lips are forming that grimace. "Maybe he likes killing women now. Who's next? Me? You? Some random woman he picks up in a bar?"

There's nothing I hate more than seeing a woman cry twice in one day, probably because I've done some of it myself lately. Plus, she could be right. She knows her husband, and she has the real-estate shark's knack for reading people.

"Where is he?"

"He's borrowing a penthouse suite at the Birdstone."

"The Birdstone?" I suck in a whistle of admiration despite myself. The Birdstone is the most expensive golf club in the Palm Springs area. Last time I had reason to check, the initiation fee was a quarter million. And the place runs its own personal jet service for members.

"Of course," Rachel says with an annoyed look. "Julian is on the board. When I kicked him out he borrowed the unit from the Friedmans, who are summering this year...let me think...oh, yes, at their place in Wyoming. So he's landed on his feet again, the bastard."

Golf and real estate are the two main religions out here, followed closely by plastic surgery. With the Birdstone membership, the Bartells have hit the trifecta.

"I could poke around," I say. "I get seven-fifty a day."

Rachel begins writing. "How about a week's retainer to get us started?"

Chapter Twenty-Five

— • —

I watch from the window as Rachel backs out of the driveway and disappears down Cahuilla Drive. Then I study her check. A week's retainer is almost four thousand bucks.

But is it enough to justify wading back into this nightmare case, based on nothing but the suspicions of an enraged alcoholic willing to do what Rachel Bartell did to a corpse the night of Jennifer Williamson's murder?

I start to tear up the check and text Rachel to forget about her husband and concentrate on getting sane in rehab. But my neck hair stops me.

One call, I promise myself. One call. If it doesn't pan out, I tear up the check.

The call is to a guy named Tommy LaSalle, the county's chief medical examiner. I know him from my days with the sheriff's office.

I try his direct line at the morgue. Today is Saturday, but Tommy's likely to be at work. He is, as he puts it, more comfortable with the departed than with most of those still present.

He answers on the first ring. "Dana," he says. "Couldn't hardly believe my eyes when I saw you on the caller ID. Long time no."

Thank God he doesn't say more. The subject of our last conversation was the autopsy he did on Frank and I don't want to go there again.

"It has been a while, Tommy. How's business?"

"What can I say, the customers are dying to get in."

"Good one, Tommy, never gets old."

He chuckles. "But old jokes are not why you called. What's up?"

"It's about that suicide a couple days ago. Chelsea Miller?"

"Did I hear you found her body?"

"I did. Got a couple minutes? I'd like to come down."

"I'll be here," he says.

Half an hour later, I pull in at Tommy's office in Indio. It's in a low-rise business-industrial complex made of khaki-colored sandstone. It looks like a desert outcropping, except for the windows.

Tommy meets me at the employee entrance and takes me to his office, which is as sterile and industrial as the outside of the building. White walls, gray tile floor, cream colored plastic furniture.

He's in his early forties, I'd guess. Double chin, thirty extra pounds, widow's peak, glasses, face remarkable only for its ordinariness. You'd peg him as a produce manager at Albertson's, not someone who spends his days with the dead. He has a picture of his golden retriever on his desk, and a sign that says "Welcome to the real Slab City."

I take the seat across from his and he hands me his report on the death of Chelsea Miller. He works at his computer and listens to NPR on the speakers while I go over the report.

It reflects what Avila said: Cause of death, gunshot wound to the head. Manner of death, suicide.

"She's a popular girl," Tommy says as I close the report and lay it on his desk. "Gary Avila called about her last night just as I was closing up."

"What did he want?"

"Apparently Rachel Bartell is claiming her husband hired the Miller woman to kill Jennifer Williamson, then he killed Miller to cover it up. Avila called to ask me what I thought."

"And that was?"

"I told him the available evidence is consistent with suicide, just like in the report. But homicide can't be ruled out. Or for that matter even accidental death. I asked if he wanted a formal inquest. He didn't. He said things are usually as simple as they look."

"He says that a lot." I pick up the report and flip through it again. "Any chance it wasn't suicide?"

"Meh."

"Meh is not zero."

"Not quite. You want to take a look?"

I don't, but I nod.

Tommy leads me down a hallway into the morgue. It's a cold room, all stainless steel and fluorescent lights and heavy-duty air-handling equipment that makes a lot of noise and keeps the place mostly smell-free. In the middle is a big autopsy table equipped with hoses and drains where the actual work of the morgue takes place. Thankfully, it's unoccupied.

The bodies are kept in refrigerated lockers along the wall. I follow Tommy to one of them, where he checks the nameplate on the door, then opens it to reveal two bare feet with a tag on the left big toe and a silver ring on the right one. The tag has Chelsea's name on it, followed by several lines of identifying information and a case number.

The body's on a metal shelf—the actual 'slab' in a morgue—that slides out on rollers when Tommy pulls on it. And there's Chelsea, covered by a white sheet except for the feet. Tommy rolls the sheet down to her collarbone. She looks the same as when I found her, except colder, grayer, and deader.

Tommy runs down all the reasons why her death is consistent with suicide. Part of it is the way I found her, alone with her nine-millimeter.

"Gunshot residue on the right hand, like you'd expect, and no sign of a struggle," he says. "No bruises, no scratches, nothing unusual under the fingernails, no injuries at all except what happens when you put a nine-millimeter through your head." He points out the entry and exit wounds, then pauses.

"Pretty girl."

"She was, but don't go Uncle Creepy on me, Tommy."

"I'm making a point."

"And that is?"

"The most common way women kill themselves is by poisoning or overdose," he says. "Not by gunshot. I understand women about like I do bitcoin, but I'm guessing it's vanity. They want to look good in the coffin, so they don't blow their faces off with bullets, especially the pretty ones."

"I hate to admit it," I tell him, "but a woman might think like that."

"So," he says, "why would this girl shoot herself rather than just take too much of something and float away on a cloud? They found a bottle of OxyContin 80s on the nightstand and she had enough in her system that she was probably feeling pretty mellow when she died, so why use the gun? Why not just take a few more pills?"

"Huh."

"Yeah. But that's another question, not a fact. And a question is not evidence."

My neck hair bristles again. It tells me I forgot something. Something about when I saw Chelsea in the back room at Coffi. She was cutting open a box and then we shook hands. With our left hands.

"Do people ever shoot themselves with their non-dominant hand?" I ask him.

"Eh?"

"Chelsea was left-handed."

Tommy pulls back the sides of the sheet and looks at her left hand, then her right hand, where he found the gunshot residue. "Really."

"Yep." I tell him about the encounter at Coffi. "You can't tell a victim's dominant hand in a post-mortem examination?"

"Not reliably," he says. "To your question, though, it's rare for people to shoot themselves with the non-dominant hand. But it's not unheard of. You never say never when it comes to suicide. Somebody at that point, they're by definition in an altered state."

"But it at least raises another question?"

"But, again," he says, "a question is not evidence. Even two questions. Although they're both interesting. That I admit."

"Interesting enough to change your conclusion about the manner of death?"

He thinks it over, then shakes his head, no. "But interesting enough that I'm going to revise the report and add a couple of footnotes."

He covers Chelsea up and slides her slab back into the locker. The last thing I see is the dyed auburn hair she hoped would make her be like Jennifer.

"I don't suppose you know any of her people?" Tommy asks.

"She's got an ex-husband back in Nebraska and I think an aunt in Chapel City."

"Them I know about. They don't want her."

"What?"

"Nobody's claimed her body, and apparently nobody's going to. Once Homicide releases it, we'll have her cremated and eventually I'll scatter her ashes in the Salton Sea."

"You personally?"

He looks embarrassed. "I do it every year on Easter with the unclaimed cremains. We're supposed to ship them to a place in Arizona for disposal but I just...well, everybody deserves some kind of sendoff, you know?"

Back in my Jeep, I sit in silence with the AC off and the doors closed. The interior is like lava from being in the sun while I was with Tommy. But right now, I need the warmth.

After a few minutes I dig Rachel Bartell's check out of my purse, sign it on the back and fill out a deposit slip in my checkbook. Then I look up the nearest ATM with the map app on my phone, and pull away.

CHAPTER TWENTY-SIX

— · —

A fter I finish at the ATM, I park in the Wells Fargo lot to think it over.

I could confront Julian Bartell, and have no better luck than Avila did. Then I remember the story in the *Herald* from this morning, and start for Chelsea's place in Chapel City.

Twenty-five minutes later, I pull the Jeep around the main house at 35220 Fan Palm Drive and steer my way down the side to Chelsea's garage apartment in the rear.

Sure enough, an old green Ford minivan is backed up to the door with the doors open. It's half filled with bulging shopping bags and some of the taped-up moving boxes I saw in the place when I discovered Chelsea's body. As I walk past, I see a Del Taco cup in the console, a black purse on the front seat, and a pile of clothes on the rear bench. Most of them are still on hangers.

Aunt Vivian from the *Herald* story comes to the door as I reach the stoop. She's a heavy-set fifty-something with gray braids and a face to match. She's in khaki shorts, sneakers, and an "I GOT SCALPED" T-shirt like Edgar's.

"I thought I heard somebody pull up," she says in a smoker's rasp. "Can I help you?"

"You're Vivian, right? Chelsea's aunt? I'm Dana Forsythe. I'm investigating her death."

She extends her hand. "Vivian Miller," she says as we shake. "Chelsea's father was my brother."

I hand her my card. She studies it for a moment.

"You're a private investigator? For who?"

I debate how much to tell her, and decide it won't hurt to plant a seed. "I can't disclose the identity of my client, but I've been hired to do some basic checking to confirm that Chelsea's death really was a suicide."

Aunt Vivian heaves a sigh and says "Come on in."

The living room sofa still has moving boxes, though not as many as before. The sofa seats are free again.

The calico cat I saw before eyes me from atop the refrigerator, then folds a front paw and licks it. On the kitchen counter is a small moving box with the flaps open. Beside it are two more that are taped shut but not yet labeled. The cupboard doors are open and the shelves are almost bare.

"Grab one of these, willya?" Aunt Vivian points at the sealed boxes on the counter.

I do, she grabs another one, and we carry them to the minivan. They're not big, but they're heavy because they're full of dishes. We load them in.

She stares at the two boxes as we stand in the sun and the heat, then pulls a Sharpie from a hip pocket and writes "DISHES" on the boxes.

"That Jennifer woman was the last straw," she says with a shake of her head. "If Chelsea never met her....ah, hell, I could use a beer. How about you?"

I don't but I say I could.

She leads me back inside, pulls two cans of Budweiser from the refrigerator, and waves me to a seat at the dining table.

She drops into the chair across from me, cracks the tab on her Budweiser, and sucks down a long, slurpy drink. I open mine and take a fake drink with fake slurps that lasts almost as long. She doesn't notice, not that I can see.

"So, Chelsea met Jennifer..."

Aunt Vivian nods. "Almost as soon as she got out here after her ex took the kids in the divorce. She stayed with my boyfriend and me for a while, then got that job at the coffee place and that's where she met Jennifer. Jennifer worked next door at the Chamber of Commerce?"

"Uh-huh," I murmur. It's usually best to say as little as possible once a witness gets rolling on a story.

"Pretty soon, she's got this place." Aunt Vivian waves at the clutter around us. "It's not much but it was hers, you know? She made enough at Coffi that she didn't need any, ah, work on the side like she had to do back home?"

Aunt Vivian stops with the question on her face, do I know what she's talking about?

"Yeah," I tell her, "we did find some of that in her background check. A woman does what she has to, right?"

"Damned straight," Aunt Vivian rasps. "I don't approve, but I do understand."

"Copy that."

"Anyway," she continues, "Chelsea meets Jennifer and she--what?—falls under her spell. Chelsea was as straight as they come, but Jennifer, she, she..."

"I've heard she had that effect on people."

Aunt Vivian takes another loud drink from her Budweiser. I fake another one from mine.

"Yeah," Aunt Vivian says. "Every man she met wanted to sleep with her, every woman wanted to be her, including Chelsea. But she never figured out that wasn't gonna happen. She even dyed her hair to be like Jennifer's. Sure, Chelsea was hot enough, and plenty willing. But, but..."

"But if you aren't born with what Jennifer Williamson had, you'll never have it."

"Exactly," Vivian says. "It wasn't too bad for a while. Chelsea was getting by on the pay and tips from Coffi, she was up on her own two feet here in her little place, she adopted Nemo there from the pound." She waves at Nemo, now curled up asleep atop the fridge. "You don't by any chance need a cat, do you?"

"My German Shepherd would probably eat him."

"Then he's going back to the pound. My boyfriend has a pit bull."

Now the conversation has stalled. Sometimes a detour will do that. "So Chelsea was doing okay for a while?"

"And then that cop boyfriend of Jennifer's got shot." She stops, looks at my card again, and recognition dawns on her face.

"Oh, no, you were in the news, he was your- -"

"It is what it is," I say. It's the emptiest phrase I know, which is the point. Aunt Vivian gets back on track.

"Jennifer turned into a vampire after that. She was bleeding Chelsea dry, borrowing money from her all the time and never paying it back. Poor Chelsea, she started, started - -"

"Doing business in Desert Hot Springs?"

Aunt Vivian gives a vigorous nod. "And then Jennifer's new boyfriend came along, that plastic surgeon, and she was bleeding him, too, and not just for money. He was their source for oxy. God, it was awful."

"They were both using oxy? I heard Jennifer liked cocaine."

"Whatever," Aunt Vivian says. "I got the impression Jennifer mostly stayed clean except when she was partying. But poor Chelsea, he did some free work on her jawline because of Jennifer, she got a couple of prescriptions for the pain and then ..."

"Yeah."

"She was such a mess, I wasn't surprised she killed Jennifer, in a way I almost didn't blame her. And then the suicide...she was always hoping to move back home and get with her kids so she was about to go back to Nebraska and clean up her act and try for at least shared custody. But even dead I guess Jennifer still had her hooks into Chelsea and eventually Chelsea just..."

"So you two were pretty close?"

"I was about all she had. Other than Jennifer."

"You know nobody's claimed the body, right?"

"I'd like to," she says. "But I can't afford a casket and a burial. I house-sit and clean motel rooms for a living and - - well, I heard the state will cremate her?"

"The county, actually, but, yeah. And after a while, if nobody claims the ashes, they'll spread her over the Salton Sea."

Aunt Vivian brightens. "Chelsea loved the Salton. We'd drive down there sometimes, get beer and burgers at that place in Bamboo Beach with the dollar bills all over the walls."

"The Surf Inn."

"Yeah, and then we'd walk up on the dike and look out over the water in the sunshine and there'd be those fish rotting on the shore and she'd say, 'How can something so beautiful be so dead?'"

She's silent for a while. "Yeah, I think she'd like that, ending up in the Salton."

"What are you gonna do with her stuff?"

"I'm taking it to Goodwill. Except the TV. Mine is on its last legs, so I was thinking I'd keep it."

"So you think it was suicide, then?"

"What else?" she says.

"It's just that Chelsea told me the same thing she told you, about going back to Nebraska. Like she was getting her life together, she was making a big move. She even said something about hiring a lawyer on the child custody issue, so it seems like her plan was pretty expensive. Any idea how she was going to pay for it?"

"None whatever," Aunt Vivian says. "Maybe she figured she'd go back to turning tricks if that's what it took."

"But that could complicate the custody situation, right?"

Aunt Vivian raises the Budweiser to her lips and studies me over the rim. "So your client doesn't think it was suicide?" She drinks from the can and sets it down.

How big a card to play? I decide to show my ace in the hole.

"The fact is, my client thinks Jennifer's boyfriend, the plastic surgeon, hired Chelsea to kill her because she was bleeding him, too, and threatening to tell his wife what was going on. And that he killed Chelsea and made it look like suicide to cover it up."

Aunt Vivian is silent for a long time. "So your client must be his wife."

I don't answer.

"Nah, I don't buy it," Aunt Vivian says. "I think Chelsea killed herself from guilt and grief, with the same gun she used on the woman she wanted to be."

"My client's theory would explain how she got the money to pay for her new life plan."

"The police went through this place pretty good once they figured out she killed Jennifer. They didn't find anything suspicious about Chelsea's suicide, right?"

"I just wonder if they could have missed something. You don't mind if I look around as long as I'm here?"

Her face says she does, but she waves at the remains of Chelsea's life around us and says, "Knock yourself out."

She tosses her Budweiser empty into the trashcan by the refrigerator. I drain mine into the sink and toss it in, too.

Then I start my search. I go room by room, because you don't take anything for granted.

In the kitchen, nothing that matters. No food in the refrigerator—Vivian tells me she threw it all out because what wasn't spoiled wasn't worth taking home. The food containers still in the cupboards hold nothing but food and the remaining dishes are just dishes. The bag of kitty litter under the sink contains only kitty litter. In the trashcan, the food from the refrigerator, a box of regular Tampax Pearls with nothing in it but tampons, and the two Budweiser cans we threw in.

Same for the living room--nothing of interest, except for Chelsea's phone on the coffee table. It's unlocked and devoid of anything of significance. I pocket it anyway, figuring it can't hurt to have Lita take a deeper dive.

The bedroom is likewise unproductive. Nothing that matters between the mattress and the box springs, or under the bed, or in the closet, or in the dresser.

The nightstand has a couple of books on it. One is "New Moon" from the Twilight vampire series. The other is "The Addiction Recovery Workbook." Sitting on top of it is the lid of a peanut butter jar.

It holds a pile of powdery ash and a roach smoked down to the size of a pencil eraser.

In the drawer of the nightstand, there's a bottle of sleeping pills and another of kratom capsules, which addicts use for self-treatment. Also, a box of condoms and a vibrator shaped like a giant silver bullet.

In the bathroom shower, a mat of hair over the drain, and shampoo, conditioner, and liquid soap on the ledge below a window of frosted glass. In the medicine cabinet, makeup from low-end brands like ELF and Maybelline, except for some blush and highlighter from Clinique. On the sink, an electric toothbrush, a box of whitening strips, and a crumpled tube of whitening toothpaste.

When I'm done in the house, it's time to look through the boxes Aunt Vivian has packed up. I take a steak knife from a kitchen drawer, and go out to the van, figuring to start there and work my way back in.

Aunt Vivian follows me out, grabs her purse off the front seat, pulls out a pack of Marlboro Lights and fires one up. She sits on the stoop, smoking and watching as I slice open the boxes and rifle through them. She coughs and says, "You gonna tape those back up?"

"Yeah, sure," I say.

When I'm done with the van, she follows me back inside and puts the black purse into a kitchen cabinet beside a half-dozen water glasses.

I start on the boxes in the living room, but that purse she's taking such good care of is on my mind. I walk into the kitchen. "I could use a glass of water," I say as I open the cabinet door and knock the purse onto the floor.

Aunt Vivian starts and makes a grab for it, but I get there first and hold it up between us.

"Nice purse," I say. "Mind if I take a look?"

"Of course I do." She tries another grab, unsuccessfully. "What's in there is none of your damned - -"

Too late. I'm already opening the purse and dumping it out on the counter beside the refrigerator. A packet of hundred-dollar bills falls out with the clutter from Aunt Vivian's purse. A packet secured by a green rubber band.

Aunt Vivian makes another grab, but I'm faster. I stuff the packet into a hip pocket.

"Give me that," she says. "It's mine."

"No, it's evidence in a murder case. Where'd you find it?"

She shoots me a disgusted look and points at the Tampax box in the trash can. "The money was in that. It was under the bathroom sink."

"Huh," I say.

"Uh-huh," Aunt Vivian says.

"I gotta hand it to Chelsea. A man wouldn't look in there. Not a cop, not a plastic surgeon."

"Nope."

"How did you happen to find the money?"

"That box was heavy. Like twice as heavy as a box of tampons that size should be. And kind of off-balance when I shook it. "

I wave the packet in front of her nose. "Ten thousand dollars and you can't afford a casket?"

As I drop the money into the Tampax box, Aunt Vivian says, "It's not like she was gonna know."

"And that's why I needed some twin time," I tell Lita an hour later at Toddler Town. I've just told her about my encounters with Tommy LaSalle at the county morgue and Aunt Vivian at Chelsea's place, and the ten thousand in the Tampax box.

"*Dios mío!*" Lita exclaims. "That poor woman, she had no one good in her life."

"Apparently not." I sip from my latte and rest my eyes on Sonny and Rose at play. Sonny's in the ball pit with a couple of other little boys, giggling and shrieking as they dive and surface and dive again like baby porpoises. Rose, meantime, has found a friend who also wears a princess dress. They're side by side on the dolphin and the unicorn.

"So now you take it to the police," Lita says. "*Si?*"

I don't answer. She catches my expression and her eyes widen in alarm.

"Dana!"

"They already had their run at Julian Bartell," I say. "And he wriggled off the hook. I'm gonna handle it myself."

"*Amiga*, no! If you're right about him, he's a deadly man."

"He's staying at the Birdstone, according to his wife. He won't try anything there."

CHAPTER TWENTY-SEVEN

The next morning, I take a picture down the canyon from my house and put up the standard "beautiful day in the desert" post on Facebook.

Now there's nothing to do but wait.

Duke and I venture out for a very short stroll. It's already 102 degrees on the patio, and my phone says we're in for a high of 117 today. Duke does his business, checks his pee-mail on the cacti and brush, and gives me a look that says, "Why are we still out here?"

Back inside, I hit the Peloton for my daily thirty, then shower and prep for the Birdstone.

For once, I'm intimidated. The Birdstone. People with so much money they don't have to think about it any more than they think about the air they breathe.

But what to wear? Something that'll let me fit in without saying say "trying too hard." Something I can carry off. Something that...

Ah, to hell with it. I pull white jeans off a hanger, top them with a cream shirt, and dig out the rose Gucci slides Frank got me for our anniversary a couple of years ago. I'm arrayed for conquest.

Except I haven't heard from the Chaplain.

Time for a news cruise before I hit the Birdstone. There's nothing new that matters. Reporters appear to be bored with the Jennifer Williamson murder. There's not a single story about it today.

Facebook is still aflame over the Forever Marilyn statue. An activist named Catherine Bennett complains about plans to install it in front of the local museum, with its backside to the door.

"Marilyn will literally be mooning the museum," Catherine says. "It's appalling."

In Slab City—the one by the Salton Sea, not the one at the medical examiner's office—a guy named Ouroboros is begging for antibiotics. "I might have dysentery," he says. "What I don't have is money to pay for meds or go to the hospital."

Finally my phone chimes with a number I don't recognize. I hope it's the Chaplain on a new burner, but you never know. I answer with a neutral "Hello?"

"It's Luther," the Chaplain says.

He's using his government name now? If it's an opening, I don't know how to dive through it. So I get down to business.

"You available tonight?"

"Please, Dana."

"Not for that. It's for work."

"Yeah?"

I lay it out for him. A long silence follows.

"You sure about this?"

"Never more so," I tell him. "Son of a bitch had the mother of my husband's kids killed."

"What if he doesn't take the bait?"

"Then I go to Avila. But first I want to see his face when I break the news."

Another long silence from the Chaplain, then. "I'm in. Take me through it again."

To believe the Birdstone Golf Club, you have to see it.

Which I do every time I drive down from my perch on the highest inhabited ridge in the Cahuilla Hills. The club is several hundred feet below me and in the next valley over. It has not one golf course, but two. They're draped across the valley floor, green and shiny in the morning sun like a carpet of money. It's a short trip in distance, less than three miles. But in class and status? A million light years.

As I follow the curving drive to the clubhouse past a valet lot full of Beamers, Mercedes, Corvettes, Audis, and even a silver Rolls, I notice a big fountain in the courtyard. It's so big that its spray is carried onto the drive by the desert breeze. The result is a gray wet spot in front of the tall double doors etched with the Birdstone's *B/G* logo in gold.

The fountain's sensors detect my approach and stop the spray as I pull up. A uniformed valet glides out from behind his brushed aluminum podium and comes around to take my keys. His nametag says he's Jorge. His face says, "A Jeep at the Birdstone? Really?"

"Lambo's in the shop," I tell him.

Inside, a quick scan of the lobby turns up a concierge desk off to my right. Like everything else in the place, it makes a statement. Black front panel with the gold logo, a bouquet of white lilies and carnations on the counter in a fluted crystal vase, icy blond at the counter in a gold top and a gold nametag that says "Bianca."

"Morning, Bianca," I say. "Can you let Dr. Bartell know that Dana Forsythe is here? I believe he's in the Friedman penthouse. He's expecting me."

I figure if I show Bianca how much I know about Julian Bartell, maybe she'll believe he really is expecting me.

"Actually," she says, "I think I just saw them go out onto the Terrace for brunch." She points at two doors with gold logos on the front and a black and gold sign above saying "Canyon Terrace."

Them? This should be interesting.

Inside the double doors, a silver-haired maitre d' at another black and gold podium requests my name.

"Actually, I'm with the Bartell party," I tell him. "Dr. Julian Bartell?"

Perry, according to his nametag, scans the screen of an iPad. His face frosts over. "I'm afraid the reservation was for a party of just two. Can I seat you at the bar?"

"There must be a mixup," I say. "Perhaps you could take over my card?"

"Of course."

I pull a Jacinto Investigations card from my purse, think for a moment, and ask to borrow Perry's pen. He passes it over—it's black and gold, of course--and I write, "$20,000?" on the back of the card.

When I hand him his pen and my card, he studies the inscription on the back and the frost deepens. "If this is a business matter, I'm not sure Dr. Bartell would - -"

"Oh, he definitely would. Just ask."

Perry frowns, crosses the bar, and disappears through an archway that opens onto the terrace proper.

In a moment, he's back with a puzzled expression. He beckons me to follow, and escorts me through the archway and heads for the outer edge of the terrace.

It's a perfect spot for brunch. The sun is behind the clubhouse and the terrace provides a grand overlook of the valley below. With the temperature well above a hundred now, it's not cool on the terrace, but neither is it the unbearable heat of late July in the open desert.

The terrace is shaded by a portico with misters lining its outer face. A soft, cool fog drifts down over the diners. A blond pianist in a long blue cocktail dress is playing smooth jazz loud enough to enhance the ambience, not loud enough to interfere with conversation.

As we come through the tables, I spot Bartell with a Latina immersed in her phone. She looks familiar, but not enough so that I can place her. They're nursing margaritas in big frosty glasses with lime wedges and salt around the rim. Perry seats me and glides away.

Bartell looks at me. I look at him. His dining companion looks up from her screen with a confused expression. Then I recognize the plastic face and perfect boobs. She's Ariana Vega, the receptionist from Bartell's clinic. They're in sleek, expensive-looking golfing togs—matching white polos and sand-colored shorts. Her shorts are shorter. Much shorter, and dazzling against the golden tan of her legs.

I catch her eye and put out my hand. "Dana Forsythe. Pleasure to see you again, Ariana."

She declines my hand with a tight nod. "Ms. Forsythe."

"Did your date show you that card the maitre d' brought over?" I ask her.

"Julian said not to worry about it."

"I have to disagree. You should be very worried. He had his last girlfriend killed, then he personally killed the woman he hired to do it."

Ariana looks from me to Julian and back again. "No, I don't believe - -"

"Don't worry, Honey," Bartell says. "This woman's crazier than Rachel." He hands Ariana a key card. "Why don't you wait in the suite? I'll have our order sent up and join you there after I deal with this. I won't be long."

She opens her mouth again. Bartell holds up a hand to stop her. She closes her mouth, grabs her margarita, and leaves without a word.

Bartell holds out my card, so the scrawled "$20,000?" on the back faces me. "Rachel's doing, right? Talk about hell having no fury. First she sics the cops on me and now you."

"I'm not the cops."

"Doesn't matter." He pockets my card. "I'm telling you what I told Lieutenant Avila. I did not pay Chelsea Miller twenty thousand dollars to kill Jennifer Williamson. That money was right there in our home safe the whole time. I showed it to the police and I'd show it to you if Rachel hadn't kicked me out. Nor did I kill Chelsea Miller. Now stop harassing me or I'll get a restraining order."

He points at a silver-haired black couple picking at fruit salads two tables away. "You see those people? That's Judge James Artemis Harris and his wife. He's the man I will ask for the restraining order. He is on the board here, as am I. We golf together twice a month, and I let him win. When I ask for a restraining order, my friend Judge Harris will listen carefully. Very carefully. Understood?"

I don't answer. Instead, I pull my purse from my lap and lay it on the table. He watches in silence as I open it and tease out a ziplock bag just far enough to show the corner of a packet of currency. He can't see the denomination yet, nor the green rubber band securing the packet. But he can see it's cash.

He says something under his breath that sounds like "Shit."

"Any guess what that is?" I ask.

"Money, obviously. But anybody can - -"

He stares as I slide the ziplock out far enough to show the money is hundred-dollar bills wrapped in a green rubber band.

The "shit" is louder this time.

"Did you know," I ask, "that money is really good at picking up fingerprints?"

Bartell's hand crawls across the table toward the ziplock like it has a mind of its own. I slide the ziplock back into the purse, and drop the purse into my lap. The hand returns to the margarita and pours quite a bit of it into Bartell's mouth.

"That money probably has dozens of fingerprints on it," he says.

"True. But the cops only need one. I'll be waiting in Lieutenant Avila's office tomorrow when he shows up for duty, and then his forensics people will work their magic."

"How did you...where did you..."

"How did I find the money? I didn't. Chelsea's aunt did. And where did she find it? You know, junkies get pretty good at hiding things, and Chelsea was smart enough to put this money somewhere no man would look."

I take out my phone and bring up the picture I took of Chelsea's Tampax box with the ten thousand dollars peeking out the top.

"Shit," Bartell breathes again.

"My only question is how did you get her to lie still long enough to shoot her in the head? That was a contact shot, according to the medical examiner, and no sign of a struggle."

"You should get out of here," Bartell says.

"And you should probably get upstairs." I rise and sling my purse over my shoulder. "Ariana's waiting."

I point at Bartell's golfing buddy two tables away. "Or perhaps you'd prefer to go over and discuss that restraining order with Judge Harris first?"

Chapter Twenty-Eight

—.—

I walk to the terrace and take a phone shot overlooking the money carpet of the Birdstone courses. Outside, I hand Jorge my valet stub. While he retrieves my Jeep, I put the photo up on Facebook with the standard caption: "Another beautiful day in the desert."

Jorge returns and I hand him a fiver as he holds the door open for me.

Jorge looks at Lincoln's picture on the bill, then at me. "They still make these?"

"Sell it on eBay," I suggest.

The Chaplain calls three minutes later.

"Did he take the bait?"

"He took my card."

"Still sure you want to do this?"

"Definitely," I say. "He's a sociopath."

"I'll be in position by dark."

"Me, too."

Back home, I spend the rest of the day getting ready for the night's work.

The first step is to rig the bed so it'll look occupied in the dark. Dark is really dark in the desert, so my fake version of Dana doesn't have to be great, just good enough.

She should lie on her side facing away from the bedroom window, I decide. I arrange a collection of cushions, towels and blankets on the bed to resemble a sleeper under the sheet.

The final touch is the head. I find a throw pillow from the sofa that will work, except it's bald.

Then inspiration strikes: The time Frank and I went to a New Year's Eve party as each other. I wore his Stetson and smoked a Partagas; he stuffed himself into one of my dresses, carried my purse, and wore an ash-blond wig we bought in a second-hand store.

I dig the wig out of the midden heap of junk not quite useless enough to toss that fills the top shelf of my closet. Once the wig is draped over the pillow and a sheet is pulled up over most of it, Fake Dana is ready. With the blinds down and the lights off except for the night light plugged into a wall socket, she looks to be in a deep sleep.

After that, there's not much to do but wait. I station Duke at the front window to watch the road coming up from the valley below, then while away the afternoon with a few episodes of Joe Kenda, followed by a workout on the Peloton and a shower. Then I eat a Cobb salad out of a plastic container as I watch the evening news.

The news is grim tonight. A trans kid named Myriad has been found dead of seven stab wounds in an irrigation canal along the northeast edge of the Slabs. And someone identified only as an adult male has been found dead of apparent heat exposure on a hiking trail in Palm Springs.

Finally the sun slides behind the ridges back of my house and the valley my feet settles into darkness.

I pack my gear into a green canvas gym bag, turn off the lights in the house, and take a surprised but happy Duke out for a walk as the desert cools and a velvet blackness drapes the hills.

The moon's not up yet, but it's lovely out. To the east, Jupiter and Saturn are already clear of the horizon over Joshua Tree National Park. Starlight from the cloudless sky makes for an easy walk along the familiar trails near my place.

Duke and I climb a little hill that offers a view of the house and the road leading up to it. I tell Duke *"Pass auf!"*—"Watch!"—and check the knoll for snakes and scorpions. Then I unroll a sleeping bag on the sand.

Somewhere down the hill, somebody's having a party. The patio and back yard are lit up like Las Vegas. Car doors slam, people laugh, music plays, dancers shout to make themselves heard. In the brief snatches of quiet, random phrases float up the canyon on the night breeze: "...stop dating girls with the same name as my mother...she had a lovely touch and didn't mind my mastectomy..."

I drink from a water bottle, pour some into the bowl I brought for Duke, lay my head back and gaze up into the starscape.

A kind of inversion happens in my mind and suddenly I'm looking down, not up, into a deep pool of dark water that mirrors the sky. The stars are tiny flecks of phosphorescence on the surface of the pool and time passes like a river flowing and I sink into it. Am I a mile downstream now, or two miles, or ten?

The sounds of the party fade and I'm at the windmills again with the Chaplain. We're on his Harley, he's smoking a Partagas. We pull around the no-trespassing sign and park under a windmill. I'm wearing something flowing and filmy with nothing under it but skin. The breeze plays across it like fingertips.

There's no sound except for the thrumming of the generator at the base of the windmill. It's more powerful than before, a deep, slow throb that settles in the pit of my stomach. The Chaplain swings off the Harley, flicks the cigar into the darkness, and puts out a hand to help me off the back seat. But when I reach for it, he takes my arm and throws me over his shoulder with such ease that I feel weightless. He doesn't speak and I can't.

He stalks out into the desert and pours me onto the sand and - -

And I jerk upright as Duke woofs a second alert. He's on his feet now, staring down the hillside.

I shake off the dream with a deep breath and a shudder and follow Duke's gaze. A pair of headlights wink out about a quarter mile below. The interior lights of a car come on briefly, then fade, and I hear the distant click of a car door being eased shut with maximum silence. I don't know how long I was out, but the party downhill is over. Now it's just us and the stars.

I pull infrared binoculars from the gym bag and point them at where the car was before the lights went out. I can see the shield-shaped Porsche emblem on the grill of the SUV. And despite the dark clothes I recognize Julian Bartell as he starts up the slope.

I text "he's here" to the Chaplain's burner.

"Got him," comes the response.

Through the infrareds, I watch as Bartell walks up the road to the house, circles it twice, and stops at the patio door. He pulls some sort of tool from a pocket, pauses for a moment as if thinking, then tries the knob. It turns, because I've left it unlocked. He pockets the tool and eases inside.

Duke and I make our way down from the hill, I pull Miss Kitty from the duffle bag, rack the slide to put a round in the chamber, and we start for the house.

From inside I hear the "pop!" of a gunshot, a moment of silence, then Bartell screaming, "My arm!"

Then I hear the sound of a struggle or maybe I don't. It's hard to tell from outside the house. Next the bedroom blinds glow as the lights come on inside. My phone pings with an incoming text. I check it. It's from the Chaplain's burner. It says "all clear."

Duke and I cross the patio and move through the darkened house to the light pouring from the bedroom doorway.

"*Sitz!*" I tell Duke. He parks himself beside the door and watches with pricked ears as I go in.

Julian Bartell is asleep on his back on the floor with his wrists zip-tied to his belt loops. His right forearm shows a raised red welt. The Chaplain stands near his head.

I point at the arm. "Hammer work?"

The Chaplain grins and pats the ball-peen hanging from his belt. "Just a love tap after he shot your bed. I was waiting in the corner. He never saw me coming."

"And you have his gun?"

The Chaplain pulls it from his vest and shows me. A dark-gray semi-automatic, probably a Taurus thirty-eight.

"Break the arm?"

"Hope so."

"And how exactly did he become unconscious?"

The Chaplain grins again. "He tried to look at me. I laid the hammer handle alongside his head to discourage him."

He points and I see beads of blood in the hair over Bartell's right ear.

"Any chance of permanent brain damage?"

"A headache for a day or two, maybe. I knew you'd want to talk to him."

"So he didn't see you at all?"

"I was never here."

"He might be uncooperative when he wakes up."

"He can try." The Chaplain points toward the bedroom corner where he awaited Bartell's arrival and I see the ash bucket that normally sits beside the fireplace that's been used exactly twice since Frank and I bought this place.

"Huh."

He retrieves the bucket and lowers it over Bartell's head. The back of the rim rests on the floor; the front on Bartell's chest.

"Ah," I say.

"So now we wait."

I squat beside Bartell. Three or four minutes pass. He groans a little, falls silent for another minute, groans again, and tries to lift his hands to the bucket covering his head. The zip-ties make that impossible. He jerks his hands once, twice, then slurs, "Wha the fuh?"

He tries to dislodge the bucket by rolling onto his side, but a very large motorcycle boot holds it, and him, in place.

"What the fuck?" The bucket says it more clearly this time.

"Mr. Bartell," I say. "I think you shot my pillow."

Silence from the bucket for maybe fifteen seconds. Then "Who..."

"Dana Forsythe. We ran into each other at the Birdstone yesterday? You were with Ariana? We need to talk."

"I want a lawyer. I'm not saying one word."

I nod at the Chaplain.

He leans more weight on the motorcycle boot and whacks the bucket with the ball-peen hammer.

The bucket screams "Fu-u-u-ck! I will sue your ass - -"

The Chaplain doesn't need a nod this time. He delivers a whack that makes even my ears ring.

A dark stain appears at Bartell's crotch and the smell of urine seeps into the air. The bucket whimpers.

"First you shoot my pillow and now you pee on my floor?"

"Fuck - -" Bartell cuts himself off, but not quite in time. The Chaplain delivers a light tap to the bucket, more of a reminder than a whack.

"Ready to talk now?" I ask.

"Take this thing off and I will."

I beckon Duke over from the doorway and station him at Bartell's right shoulder. I dig Miss Kitty out of my duffle bag, quietly unload her, and point her at the bucket. I turn on her built-in flashlight and nod to the Chaplain. He rocks the bucket back.

Bartell squints in the sudden light. His eyes dart from Duke to Miss Kitty and back.

I tell Duke "*Gib Laut!*"—"Bark!"

Duke snarls and roars, fangs opening and snapping shut maybe three inches from Bartell's nose. He shrieks and the stain at his crotch expands. The Chaplain drops the bucket back into place.

"I think we'll leave the bucket on. Okay?"

The bucket jiggles, but no words come out.

"If you're nodding, I can't see it. You'll have to speak."

"Yes, leave it on," the bucket sobs. "I'll talk."

"Wise choice," I say.

"Who's that with the hammer?" the bucket quavers.

"It's just me and you here. And my dog."

I lay my phone on Bartell's chest.

"What's that?" the bucket asks.

"My phone. You're being recorded."

"You can't do that," the bucket says. "I know my - -" The bucket stops talking as the Chaplain gives it a medium whack on the side.

"All good now?"

"Go ahead," the bucket says in a small and cooperative voice.

I start the recorder on my phone.

Bartell has a broken arm, and he's wet his pants, and he's under a bucket. He's in no shape to talk, really, so it takes a while. But eventually the full story comes out, as will happen when a witness breaks.

It starts with Bartell spotting Jennifer when he dropped in at the Chamber office. He hooked up with her after Frank's death, and started supplying her and Chelsea with drugs.

At this point I ask a couple of questions about the nature of their drug use. He confirms what Aunt Vivian said. It was mostly recreational cocaine with Jennifer, but Chelsea got into OxyContin after the work he did on her jawline.

Over time, that led to a form of friendship between him and Chelsea, who complained more and more about her mistreatment at the hands of the unfairly lucky and beautiful Jennifer. Chelsea talked of going home to Nebraska, getting clean, and starting over.

This was at the same time Jennifer's demands on Bartell were getting out of hand, leading him to cut her off financially. Then she threatened to go to his Rachel, and it dawned on him that Chelsea could be the solution to his problem.

When she called for her next OxyContin refill, he set up a meeting with her at the bar where, unknown to him, they were photographed by Rachel's PI.

"I told Chelsea," the bucket says, "that I wanted to help her. I said I could let her have twenty thousand dollars to get back home and clean up. Enough to pay off any debts she had out here and cover her moving expenses."

"How did she react?" I ask.

"She cried and thanked me," the bucket says. "And I told her I was happy to do it. But I said maybe she would be willing to help me solve a problem of my own."

"And when you told her the problem was Jennifer and the solution was to kill her?" I ask.

"At first she said 'no,'" the bucket says. "But I hadn't given her the oxy yet that she called me about. I took the baggie out of my pocket, there were a dozen tabs in it, and I put it in the middle of the table. When she reached for it, I put my hand over it and I said, 'You sure you can't help me out?' She looked at me with those junkie eyes and she didn't have to say it. I knew."

Before I can stop myself, I mutter, "Jesus Christ."

"What?" the bucket asks.

"Nothing. How exactly was Chelsea supposed to do it?"

"I knew Jennifer was going to a party in Chapel City while I was in Anaheim. I told Chelsea to stake out her condo and follow her and do it when she got the chance."

"And if she didn't get the chance?"

"There's always another night."

"And how exactly was she supposed to get paid for killing her best friend?"

"Ten thousand down before I went to my conference," the bucket says. "Another ten thousand if it was done when I got back, then I get rid of her gun and the burner phones we were using, and she gets a hundred tabs of OxyContin when she's ready to leave for Nebraska. She said that would keep her on her feet till she figured things out back there and got into a program."

"Of course it would," I say. "So you were planning to kill Chelsea right from the start?"

"Of course not," the bucket says. "Too many bodies, too many questions. But then Rachel got drunk and hired Smokey Hale and that screwed everything up. Even then, it might have worked if you hadn't started figuring it out and gotten Avila involved and...well, anyway, killing Chelsea was the logical solution. If I could cut the investigation off at Chelsea it might never go any farther."

So, the bucket tells us, when Chelsea said she was ready to leave and asked Bartell for the final ten thousand and the oxy for the road, he stalled until she used up what she had on hand and started to get withdrawal symptoms. Then he took over the money and the drugs, except he brought eighty-milligram tablets instead of the twenties she was used to.

"She gave me the gun as agreed," the bucket says. "I gave her the money and the OxyContin and she popped three on the spot without checking the dosage—the tabs look just alike, except for having the dosage twenty or eighty on the back. When she nodded off...well, it was easy to make it look like suicide. I left the OxyContin for the police to find and kept the ten thousand I brought with me. But I couldn't find the first ten thousand. I had to leave without it."

"If only you checked the Tampax box, huh?"

There's a sigh from inside the bucket. "Then we wouldn't be here, right?"

"You got that right. And what was your plan for killing me tonight?"

"I couldn't let you take the money to Avila and you were dumb enough to give me a business card with your address on it. I was going to come up here, get the job done, throw the gun into the deepest arroyo I could find and cross my fingers. I was out of options."

"I was dumb to give you a card with my address on it? Is that what you said?"

"Yeah, I mean... Oh, this was a trap."

"Duh."

"Doesn't matter," the bucket says. "There's no way this crap will stand up in court. You forgot to give me the Miranda warning. Everybody knows the police have to do that."

"I'm not the police," I tell him.

Chapter Twenty-Nine

— • —

Two weeks later, I arrive at the Sand Trap for our victory party in the Jennifer Williamson case.

It's a weeknight. Business is light. Three guys at the bar, a millennial couple shooting pool on the scratched and patched felt of the Sand Trap's old table. Against the wall behind them, *Under Pressure* pulses from an ancient jukebox lit up like the Vegas strip.

Most of the tables on the veranda are unoccupied, so Ike has been able to snag one right at the outer edge. A soft fog drifts down from the misters along the eaves, so it's pleasant enough out there, even with the temperature still near ninety. There's no moon tonight, but there is a fine view of traffic beading along Palm Canyon Drive under a dome of star-speckled sky.

Ike is sitting as close as possible to Sylvia Webster, our client in the lesbian divorce. With her dark, swept-back mane and a lightweight white jumpsuit draped over her slim frame, she's as sleek as a seal.

Ike is halfway through a Dos Equis. Sylvia is working on a bottle of pinot noir positioned between them.

I watch the show for a few seconds. Ike is giving her the full-court press. Eye contact, the occasional arm touch, hanging on her every word, giving her the smile that never fails to charm a juror. But Sylvia? Her expression says 'meh.'

Lita's on the other side of Sylvia, in front of what I know will be a virgin mojito. I take the seat beside her.

Pretty soon I figure out she's on the phone with her mother, Yolanda, about our upcoming trip to Disneyland for the twins' birthday.

Rose doesn't know exactly what Disneyland is, but she does know she will get to meet Princess Anna and Queen Elsa from *Frozen*. We've bought her a new princess dress for the occasion, one that makes her look as much like Elsa as possible.

Sonny, meantime, has somehow become aware that Disneyland has a jungle cruise that runs through elephant country. When I told him about the trip, he announced, "Shoot effalunt, *tía*! Shoot effalunt!"

"Elephants are nice, Sweetie," I said. "They like peanuts. We don't shoot them."

So now it's "Ride effalunt, *tía*! Ride effalunt!"

Yolanda is worried it'll be too hot to be outside without air conditioning. Lita tells her it's always twenty-five degrees cooler in LA this time of year. Or we'll go at night if need be. "*Mamá, estará bien,*" Lita says. That seems to pacify her. Lita taps off the call.

Much has happened in Palm Springs since the night Julian Bartell shot my throw pillow.

A semi towed Forever Marilyn into town on a big flatbed trailer and now she's flashing her bum at the art museum. Tourists tough enough to brave the summer heat are happily pointing their cameras up her skirt. An op-ed in the *Palm Springs Herald* denounces her as an anti-queer slur, while a Facebook user thanks God we didn't give in to the Marxists.

Our client and guest of honor Smokey Hale comes in. He's now free of all charges, thanks to his assistance to the police in the Bartell case. He's brought along Cara, the artist from Bamboo Beach who was supposed to fence the Patek Philippe watch for him. Her baby bump is slightly larger than when I saw her standing on one leg at the Jungle House in Bamboo Beach.

They slide into chairs next to me and get introduced to Lita and Sylvia.

Rusty the barmaid comes over in her cutoffs and tank top for drink orders.

"Bulleit Manhattan on the rocks," Hale says.

"A Diet Coke," Cara says.

"The usual for me," I say.

Rusty starts for the bar.

Somebody's phone goes off and I scan the table to see whose it is.

"Dana." Lita points at my phone on the table.

I pick it up and see the Chaplain's burner number on the screen. I excuse myself and tap the call to life as I walk to a quiet corner of the veranda.

"Where are you?" the Chaplain asks.

I tell him about our party at the Sand Trap.

"Gonna be there a while?"

"Couple hours probably. Why?"

"Don't leave."

The line goes dead.

I return to the table as Hale asks us to catch them up on the Bartells.

"Yeah," Cara says. "We've been too busy to watch the news much." She leans her head on Hale's shoulder.

I try to focus on the proceedings but I'm only half present. Why would the Chaplain be headed for the Sand Trap?

"Dana, you want to get us started?" Ike asks.

I shake my head clear of the Chaplain. "Yeah," I tell Hale. "Your friend and former employer Rachel Bartell has already bailed out and started rehab up in Sonoma County. The Cerulean Center, I think it is. Hot and cold running shrinks, gourmet dining, Bikram yoga, the works."

He grins. "So she's gonna be fine."

"Of course she is," Lita says. "She's a rich blond white lady with *tetas grandes*."

When the laughter dies down, Cara speaks up. "But what about her husband? Is he getting off, too?"

"We're pretty sure not," I tell them. "Let's just say that Dr. Bartell has had a rough few days."

Ike reports that Bartell has been charged with the attempted murder of yours truly for shooting Fake Dana in the pillow.

I take them through the details of that night, minus any reference to the Chaplain's involvement.

"I did," I conclude, "provide the police with his confession and his gun, which did have his fingerprints on it. I also provided them with Bartell himself, trussed up like a Thanksgiving turkey on my bedroom floor with urine stains on his pants and gunshot residue on his right hand. And I gave them a pillow with a bullet hole, and a sworn statement as a former law enforcement officer."

"Long story short," Ike says, "Bartell is toast on the attempted murder charge."

Rusty arrives with our drinks and asks if we're ready to order dinner.

"Not quite yet," Ike says, "just bring me another Dos Equis, willya?" He refills Sylvia's wine glass without asking. Lita orders another mojito.

I take a drink from my mule and savor the night air as Ike resumes the story.

As for Bartell hiring Chelsea Miller to kill Jennifer Williamson, then killing Chelsea himself to clean up the mess, he reports, things are more complicated.

Based on background chats with the prosecutors, Ike has learned that Bartell's fingerprints were indeed present on the packet of hundred-dollar bills I found at Chelsea's place. And the money's definitely admissible in court. Chelsea's aunt let me in and gave me permission to search the place, which I interpreted to include purses.

But Bartell's confession from under the bucket? That's where the complication comes in. Bartell's lawyers, Ike says, maintain it was coerced, which I deny and which the recording does not show.

"My guess?" Ike says. "That recording will make it into evidence, Bartell will be convicted, and his lawyers will still be appealing thirty years from now when this place is too hot for anything but scorpions and tarantulas. However that comes out, he'll be spending some quality time in the graybar hotel for trying to kill our friend Dana."

Hale raises his Manhattan. "A toast to Ms. Forsythe and to the finest lawyer in Palm Springs! And the tab's on me tonight."

I smile modestly, join in the toast, and wait for the applause to die down. "You're picking up the tab? Meaning Ike will put it on the bill he sends your grandfather?"

Hale, Cara, and Ike exchange grins like three cats who just ate a pet shop's worth of canaries.

"Actually not." Hale puts his hand on Cara's wrist. "We're getting married." "Tomorrow night at the Surf Inn in Bamboo Beach," Cara says. "You're all invited."

"Which will make me the Bump's legal father when it's born," Hale says.

"Which will mean the trust is officially cracked open," Cara says.

"We'll be rich," Hale says.

"But you're not the biological father," I say. "How - -"

"Not a problem," Cara says. "I've reviewed the trust documents."

"Me, too," Ike says. "There's no biological requirement whatever."

"No DNA test, no nothing," Hale says.

"The trust only requires him to produce a grandchild," Ike says. "And for legal purposes that's exactly what the Bump will be if they're married when it arrives. Mr. Brixton Lee Hale the Third here could be worth something like eighty million dollars."

"Actually, it's $83.6 million as of the market close today," Cara says. "I checked."

"And Grandpa Brixton Lee the First agrees with this?" I ask.

"He does, albeit with some reluctance," Ike says, his canary-eating grin still in place. "His lawyers checked and discovered they neglected to include any biological provision when the trust was created. Grandpa told them they had pissed all over their white shoes and he was firing their asses. Then he hired new lawyers who told him the same thing. So we settled."

"I get half the trust when the Bump arrives in a couple months," Hale says. "And the other half if and when we produce a child of our own. Right, honey?"

"Except for the advance."

"Oh, yeah," Hale says. "The advance. Brixton the First advanced us thirty thousand bucks for the wedding."

"That's disgusting," Lita says. "People shouldn't get married unless they're in love."

"Not even for $83.6 million?" Cara asks.

Hale raises his glass again. "Here's to true love. And the law of all's well that ends well!"

We join in the toast amid much laughter and cheering. Except for Lita, we are still congratulating the spouses-to-be when Rusty returns for another welfare check.

This time we do order food, so as to soak up some of the alcohol in the next round of drinks we also order. At least I force myself to order a Cobb salad instead of the steak with cheese fries I really want.

Not so with Ike. He orders exactly that. Cara and Sylvia order salads, Hale a bacon cheeseburger with fries.

Sylvia watches Rusty as she walks away, then speaks for the first time since I arrived.

"Have you had any luck with my...my recipe box?"

"We think we know where it is," Lita says.

"But you don't actually have it?"

"Not yet," I say. "But our best operative is on it."

Sylvia frowns. "What operative?"

"Sorry, that's confidential," I say.

Sylvia smiles a sad little smile at this. "Not yet. Does that mean not ever?"

"It does not," I say. "We'll find it. He'll find it."

She splashes pinot noir into her glass and raises it to her lips.

Ike takes a long, thoughtful pull from his Dos Equis. "She was so young and beautiful to die like that."

It takes the women at the table a couple of seconds to figure out he means Jennifer Williamson. Then we glare at him in unison.

"Jesus, Ike," I say. "Level up"

"So...what?" Cara says. "It would be okay to kill her if she was old and ugly?"

Sylvia edges away from him.

Ike bows his head in surrender.

"Actually beauty was what killed her," Lita says. "Maybe Chelsea pulled the trigger, but it was beauty and bad choices that killed Jennifer. Too beautiful, too easy to get whatever she wanted from too many men. She never had to work for anything."

I take a swallow from my Moscow mule and shake my head. "No," I say. "It was my husband that killed her."

This brings a chorus of whats and nos from around the table.

"She loved Frank but he got himself shot and she couldn't drink, drug, or screw him off her mind and it killed her. He killed her. The bastard."

Ike looks straight at me. "That can happen."

Suddenly I feel like I'm about to ugly-cry. I hide it behind a slow swallow from the Moscow mule.

The food arrives and we dig in. There's a discussion of what sentence Julian Bartell is likely to get, whether the Salton Stench will gas the wedding party tomorrow night in Bamboo Beach, and whether it would be better to hold the ceremony downtown between Forever Marilyn's legs.

I'm halfway through the Cobb when my phone lights up again with the Chaplain's number. I walk to the edge of the veranda and bring up the call.

"Come out to the parking lot," he says before I can say "hello."

"What? Why?" I can't help saying. But he's gone.

I make my way around the end of the bar and down the hall to the back door of the Sand Trap.

Outside, I blink and let my eyes adjust to the darkness. Somewhere in it the Chaplain is waiting but there's no point looking for him. He'll be invisible until he isn't.

After a few seconds, a headlight flashes once from the shadows behind the Wells Fargo branch next door. I make my way across the shared parking lot by starlight until I glimpse his silhouette leaning on the rear fender of his Harley.

"Got your phone?" he asks.

"Yeah, why?"

"Turn on the flashlight." He reaches into one of the Harley's saddlebags and sets something on the seat.

I turn on my flashlight and see a little red cedar box with vines carved into the lid. When I tip back the lid, the flashlight picks out a couple inches of three-by-five index cards. The one in front is dog-eared and smudged and bears an apple-pie recipe in the graceful loops of old-fashioned cursive.

"Nothing you do should surprise me anymore," I say. "But how did you pull this one off?"

The Chaplain grunts. "I found the place in Tahoe. I talked to the help. There's a maid named Consuelo. She lost her mother to a stroke last year. Kind of like with Mee-Maw."

"Nice work."

"Always start with the help," he says. "They know everything. They forgive nothing."

I reach for the recipe box on the Harley seat, fumble, and drop it. The Chaplain's arm snakes out and he catches the box before it hits the ground. He sets it on my palm.

"Having fun in there?"

"We're celebrating," I say. "Big case, big win, big fee. I'm on my second mule and I may have a couple more before I'm done. I'm traveling by Uber tonight."

He swings a leg over the Harley. "Velasco."

"Velasco?"

"My last name. It means Little Raven."

He kicks the engine to life, pulls onto Palm Canyon Drive, and disappears into the night before I can process the fact that I now know his full government name.

I return to our table on the veranda and stand behind my chair till everybody notices and falls silent except Sylvia, who's saying something to Lita about Stanford Law.

When Sylvia notices the silence, she turns and looks up at me with an expression of mild irritation, then lifts the pinot noir to her lips. Ike raises his eyebrows in question.

I set the little cedar box on the table in front of Sylvia.

It takes her at least ten seconds to grasp what it is, frozen with her glass motionless against her lips. Then she drops the pinot noir into Ike's lap.

He says, "Jesus!" and leaps up and dabs at his crotch with a napkin as she opens the box and fans through the recipes.

Tears stream down her cheeks and she gulps out "Mee-Maw, she, she...how did you...Mee...Mee..." before collapsing into sobs.

Lita hands her a wad of napkins from the table. "I think you need a moment in the Ladies Room. Let me take - -"

"No," Sylvia sobs. "I need to go home."

She looks at Ike and says, "I'm so sorry but I just can't...I have to...you all enjoy your party and I'll be in touch when I, when I..."

She looks back to Lita and says, "Can you take me? I can't drive now."

"Of course."

They rise, collect the recipe box and their purses, and leave the bar. Lita's tapping something into her phone as they go.

Ike looks after them. "Well, I'll be damned."

My phone pings and up pops a text from Lita. It says, "dont tell mom lol!"

"Well, I'll be damned," I say.

Ike starts to get up. "I should go with them."

"No, Ike," I say, "you should absolutely not go with them."

He sinks back into his chair. "Why not?"

"Call it woman's intuition."

"Whatever." He takes a disappointed pull from his beer.

Hale and Cara have been watching this with eyes open and mouths shut.

"What was that about?" Hale asks.

"It's quite a story," Ike says.

"And a good one," I say.

So, we team up again as we work through dinner. We tell them about Mee-Maw giving Sylvia the recipe box, about Sylvia coming out as gay to Mee-Maw, about Mee-Maw dying before Sylvia could say goodbye, and about Miranda the evil ex stealing the recipe box after the big breakup.

"That bitch!" Cara exclaims.

"That is cold," Hale says. "But how'd you get it back?"

This leads to another longish tale about how we learned of Miranda's secret hideaway at Tahoe, figured the recipe box had to be there, and tracked down its location.

"All the way up in Tahoe?" Hale asks. "That's like a thousand miles from here."

"More like five hundred," Ike says. "But, yeah, it's far."

Hale looks at me. "How the hell did you get it?"

I smile, raise the copper mug, take a long slow drink.

"I know a guy."

The End

Acknowledgments

Many people helped bring THE SAND GARDEN into being. But the authors would in particular like to thank Nick Wasche and Jesica Sartell for their contributions to the effort.

www.ingramcontent.com/pod-product-compliance
Lightning Source LLC
Chambersburg PA
CBHW030619120726
47904CB00006B/1955